# THE WEIGHT OF

# NOTHING

# THE WEIGHT OF

# NOTHING

## STEVEN GILLIS

brook street press
SAINT SIMONS ISLAND

Brook Street Press
*www.brookstreetpress.com*
Brook Street Press is a trademark of Brook Street Press LLC

First Edition

Library of Congress Cataloging-in-Publication Data
Gillis, Steven.
The weight of nothing / Steven Gillis.-- 1st ed.
p. cm.
ISBN 0-9724295-5-7 (hardcover)
1. Americans--Africa, North--Fiction. 2. Murder victims'
families--Fiction. 3. Loss (Psychology)--Fiction. 4. Male
friendship--Fiction. 5. Africa, North--Fiction. 6. Young men--Fiction.
7. Bombings--Fiction. 8. Pianists--Fiction. I. Title.

PS3607.I446W45 2005
813'.54--dc22

2004018276

Jacket design by John Fulbrook III
Text design by Diane and Erich Hobbing

Printed in the United States of America

10  9  8  7  6  5  4  3  2  1

All author proceeds from the sales of this hardcover edition go to 826 Michigan,
an educational nonprofit organization in Ann Arbor and Detroit, Michigan.
For more information, please visit www.826michigan.org
and contact Steve at 826michigan@gmail.com

FOR
*my father*

*To force solitude on a man who has just come to understand*
*that he is not alone,*
*is that not the definitive crime against man?*

—ALBERT CAMUS

# AN IGNOMINIOUS
# INCEPTION

When I was six years old I found my mother in our driveway lying face down in the snow, her arms extended frail as robin's wings, arched from her shoulders above her head, her legs thrown out and bending slightly at the knee as if she was swimming a butterfly stroke and in that moment about to rise and propel herself forward through a sea of white foam. The snow was heavy and gathered in her hair and across her back. Bluish rings settled around her eyes, her once fair skin turned grey and acquiring then a permanent cold.

I ran to where she'd fallen and rolled her over just as my father stormed barefoot from the house, his large hands fisted, his meaty arms and shoulders, thick legs, and broad chest barrelling toward me. His face was contorted and red with fear. He didn't once look at me while pulling my small fingers from my mother's wrists, knocking me back with such force that I landed across the drive and remained collapsed in the snow until the sirens drew near and a man I didn't recognize scooped me up and brought me inside.

BOOK I

# IN THE BEGINNING

# CHAPTER 1

# THE FATHERS

What he saw before the others was the global metamorphosis, boundless and brilliant, as unavoidable as time tic-tic-ticking in the high pocket of a railway conductor's red vest, as bright and promising as sunlight shining against the windows on the forty-seventh floor of the Reedum & Wepe Building in the heart of downtown Renton. "Vision!" P. Harlen Kelly bellowed when rumors had him amassing his fortune through less than scrupulous means. "Vision!" he barked at anyone brazen enough to argue, and insisted, "War's the thing. Conflict and crisis create markets, boys. Human consumption is born from the illusion of want and need."

Dressed in a blue suit, silk shirt, and neatly tapered slacks, his silver hair brushed back, his neck and cheeks surgically taut and altering the shape of his eyes, P. Kelly stood at his office window staring at the skyline, delighted by the surfeit spread out before him. A shrewd investor—the riots in Pôrto Alegre helped facilitate his deal to sell farm equipment to the Brazilian government on loans guaranteed by the World Bank—P. Kelly made his first fortune just after World War II as he put his cash into affordable housing, butter and oil, automobile tires, women's accessories, candy bars, and transistor radios. He studied similar trends during Korea and Vietnam, Grenada, the Falklands, the Gulf and Iraq, observed the clashes in the Middle East, Algeria and Chile,

Colombia, Zimbabwe, Russia, Indonesia, and the Philippines, followed the opening of China and South Korea, the changes in South Africa, the dismantling of Yugoslavia, and collapse of the Berlin Wall. Year after year he employed the simplest principles of supply and demand, anticipated revolution, analyzed and profited from clever trade.

Voluble, he spoke at seminars and conferences where he extolled the virtue of turmoil, explained how each episode was part of a purposeful evolution aimed at marshalling efficiency and profit. He read up on the history of companies such as Ford, Mercedes, and Xerox—each of which cut deals with the Nazis in order to expand their market share—and concluded that business not politics made strange bedfellows. "Nothing is immune to barter! For every man a dog," he relied on this assumption and made himself rich adhering to the tenets of capitalism, which screamed at him to expand, expand, expand!

Who could not enjoy such bounty? P. Kelly set his hands upon the window in the early morning light and crooned, "God bless the new millennium!" An age of endless expanse, with 3 billion Chinese ready to buy color TVs, electric toasters, and washing machines, and with Pizza Huts and Dunkin' Donuts going up in Gaza and Iraq. He saw himself living in the lap of Eden, the land of milk and honey, where opportunity more than knocked, it whistled and howled! How easy to feel invincible on such a beautiful day, and what a surprise when he laughed then only to have the brilliance of the hour explode in front of his face, startling him while the whole of the Reedum & Wepe shook and the horizon vanished in a thick black cloud, drowning him in a thunderous roar, the windows shattering and the floor beneath his feet giving way, the walls around him groaning and tumbling down.

———

A man on a ledge, fresh to the union and newly moved from Zenith to Renton, Franklin Finne danced along high beams, remarkably agile for someone so large. His huge frame weighted through the hips, supported by a double mass of thigh, like Zeus gaping from Olympus with no fear of plunging and the women walking beneath so perfectly prime. He pranced inside the skeleton of the Ryse & Fawl Building, all hale and hooting down to the streets below, "Hey, honey, can I hang my hat on your rack?" "Sweetie, I lost my number, can I have yours?" "Baby, does a hamburger come with that shake?"

Targeting then the prettiest girl, he could not explain how he noticed her at all. (What draws a man is hard to say.) A modest figure in a short tweed coat, black hair, and green shoes, her slender arms curled and floating as she walked, he saw her as the crowd passed and she stood for a moment viewing the spectacle of girders, a hand placed above her eyes as she surveyed the site. Franklin watched in silence, and the next morning as the woman came and stared again at the construction site, he waved.

Two weeks went by with more of the same until Franklin decided to change his schedule and wait for her outside the Reedum & Wepe. She was surprised by his age, having always imagined an older man waving down at her. At work—she was a typist at Kelly & Kline—older men often made advances, saying they noticed her at her station or passing through the halls, and anxious for company they invited her for a drink. Naive in this way—she was not entirely fluent in the nuances of sexual gamesmanship as some of the other girls who knew how to manage a man and get as much as they were asked to take—she learned in time how to accept a free meal without becoming tangled up in strings, and avoided sleeping with these men even as they flattered and cajoled her and placed a hand on her knee.

Still, when Franklin came and introduced himself and asked

her to dinner she said no. He was a stranger after all, someone who'd swooped down from inside the unfinished Ryse & Fawl Building like a bird of prey, and what did it matter if his eyes were kind, his large body tender as a toy bear, and a voice that tempted her with sweet regard? He suggested as a compromise she meet him at Childe Duke, a club that showcased local musicians on Saturdays where Franklin sometimes played. The invitation appealed to her. As a student taking night classes in composition and voice, she knew Childe Duke and told him that would be fun. Brought together then, compatible in ways neither could have predicted, they dated through the summer, rented an apartment that winter, and married the following spring.

A reader of myth, the single carryover from his three semesters at Mount Farrell Community College, Franklin saw Maria as Selene, goddess of the moon, as Metis and Tyche, goddesses of wisdom, fortune, and fate. He teased her that she was a siren who drew him from the safety of his perch, and when she smiled and reminded him that he was the one who first sought her out, he joked, "Yes, but you were there waiting." To hear Maria sing at her class recitals and other nights at home, he felt such a dizzying sort of love that he literally shook. To lay with her and have her slide up onto him, bare atop his chest, left him mystified by the sheer reality of her presence; how she took him in so deeply, devouring him beyond a point he could imagine, until he stopped thinking for fear of such love fleeing, celebrating instead the incomprehensible nature of his fall.

In the second year of their marriage, they bought a house and Maria gave birth to a son, Tyler. (A Finne family, friends couldn't help remark.) Six years later a second boy, Bailey, was born, and six years after that a winter's snow brought by Persephone, goddess of death, aided by Nyx and Hypnos, goddesses of night and sleep, visited Maria and persuaded her to rest.

# CHAPTER 2

# THE SONS

Shit happens.

There's no way around it.

Bailey in the moonlight, fresh from seeing Emmitt, eyes the sky with dark glasses on.

Just after my mother died, I was sent each day following school to stay with my Aunt Germaine. A guidance counselor at South Renton High, Germaine was a spinster living over on Delmore Street, a stout old girl with sausage-shaped hands, small grey eyes, and a double chin which shook like soft rubber. My father grieved my mother's death hard and took advantage of Aunt Germaine's support to remain downtown after work where he drank himself into a convenient stupor.

I remember my mother having an incredible voice, at once willowy and soulful, arced and bluesy. She sang jazz and torch songs with spectacular range even as my father's raw accompaniment on the piano choked the melody or rushed the lyric. (I can still recall my father's shoulders hunched and enormous hands mashing, his booted feet stomping against the pedals and broad hips swerving from side to side, rocking a half-second off the beat.) A look would come over my father's face each time my mother entertained him with any of his favorites—"Black Is the Color," "Ne Me Quitte Pas," "Make the Man Love Me," "My Last Affair"—and tilting his head to the side, his eyes would squint uneasily down at his hands. A second later he'd snap his shoulders back and start pounding away at a wild rendition of "Salt Papa Blues," yelling above the din for my mother to catch him if she dared. She'd laugh and cover her mouth and my father would howl and play even louder than before.

In those days I shared a bedroom with my older brother, Tyler, whose taste in music ran from Bad Company to Warren Zevon and Uriah Heep. I, in turn, marveled from an early age at my father's music and listened intently to the would-be lyric of his flawed recitals; the mystery of the sound, how it seemed to come together out of thin air. Although I was forbidden to touch my father's piano, I couldn't help but want to try the trick on my own, and one day, with my mother upstairs, I snuck into the front room and sat down. An arrangement my father played the night before was still in my head, and bringing my fingers to the keys I performed "A Nightingale Sang in Berkeley Square."

My mother followed the sound, thinking my father was home early, though the playing she would later say sounded much different, and how surprised she was to see me there on the bench. The look on her face caused me to jump up, convinced I was in trouble and would be punished for touching my father's piano, but instead, and trembling with surprise, my mother said, "That's very good, Bailey. Go ahead then. Play something else. I don't mind."

In secret, she began instructing me on her own each day, wanting to make sure my gift was nurtured slowly, without my father overwhelmed by my talent and turning such into a sideshow event. I played what I heard with no idea what I was doing at first, my hands tiny and without initial grace. My mother helped improve my technique, had me listen more closely to the music, showed me how to break the larger chords by starting them before the beat, unable as I was to reach a minor tenth from black to white keys. She described how each piece of music possessed a natural symmetry and that it was important to identify and respect the essence of the arrangement, how music was controlled centrally by the aural image and the body was the conduit through which music's fundamental magic was transformed.

I was given picture books that demonstrated how to read the notes, was taught about staccato and legato, how to use my hands, and never to hit the keys too hard or misconstrue power for proficiency. "You want to deliver only what the music asks," my mother said. "A word to the wise," she'd smile and kiss my cheek. I was amazed by how much she knew, how well in secret she also played, and concentrating on whatever she put on the stereo, repeated the scores back to her, everything from Motown to Chopin to jazz. In playing for my mother, I was elated not by my own accomplishment but the chance to please her, and believing music mirrored the world in all its brilliance, assumed everything else in life was equally magnificent and abiding and would endure forever.

That winter, an executive at a small record company heard my mother sing at a club where my father coaxed her to perform, and impressed, offered her a chance to cut a demo at a local studio. She said yes only after the man reluctantly agreed to let my father accompany her. They were given a date for the end of the month, and ecstatic, my father insisted they start rehearsing at once. Practices were held first thing in the morning and immediately after dinner, with arrangements selected and rejected, played and replayed, again and again. On the afternoon of their scheduled recording session, my mother sat in the front room sipping a cup of hot tea. (All the long hours of rehearsal had exhausted her, though she did her best to hide as much from my father.) Restless, my father's own playing went poorly, the more he rehearsed the less compatible his fingers found the keys, and nervous, he asked my mother to sing one last song, "for luck." They did Ned Washington's "Wild Is the Wind." ("Love me, love me, say you do.") My mother started out very soft, then rose with, "Like the leaf clings to the tree, oh, my darling, cling to me." When she finished, my father got up from his piano without saying a word and went off to shower. A heavy snow was falling, already several inches outside, and standing by their bedroom window, my father complained of his bad luck.

My mother went upstairs and picked out my father's blue suit from the closet, placing it along with a white shirt and bright paisley tie on the bed. She then returned downstairs where she slipped on her boots and coat and the thinnest pair of white cotton gloves. The temperature was well below freezing and the snow was falling harder than before. I watched from the window as my mother retrieved a shovel from the garage and began clearing the drive. The absolute chill stirred her for a moment and her movements became animated, but the cold was deceptive and wrapped itself around her, bearing down until her muscles trembled and her head went light. Her lungs seized and hyperventilated as the last of her body's heat escaped, her legs buckling and giving out, the snow's pretense at softness offering no resistance to her fall.

Afterward, my father removed every stick of furniture from the house, replacing it with a cheap wooden table and mismatched chairs, a faded brown couch that sagged in the center and poked at the flesh with hard metal springs. ("Gone, gone, gone!" he howled.) I woke one night to the sound of my father shoving his piano through the side door and down the steps, pushing it into the center of the yard where he took an axe to the keys, shattering the ivory and wood, crushing the pads and wires until the legs collapsed and everything was reduced to pulp. He soaked the remains in gasoline then and ignited it all with the first match struck.

"These are the things I remember," I tell Emmitt who—as Dr. Speckridge—stares at me from behind his desk, his bird eyes black and shrinking as he removes his glasses. (He has an oval head and high voice that cracks oddly at awkward moments.) "Elizabeth?" he asks, and I roll my hands over as if to catch something about to fall, and thinking again of my father as he stormed about while the glow of the fire raged and filled the sky with sparks and ash, I picture him fully ablaze and exposed by what comes of love. Shaking my head, I say, "Liz?" and realize then as I do now the danger of wanting anything too much and how I learned so young the way to want for nothing.

Niles Kelly walked east, away from campus and in the opposite direction of the downtown district where the Reedum & Wepe once stood and his father by the window watched the universe crash beneath him.

"Sit then," the man motioned to Niles as he arrived, pointing to a large blue pillow tossed atop a red rug. Several other pillows and rugs were set in a circle around the center of the room. Niles' host was thin framed, dressed in grey slacks, leather sandals, and a long white cotton shirt. A beige cap was perched on the crown of his head. His skin was dark copper. Niles dropped onto the nearest pillow as Massinissa Alilouche offered him tea.

"You are feeling all right?" The question was asked as Niles was sweating, his shirt damp and cheeks red. "I'm fine," he explained. "I walked from campus, that's all." A long table to Niles' left was stacked with papers and books. A box filled with several small vials of medicines was stored beneath the table, tiny white labels affixed to each. Behind a half wall, the kitchen was arranged with a stove near the sink, a refrigerator no larger than a hatbox, and a round table covered with additional books and medical paraphernalia—tubes of salve and bandages, cotton balls in a plastic container, a flashlight and stethoscope, unopened packets of sterile syringes, a jar of needles, and thread all set out in no particular order. At night, the pillows in the front room were arranged for reading and sleep.

Niles glanced toward the table and the stack of books, spotting on top Camus' *The Rebel,* followed by Thoreau's *Walden* and essay on Civil Disobedience, next to Tahar Djaout's posthumously published novel, *The Last Summer of Reason.* The books were dog-eared with tabs jutting out from several of the pages. Massinissa Alilouche observed Niles staring at the books, paused a moment, then turned and retrieved a legal-size envelope from the table and set the folder down on the pillow beside his guest. "What's this?" Niles asked.

"A gift," Massinissa Alilouche answered. "All that you need."

Niles was skeptical, though he placed the envelope inside his backpack, and said, *"Shoukran."*

"There is nothing to thank me for," the older man waved him off before asking as he always did at the start of one of their sessions, "How have you been, my friend?"

"It's been an odd month."

"Tell me."

For the last two years, once every few weeks and sometimes more, Niles had come to Massinissa Alilouche's apartment in an effort to achieve a sense of closure, forgiveness and healing. That he'd chosen to discuss his troubles with a Muslim was perceived by some friends as strange, though no one was actually surprised given Niles' tendency to favor alternative perspectives. Their arrangement began some ten months after the Reedum & Wepe was reduced to rubble and ash, and in the course of their conversations Niles learned a great deal from Massinissa Alilouche about the teachings of the Qur'an, Muhammad and Allah, and how in the East a man believes his fate is set 10,000 years in advance and peace is found in accepting the ensuing order.

Recently however, their sessions together had turned querulous, with Massinissa Alilouche testing Niles' conviction, and rather than embrace the challenge and feel secure in the decisions he'd made, Niles had surprised himself with how uncomfortable and defensive he'd been. After he finished recounting the events of the last month and what had him struggling to move forward, Massinissa Alilouche offered encouragement, only to say, "Perhaps your desire to reach a state of grace through acceptance is a false prophet. How can you have faith in what you're doing if you're not at peace with your decision?"

"But I am at peace."

"*Sahbee.*"

"It's true."

"Then how do you explain?"

"That's different," Niles interrupted.

"Ibnee."

"I understand forgiveness is necessary."

"Ahh. So you feel obligated?" the man placed his hands on his legs, and shaking his head, inquired, "You are compelled?"

"To do what's right, yes."

"Then you are acting out of a sense of virtue, is that it?"

Once again, Niles was confused by the man's question, and shifting about on his pillow, answered, "I'm doing what I think is best. What anyone else would do in my situation doesn't matter."

"Perhaps," the older man moved his chair closer and sat now directly in front of Niles. "Then again is it not possible what you are doing is avoidance? Perhaps you are rebelling against a more human impulse."

"Forgiveness is a human impulse."

*"Fehemt,"* Massinissa Alilouche maintained a sober tone, and reaching for the top book on the table, offered a quote from Camus. "The logic of the rebel is to want to serve justice so as not to add to the injustice of the human condition. . . . (Nihilists) kill in the fond conviction that this world is dedicated to death. The consequence of rebellion, on the contrary, is to refuse to legitimize murder because rebellion, in principle, is a protest against death."

"That's right."

"So then you're a rebel," Massinissa Alilouche leaned forward in his chair and touched Niles gently on his folded knee. *"Dafee kwiyis.* A minute ago you were the Lone Ranger. If you are a rebel, my friend, then you must believe in virtue. True rebellion must be noble at its core, and yet here is the problem, for rebellion is not innocent, and therefore virtue is not always easily resolved." He flipped through the book once more and made his point by quoting again from Camus. "If rebellion exists, it's because falsehood, injustice, and violence are part of the rebel's condition. He cannot, therefore, absolutely claim not to kill or lie, without renouncing his rebellion and accepting, once and for all, evil and murder. . . . Thus the rebel can never find peace. He knows what is good and, despite himself, does evil. . . . His only virtue will lie in never yielding to the impulse to allow himself to be engulfed in the shadows that surround him and in obstinately dragging the chains of evil, with which he is bound, toward the light of good."

Niles shook his head. "The type of rebellion you're referring to has nothing to do with me. I'm not trying to change the world. I only want to get beyond what happened and move forward.

"And yet you haven't," Massinissa Alilouche pointed a finger as Niles tugged at the sleeve of his shirt. His voice remained soft, and setting the book back on the table, he invited agreement where there might otherwise be none. "We are all seekers in our own way, don't you think?" The expression on his face was tranquil enough to put Niles at ease even as he cupped both his hands around the younger man's face. Niles returned the man's gaze, then slowly pulled away. Massinissa Alilouche smiled, and continued their conversation by asking, "As a student at the university you are hoping to discover what, a greater understanding of the world or of yourself? Perhaps a combination of the two, for they are rather difficult to separate, like salt from the sea, no?"

Niles shifted sideways on his pillow. "The two together, yes."

"A sense of Truth?"

"A small sampling."

"It is all we can ask," the man rolled his head forward again. "And yet, sometimes truth involves more than forgiveness, no?"

Niles chose not to answer, did not understand why his host had taken this tact the last few sessions, and annoyed, clasped his fingers together tightly. Seeing this, Massinissa Alilouche leaned down from his chair and undid Niles' grip, in the process speaking again advisedly. "In this world, circumstance is often uncooperative. Life tends to demand swift adjustments and even a complete transformation from the person we might otherwise think ourselves to be."

No longer interested in debate, Niles wanted only to leave and reached for his backpack. Before getting up however, he couldn't help but respond, and said, "Sure, circumstance has a way of jerking and twisting everyone around, but people don't morph into something new because of it. That sort of reaction is too easy. A person has to know who they are and maintain themselves despite external factors." He gave as an example a baseball sitting inside a pitcher's glove, then heaved forward, and an instant later launched by the swing of a bat three hundred feet in the air. "At no time does the ball become anything but what it is despite how much circumstance changes."

"And yet men are not balls, are they?" Massinissa Alilouche challenged him again. "A man has the ability to choose his trajectory while a ball is there merely to be acted upon."

"But everything is acted upon, you said so yourself. Circumstance sets the tone. The reason I'm here is because of things that have happened and still I'm free to respond."

"With forgiveness."

"Yes."

"But your impulse after all this time has not brought you peace."

Niles got up and stepped toward the door. He was holding his pack against his chest, his otherwise slender frame puffing a bit in order to show how eager he was to invalidate Massinissa Alilouche's contentions. "No one said it would be easy," he grimaced, realizing as soon as he said as much how foolish he sounded, yet unable to think of anything else, he fell silent and made his exit, no longer trying to explain what exactly was difficult for him and had continued to allude him month after month for nearly three years running.

# CHAPTER 3

# THE WAY THINGS HAPPEN

"So?"

"What?"

"Bailey, you need to cooperate here."

"OK. I'm ready."

"Tell me what you remember."

"The dark."

"Of course."

"And the light."

"When?"

"In dreams."

"I see," Emmitt writes this down in his notes, his stubby fingers curled around his pen, his hand inspiring black ink to fill the page with a sequence of tilted marks assembled into words counted on to give meaning to whatever I have to say. "Tell me about your dreams then, Bailey."

"I thought you didn't subscribe to that sort of therapy, Dr. Speckridge."

"Fair enough. Tell me about the light."

"Elizabeth," I say.

"Yes."

"And Niles."

"They were in your dreams?"

"Again, Emmitt?"

"I'm trying to determine what happened."

"You want to know what I remember?"

"That's right."

"But wasn't I supposed to forget?"

"I see you haven't lost your ability to be difficult."

"A flaw in your theory?"

"To the contrary. Not all things are meant to change. I told you that before we started."

"The permanence of the particular."

"That's correct."

"And as for what needs to be unremembered?"

"You tell me."

And so I did.


At one-fifteen in the afternoon I was still in bed, my right hand tucked deep into the waistband of my shorts, the rope attached to my left wrist running through the floor and down to Niles' apartment. A Thursday, I didn't have to teach though I was scheduled to meet with my committee at three o'clock to discuss the status of my dissertation and explain once more the cause of its delay. (After so many years of carrying on as a contented if uninspired adjunct, with false promises to complete my dissertation in Art History while playing piano a few nights a week at Dungee's Bar and Grill, these occasional demands that I do more, when nothing suited me better, were unwelcome distractions in my otherwise safe routine.) I shifted onto my side, my back to the space where Elizabeth used to sleep. The emptiness was palpable, the idea of getting up too hard; I stared at the floor and the shadows that filled my apartment.

After a few minutes, I managed to untie my wrist from the

rope and go off to shower. My apartment was small, with a space for the bed, a desk and chair and books, a kitchenette, bathroom, and closet. The dresser was set along the far wall, while to the left, beside the stereo and otherwise dominating the entire space was Aunt Germaine's old upright piano. Teak with pale white ivory, the piano was perfectly tuned and reasonably unblemished, carried up the stairs several years ago by six friends inspired by offerings of whiskey and ice served in jelly jars and plastic 7Eleven cups.

I dressed in a T-shirt and jeans, then sat at the piano and played a slow version of "You Don't Know What Love Is" while thinking of Elizabeth. Angry with myself, in order to become all the more miserable and as I deserved, I played next Dinah Washington's "Bad Luck." The tune had history, never failed to inspire the worst memories, beginning with the night I was forced to wait later than usual for my father to come get me from my Aunt Germaine's. I fell asleep on the couch in her den, waking in the dark to angry voices from the front lawn. "Get out of the way, Germaine."

"I will not."

"This doesn't have anything to do with you."

"Doesn't it though?"

"I said move."

"I'm not letting Bailey go home with you, Frank. If you can't show up sober and at a reasonable hour, I'll have the boy move in here permanently with me."

"Take him, yes!" my father wasted no time responding. "That's perfect. Why don't you? After all that's happened to me, why should I care?"

"What's that?" my aunt in turn. "How can you stand there and think about what's happened to you when the boy's lost his mother?"

"His mother, don't I know," my father pounded his fist against his chest. "And what have I lost?"

"We're not discussing you, we're talking about Bailey."

"A child. Children are born to leave their mothers. It's my loss that goes on forever."

"My God. You can't be serious."

"You know damn well it's true."

"I know nothing of the kind."

"Hell. Hell!"

I turned over on the couch and buried my head beneath my arms in an attempt to drown away the noise, but I could still hear the thunder of my father's voice as he shouted outside, "What is it you think he wants from me? What does he expect? Goddamn, Germaine, Maria's gone!" he howled this as if such had never been said before. "The best thing I can do is let Bailey see the world for what it is. We have no control. Fuck! I can't do anything more for him. There isn't any more, do you understand?"

The sting of my father's howl made me ache, and angry, I tried to think of something equally cruel to say, a weapon I could wield to let him know how disgusted and hurt I was by all his self-possession and singular sense of grief. Unable to put such feelings into words however, I chose another plan, something intended to shock my father into silence. As he rushed from the lawn and stormed up the steps, I hurried to the piano where I played "Bad Luck" from start to finish. My father burst into the room and nearly fell over. Germaine in the doorway covered her mouth in complete amazement as my hands moved expertly across the keys, filling the air with lush, plaintive tones, introducing riffs and flats and harmonic minors exactly as my mother taught me. (In heeding my mother's advice, I had kept my talent a secret, preserving in this way the intimacy we shared while practicing only on the sly and when no one else was around.) As I finished, I came from the bench and stood in front of my father. His face was gape mouthed and pale as he said, "Bailey?" and louder then, "Bailey!" releasing a loud laugh, his huge arms swinging above his head as he asked me then to play more. "More! More!"

But I refused.

I moved off, defiant and cheerless, determined to show my father what it felt like to be denied, and shaking my head slowly from side to side, I declined his request absolutely.

In the days following, my father hounded me with constant appeals and supplication, insisting my talent was not the sort of thing I could keep to myself, that such was obviously a gift from my mother, and "It's her talent you're keeping from me. It's all we have!"

I feared his harass, yet resented more his sudden interest in me and continued to spurn his petition. "Leave him be, Frank," Germaine tried to intervene as my father came each evening now to my aunt's house and chased me about, demanding I play for him. "You must!" he insisted, becoming enraged each time I said no. One night he arrived in a particularly foul temper, and as I refused him again he stormed off to the garage, returning a moment later with a hammer, threatening to pound the piano to pulp if I didn't do as I was told. Such intimidation produced yet another nervous rejection—"No, Daddy"—at which point my father pulled six long nails from his pocket and charged the piano with menace. "Damn you then!" he wailed and drove the first nail down into the lid. "So help me God! If you won't play for me, there'll be no more! Do you understand? If not for me, you won't play at all!"

Germaine pushed my father out of the house and across the lawn, yelling, "You're a no-good drunk, Frank! A no-good drunk!" The nail was removed, though the mark remained, and for the next several weeks I did my best to avoid my father. My effort proved in vain however as, undaunted, my father persisted in his demand, waking me in the middle of the night, tormenting me with threats and woeful pleading, referring to the world in tones of bleak and black reflection while speaking of my talent in forlorn references to his dear Maria. Such abuse took its toll and I turned for solace to my brother.

"Shit," Tyler laughed, a burly boy back then, man-sized at thirteen, built like a stevedore with meaty arms, barrel legs, and the square-jaw look of a brawler. "What did you think would happen?"

"Yes, but?"

"You never should have played for him."

"But . . ."

"What? Hell, Bailey. Do you really think he'll leave you alone now?" Here then was the sympathy I received, and disheartened, I retreated even as my brother called out, "I'm just telling you, for Christ's sake." We were, even then, quite different, Tyler and I. While I spent my time after school with Aunt Germaine, Tyler was six years older and balked at such supervision. His mood following our mother's death was truculent and brutal. He fell in with the wrong crowd and undertook a course of serious mischief: petty thefts and break-ins, the trashing of parked cars, shooting pellets into the heads of dogs, uprooting mailboxes and traffic signs, twice slipping into warehouses to see what he could cart off, and once entering a mini-mart with the stock end of a rifle tucked into his belt. "For a laugh," he said and cursed the cops who came to get him.

Absent our father's succor, and with our mother dead and buried, I retreated into myself, became timorous and developed a stutter. Tyler, in turn, stormed about, at one point dragging his mattress, his clothes and lamp, and forty-pound dumbbells down to the basement in order to separate himself from all things familiar. Confused by his distance and how he refused to demonstrate a fraternal interest in getting through our mother's death together, I tried just the same to distinguish between Tyler's rage and that of our father. Unlike the barriers our father put up with thorns and thistle meant to do damage, Tyler's hostility seemed a nervous defense, more fear than animus and like a sad dog barking.

Three days after I spoke with my brother, I was surprised when he showed up at Germaine's and hollered from the curb, "Tell Aunt Fat you're coming with me." A minute later I was giving chase through the neighborhood and out across the avenues where Tyler quickened his pace, cut down Ninth Street before disappearing into the shadows of the alley behind the old Haptree Theater. (A one-time hot spot for musical reviews and cabaret revivals, the Haptree closed years ago as the demographics of the city changed and audiences sought out different forms of entertainment.) Most of the windows were broken and boarded over, the blue paint peeled and the brick beneath grizzled and crumbling. Tyler stood atop a wooden crate and shoved back the boards. "Come on, come on," he climbed inside and waited for me to scramble after him.

A musty smell of rotten wood and dirt greeted us as we moved behind the stage. I followed the beam from Tyler's flashlight toward the basement stairs where a labyrinth of corridors stretched out in front. The lower halls were filled with broken furniture, additional crates, and garbage. Tyler stopped at the end of the final passage and handed me the light. "Go on, go on," he pointed to an open door and pushed me through. I aimed the light at the walls, which were bare and milky grey. The cement floor was cracked down its center as if an enormous force had tried to gain entrance from below, and taking another step inside I stared over to where a solid form caught the light.

An upright piano at least five feet high, larger than Aunt Germaine's, built of dark wood with a long bench and extensive sounding board sat against the wall. "They must have used it for rehearsals and didn't figure it worth carrying up when the theater closed," Tyler said. "Go on, play something."

Amazed, both excited and startled by the gesture, nervous—for this was the first time Tyler asked to hear me perform—I walked to the bench and set the light on the floor and tested the keys by playing "Take Five," which I thought my brother would like. The piano didn't cooperate initially and a few of the notes were off, though taken as a whole the instrument worked better than expected. My hands moved in perfect consonance with the music, my effort echoing nicely off the walls. As I finished, I turned to look for Tyler but he was already gone.

That night I lay in bed thinking about my brother's gift and the unexpected kindness extended. I was deeply touched and at the same time confused by Tyler's charity, which seemed to incorporate into its benevolence the joy of deceiving my father. Early the next morning I gathered up what few dollars I had and bought a box of candles before returning to the Haptree Theater. The flickering glow made the space feel warm and liquid, and seated again, I treated myself to a glorious recital. Over the next several days I cleaned the piano's wires and pads with oil and rags, removed the dust from its wood, and used toothpicks to scrape the grot from between the keys. I knew nothing about tuning and was ignorant of the physical intricacies involving the piano's construction, but the notes somehow returned to form the longer I played, and more comfortable by myself in the basement than I was at first, I explored dozens of different compositions exactly as my mother taught me.

Tyler joined me from time to time and on such occasions I switched from classical to rock, Aerosmith and Utopia or something else heard blaring from his stereo the night before. The piano sounds carried remarkably well throughout the hollow of the old theater, and Tyler would wander about, returning every now and then with some new treasure found: a costume from an old production, a sailor's cap or leather boot, a woman's silk undergarment, or rubber knife used as a prop.

At the end of summer, I began coming to the theater straight from school, contriving stories for my aunt while eating apples and carrots as my evening meal. That October my father was working on a minor Kendrecke Construction project, patching the roof of an apartment complex on Ninth Street. His drinking and erratic fits of temper had forced the company to assign him lesser jobs, far from the days he helped build the Ryse & Fawl and danced on girders five hundred feet above the city. For dinner he bought a half-pint of whiskey at a nearby party store and slipped into the alley behind the Haptree where he drank down several shots. At first, he must have thought the sound he heard was only in his head, a soft retelling of "Blue Gardenia," faint and echoed yet recognizable, sliding up from beneath him somewhere, but after a minute the melody changed, became yet another old favorite—Dinah Washington's "Bad Luck," of course—and oddly certain, he followed the sound to the boarded window, pushed aside the planks, and traced the music down.

Absorbed in my playing, I didn't hear my father moving through the hall and continued to perform even as he came to stand just outside the door. I suspect, in hindsight, that he was captivated again by my facility, as mesmerized then as he was several months ago at Aunt Germaine's, and wound up melancholy as he heard "Stardust" and no doubt thought of my mother singing. The whiskey in his chest and music in his head confused him, and yet before he could speak and tell me things he hadn't said since my mother died, his shadow fell over the first row of candles. I stopped playing and spun around.

What else was I to assume as my father took a quick step toward me? I'd already recoiled and toppled backwards off the bench, crying out, "I'm sorry! I'm sorry! I won't play anymore!" while landing on a row of candles which hissed and burned my hip and arm with hot wax. I heard my father say my name, softly first and then louder, but I paid no attention to what he was trying to tell me and squirmed away as he rushed forward and kicked through the remaining candles until the room went black. I rolled toward the far wall, hoping to crawl around and get out the door, only somehow he found me and scooped me up before I could escape, pulling me in against his chest, trying to quiet me and muffle my cries, saying something I couldn't understand, his words coming out in a tangle, the loudness pitched above my pleading, the sound unclear as he implored me to, "Listen, please!"

The moment seemed to go on forever, both of us trapped in the smoke from the extinguished candles and the darkness thick, until suddenly we were falling, dropped to the floor by a blow I didn't see delivered and with my father crumbling as I slipped off and tucked myself beside the piano. A second later the glow of Tyler's flashlight filled the room, freezing everyone in the aftershock. Tyler set his flashlight down and waited.

"All right," the earlier spell broken, no longer interested in conciliation, all the clashes had in the time since our mother's death, battles over my father's distance and maddening self-pity, incidents with social service, and Tyler being brought home by the police, culminated then with my father setting his feet and signaling with his fingers curling in and out of his palm. "You want this? Come on. Come on."

Tyler took the first step but it was our father who made the swiftest advance, charging as all his vitriol and grief returned, howling, "Damn you both!" he delivered a vicious blow to the center of Tyler's chest. A series of wild punches followed. Tyler was served by the agility of youth, his ability to sidestep and duck and break our father's hold. Still, he was a boy, and however large and powerfully built, he did not yet possess a man's strength, was not as ruthless or desperate from age, was outweighed and out-muscled as the battle swept across the floor. I watched from beneath the piano as Tyler stumbled and our father cocked his fist and struck another blow that staggered my brother severely. He fell and was pinned to the ground by knees pressing down, our father reaching for the light which he drew above his head, screaming, "I'll kill you! I will!" stopping only as I jumped and caught his arm.

In struggling against my weight, he saw Tyler's face below, heard the music in his head no doubt, and suffered a trembling in his hand. For a moment all was still, like a wave before it breaks, but then Tyler shoved our father off, and snatching back the light, cursed savagely, as fierce and final as the punches just thrown. "Fuck you!" He was determined not to weep in front of us, resigned to say nothing else, and cursed again, "Fuck!" With the blood on his lip and a welt rising beneath his left eye, he turned and ran out the door, taking with him the light, leaving everything afterward in the dark.

He did not return home again, moved out of the house that same night, lied about his age, and got a job at Penderson's Lumber while renting a room across town with Turk Nerstle, a thimblerigger ten years Tyler's senior who ran a series of card games and other assorted enterprises on the east side of Renton. (There was in Turk's line of work much use for a burly boy as tightly wound as Tyler and he was more than happy to take him in.) After the events at the Haptree, my father and I occupied our house in a steely silence. Left on my own, I developed a stoic resilience, learned to harden myself against all future tides, to take what money I needed for food and clothes from my father's wallet, to cook spaghetti and hamburgers, bake potatoes, and boil corn. I saw Tyler infrequently, and then not at all.

Later that winter, on the anniversary of my mother's death, my father got very drunk and spread himself out flat in the driveway while the clouds produced a bone-chilling snow. I stared from the window, then went outside and screamed for him to get up, while he whistled songs Maria used to sing—"I Put a Spell on You," "Bad Luck," and "A Bad Case of the Blues." Eventually one of the neighbors came and helped drag my father inside.

Aunt Germaine kept a watchful eye over me but her involvement was itself a reminder of how terribly wrong things had gone, and for the most part I kept to myself. I could have played piano at my aunt's, my father didn't bother me anymore in that regard, but I continued going to the Haptree every day until the property was sold and the building torn down. "I was sixteen," I tell Emmitt, and describe how I stood across the street and watched as the huge iron ball swung on its crane and crashed through the front, the brick shattering and the beams collapsing straight into the basement. Later that night, I snuck into the high school, where I sat and played pieces by Chopin and Dave Brubeck, Tchaikovsky, and Ellington, Steven Tyler and Henry Dixon Cowell, waiting to forget everything and become absorbed by the sound.

"And afterward?" Emmitt as always wants to know more, to force me to press further and connect then to now. I skip ahead, let him know how little changed over the next few years.

"By the time I entered the university, leaving my father's madness at eighteen, outfitted with a suitcase and duffel, a small student loan, partial scholarship, and minor allowance from my aunt, I wanted only to be left in peace. I came to enjoy my new life, my classes and lectures, the museums and concerts, friends made and women dated. As a junior, determined to savor these days, I reduced my course load to a minimum number of hours, and playing piano then at Dungee's to make ends meet, I delayed graduation further by taking every other semester off. I wrote my only published article at twenty-three, an interpretive piece on the paintings of David Bomberg, which appeared in a small journal. The essay enhanced my application to graduate school and served as a barometer by which others mistakenly measured my ambition.

"I didn't complete my master's and class work for my doctorate until my student loans became due, and landing a position as a graduate instructor, managed to hold on to the job based in large part on cajoling my students into good reviews and misdirecting my committee. Resisting then the normal course, enamored of sloth and languor and wary of disappointment, I did what I could to make myself happy, moved placidly from day to day, watching with good humor while classmates competed for positions, applied for postdocs and courted professors' favors, vying for recommendations, desperate to graduate with honors and advance their careers. Impervious to their success, I invited friends for drinks and sang hearty well wishes as they ran off to interview for jobs in cities they'd never visited before and packed their bags with great uncertainty and nervous last regards. 'Be happy,' I raised my glass in toast of nothing, and after they were gone, turned back to my piano and played a merry song."

# CHAPTER 4

# COME TOGETHER

Leaving Massinissa Alilouche's apartment, Niles headed east in the direction of campus. A hot day, he considered catching a bus but eventually decided another hike would do him good. Along the way he thought about the envelope Massinissa Alilouche had given him, considered everything the man had said about the consequence of circumstance and situations impossible to control, and tracing back to a point prior to the collapse of the Reedum & Wepe, he concentrated on the image of Jeana, and then his father, P. Harlen Kelly, who, after two marriages without an heir, still anxious at the age of fifty-six for a child, paid a surrogate to whom Niles was born.

The process was practical, logical, and efficient, as far as P. Kelly was concerned. After a sequence of interviews and tests to gauge intellect, character, and genetic makeup, a candidate was hired, paid a specific sum in advance and a large sum upon delivery. (The only condition was that the exchange could not be manufactured in a test tube but had to take "the old-fashioned way," P. Kelly convinced the vigor of a good fuck would do the child better than seeds and eggs slipped from cold plastic onto glass.) There was no further contact with the woman after that, no visitations nor mentioning of her name by the father to the son. Cared for by nannies, Niles was raised under his father's watchful eye. A firm taskmaster with old-school convictions rooted deep in Protestant ethics, no one doubted how the senior Kelly would rear his son.

Niles was enrolled at an early age for lessons in mathematics, history and politics, economics and high finance. He accepted his lot with every intention of making his father proud and did not expect his attitude to change as he entered his teens. Inspired nonetheless by books not assigned in school, by experiences witnessed and had, conversations with friends and one particular au pair whose pierced navel and green turtle tattoo were exposed at the asking, he came to question his father's views. As a sophomore in high school his interest in philosophy took hold, the ideas of Schopenhauer, Kierkegaard, and Sartre and Camus, works dismissed by his father as collective pap.

"What's this?" P. Kelly summoned Niles to his study, demanding an explanation for the alteration to his curriculum and why he quit reading Phyllis Deane and Adam Smith.

"I appreciate the books you gave me," Niles answered, "but I like these better," a reply which caused his father to snap, "Nonsense. A man must stake his claim!" P. Kelly sat in his straightback leather chair, red and large as a throne. "A person can't go about willy-nilly pursuing whatever he likes. You can't spend the dividends before you buy the stock, and you can't buy the stock until you've earned the cash. Anything else is putting the cart before the horse, which is just plain foolish and won't get you anywhere at all."

To such advice, Niles built his argument slowly, his demeanor in his father's presence deferential and cautiously contradicting. "I understand," he began, "but I thought I might pursue my own interests for a while."

"Romantic prattle," P. Kelly rejoined, and determined to

educate the boy before such childish balderdash became permanently set in his brain, he barked, "You're thinking short-term. The journey is all well and fine as long as a man knows where he's going." He stared at his son, who had his mother's small mouth and fair, porcelain features, wild brown hair, and green eyes, though where he acquired his guilelessness the old man had no idea. He'd always imagined a big-boned son moving powerfully through the hallways of Kelly & Kline, a man whose physical presence alone inspired awe and enhanced the genius he was sure to possess, and yet here was Niles, all narrow shouldered and thin limbed, a minor figure as innocent as a pup, so light framed that one stiff breeze could easily knock him into next week. Befuddled by the boy's quixotic bent, he set his aging hands on the arms of his chair and extended his neck like an old lion, growling, "In order to make a mark in this world, a man must earn a sufficient amount of capital. Money is the root to all progress. The world demands its sustenance. There is work to be done and how selfish for a boy with your opportunities to bring it philosophy instead."

"I understand," Niles repeated, "and that's fine for you. I respect your accomplishments, but I don't see making money as my ultimate ambition."

"Spoken like a child born to wealth who can afford to believe having cash in his pocket is immaterial," P. Kelly continued to argue against his son. "Your innocence never ceases to amaze me, Niles. You think people don't need lucre to survive, that the world turns on an axle that isn't greased? All things, including charity, are driven by the flow of cash. Just try going two days without a dollar in your pocket and see where your romantic notions get you." He was, as always, firm with his son, and for further emphasis said, "This is America. A man with opportunities such as you've been afforded has a responsibility to the world around him. Failing to fulfill one's promise is a sin against our very liberty. Our very country. It's a sin against God!"

Such arguments went on this way, back and forth throughout Niles' high school years. At one point P. Kelly resorted to presenting secret research and quoted a paragraph from Niles' favorite writer. "What I've noticed is that there's a kind of spiritual snobbism in certain superior beings who think that money isn't required for peace of mind. Which is stupid, of course, which is false, and to a certain degree cowardly. Weak men renounce what is theirs by right of birth as a way of appearing great but then such men are all frauds." All of which Niles took in stride and explained to his father that he was misinterpreting Camus's intent, a claim P. Kelly rebuffed with a bark of "Nonsense! I know what I read!"

Upon entering his final semester of high school, having already been accepted at a top university where his father assumed he would study economics, Niles announced he planned to pursue a more liberal concentration in philosophy and literature. Immediately, P. Kelly threatened to withhold his son's tuition. "You're wasting your time filling your head with so much balderdash and babble. Why should I pay for your foolishness? If you're convinced money bears no significance to your needs, go ahead and study what you like. Put yourself through school. You'll only wind up proving my point by having to work for what you want." In placing money at the center of Niles' revolt, P. Kelly believed he'd won the argument, and was stunned when the boy chose that moment to reveal he'd applied on his own to the University of Renton and that he was prepared to accept a scholarship where he would major in his chosen field while working odd jobs to make ends meet.

That summer, Niles moved onto campus. Several months went by when he and his father didn't speak. He finished his first semester at the university, and just as P. Kelly decided things had gone on long enough and sought to reconcile the situation, convincing himself that Niles' undergraduate studies were immaterial in the long run and a graduate program in business was still to come, he made arrangements to reinstate financial assistance to the boy only to discover things by then had gone from bad to worse.

At the campus bookstore, at the start of second semester, while buying Thales of Miletus in paperback along with a fresh supply of notebooks and pens, Niles stood in the cashier line with a young woman purchasing Robert Coover and John Hawkes for a class on postmodern literature. Typically reserved around pretty girls, he couldn't resist and wound up commenting on the books in her stack, hoping to impress her and going so far as to mention having read Hawkes last summer, recalling a line from *Death, Sleep, and the Traveler*: "The sleep of reason produces demons, but I love my sleep."

Jeana corrected him, smiling in that disabling way she had. "But I love my demons," she said.

The phone rang as I was sitting at my piano, and reaching toward the table, I hoped as always it might be Liz but then I heard the voice of Dr. Freidrich's secretary reminding me of today's meeting. I waited a minute, then headed outside, covering the familiar walk to the School of Art in fifteen minutes. As a musician, which is to say given the gift I was born with and as my mother taught me early on, in light of all the conflict my playing piano caused, I could not come in any purposeful way to make music my career; this though I love piano and can scarcely go a day without sitting down to practice and perform. Instead, I turned to Art as a solution to my otherwise vague sense of career.

My first exposure to the Moderns came in the days just after my mother's death when, sitting in my Aunt Germaine's front room, I was kept company by a print of Jean Dubuffet's *Corps de Dame*. The work was a peculiar piece all done up in startling shades of violet and blue and pink, the bloated figure of a woman with the most beautifully grotesque arms expanding slenderly outward through a backdrop of pale purple sea. I stood in front of the print, fascinated by its strange appeal, hoping at any minute the woman might scoop me up in a warm embrace. (When Aunt Germaine discovered my preoccupation she took the painting down, thus guaranteeing my interest in Art forever.) In my classes, having studied on my own before entering the university, covering most of the Moderns, Bauhaus and Dada, Cubists, Impressionists and Abstract Expressionists, Picasso and Morris Louis, Gorky and Avery, Klee and Pollack, Diebenkorn, Bacon, and Miró, I could explain the subtle variances and influences in pieces as diverse as Jean-Paul Riopelle's *Encounter* and Jules Olitski's *Feast,* and simultaneously impress and infuriate professors with opinions often in conflict with their own. The work I turned in was first-rate however, and earned high marks on all projects, papers, and exams. Despite my minor ambition in ever actually pursuing a career, I moved through the challenges of academia with a snakelike charm.

The School of Art is an antiquated, box-shaped building with six long cement steps leading up to an unadorned arch. A flat inlay of off-yellow tiles worn smooth as glass ran through the halls and inside a series of moderately sized classrooms, studios, and offices stationed in random sequence up and down the four separate floors. In the basement was a minor auditorium for showing films and slides, a storage area and library where research documents and manuscripts were housed. Built in 1919, the brick building was the third oldest structure on campus, tucked between the new Engineering annex, the Department of Social Humanities (SHsshh for short), and the east wing of the Graduate Library.

I walked across State Street and sat outside on one of the wooden benches, watching absently as groups of students hurried off in different directions. I thought about my upcoming meeting, wondering as always what would happen if I failed to show, and debated heading over to the Music School and looking for Liz. The possibility of doing precisely this unsettled me however, and anxious, I distracted myself by going through the contents of my backpack. Inside were none of the promised chapters for my dissertation but rather the following: a deck of cards and cigarettes, one harmonica and two plastic lighters, Knut Hamsun's *Hunger,* three new reviews of recent gallery shows and exhibitions, a pack of gum and pad of paper, six pens, two pencils, one Hi-Liter, a transistor radio, a pocket watch, composition paper and Kleenex, a small blue phone book, and 97 cents in loose change.

I rooted around inside my bag, searching for nothing in particular, waiting for the moment I felt ready enough to go off to my meeting. An old plastic bookmark with a picture of Robert Motherwell on the front caught my eye and I pulled it out. The marker was a gift from Niles, given to me recently when I stopped by to see him at Ebertine Books. We met almost five years ago when Niles audited a class I was teaching on the Postmoderns. At the time, he was looking for a bit of constructive diversion from his studies in Philosophy, and wrote his final paper on the artist Alberto Burri, an Italian army doctor captured and sent to a Texas prison camp in 1944 where he began painting works of abstract expressionism composed of old sacks and rags he said reminded him of the bloodied bandages he saw too much of during the war. About Burri's art Niles wrote: "His use of personal materials grounds his work with an intimacy unique to the time, and in this way makes his canvases at one with the universe's most irrepressible forces."

We became friendly and spoke often after class. I was only a few years older, and despite my status as Niles' instructor, the initial formality between us immediately broke down. We met for drinks and late-night conversation, and at some point Niles introduced me to Jeana. In the short time I knew her, she came across as bright, sincere, and vibrant, devoid of vanity and pretention, dauntless as an ancient force of nature, and very much in love with Niles. The three of us got together for lunch, for cheap dinners, and to check out the clubs around town. On nights I played piano at Dungee's, they sometimes came and listened to me perform. I enjoyed their company, was happy for Niles, and devastated the day Jeana died.

I went with Niles to her funeral—Jeana's family lived in Chicago—and in doing so, our friendship acquired a sense of permanence. Late the following summer, I mentioned my plan to take a bus trip to Chicago and check out a new Rothko retrospective and Niles said he'd like to come along. We rented a room at the Landmark Motel, and hungry from our trip, decided to get something to eat. Niles showered first and changed his clothes, putting on a pair of pressed slacks, shined shoes, and clean dress shirt. It was the first time since the funeral that I saw him in anything other than jeans, and when he said, "There's a stop I'd like to make first," I wasn't surprised and agreed to go with him.

We took a cab across town. The cemetery was surrounded by black iron fencing, the tall gate open as we drove through. A thin woman in a white dress, her blonde hair done in a series of French braids, moved between a row of headstones, managing to push a middle-aged man in a wheelchair. The evening was cool.

A small plane flew overhead. Niles knelt beside Jeana's plot for several minutes as I hung back by the cab. A half hour later we were sitting inside a restaurant across the street from our motel. Much of our meal went by in silence and we returned to our room shortly after midnight. I stayed up a bit to read, but at some point fell asleep, and when I woke later to turn off the light, I saw Niles walking from his bed across the room toward the window.

In the time since Jeana's death, Niles had suffered all the more classic bouts of depression. He lost his appetite, was distracted and sullen, had a tendency to disappear on long walks, and once flew to Florida, and later New Jersey, for three days without saying a word. He wore darker clothes, long-sleeved T-shirts and jeans winter and summer, was disinclined to look at other women, and turned an unsightly shade of grey whenever something unexpected reminded him of what he'd lost. Even with this however, I was never overly concerned. He remained in school, kept his job at Ebertine Books, resumed his focus on his studies and other outside interests, and seemed to be making the necessary adjustment. As such, I'd no reason to feel alarmed as I watched him move past me in a pair of baggy blue pajamas, his curled hair stacked atop his head, his hands slack and hanging down at his sides. He walked in a flat, uneven shuffle, his bare feet dragging softly across the floor as he went to stand and stare out the window.

I said his name, studied his features in profile against the mix of shadow and moonlight, whispered again "Niles?" and finally understanding the situation, got up and positioned myself behind his shoulders, tapping left and right in order to guide him back to bed. No sooner did I return to my own bed than Niles was up and walking the same as before. I waved at him this time, causing him to stop suddenly and say, "Sorry. Did I wake you?"

"Funny I was just about to ask you."

"Me? Why?"

"Where are you going now?"

"To the bathroom," he looked at me a moment. "What do you mean now?"

"You were sleepwalking."

"Was I?" I watched him as he went and sat in the chair.

"You don't seem surprised."

"It's nothing."

"You do this often?"

"Occasionally. Where did you find me?"

"By the window."

"What was I doing?"

"Standing and staring outside."

Niles glanced down at his hands. "It's nothing," he repeated. "I'm a poor sleeper, that's all."

"Lots of people are poor sleepers. Not everyone takes a stroll around the room."

"Somnambulism's a funny thing."

"Are you telling me this is some sort of affliction you have?"

He pulled at his pajama sleeve. "It's a condition I'm apparently predisposed to experience."

"Meaning something has to trigger it."

"Yes."

"What?"

"It would take too long to explain."

"Is it neurological or psychological?"

"That depends."

"Jeana?"

"It isn't that simple."

"You're here in Chicago. We went to the cemetery. There has to be a certain amount of anxiety."

Again, "It's more complicated. There's more to it than that."

"More than what? What do you mean?" I waited then, half expecting Niles to launch into a philosophical treatment on the subject, comparing his somnambulism to a quixotic quest in which his pacing through the darkened hours was a hunt for lost love transformed into ghosts, but he surprised me yet again, and standing, removed his pajama top, exposing a series of welts and bruises, punctures and scars and burns, old and new avulsions covering the surface of both arms and the whole of his belly and chest. I stared at his torn and fractured flesh, discolored in various shades of red and pink and brown as if gnawed by the hot fangs of some savage beast, and jumping up, I grabbed hold of Niles' wrists, turned his arms over, and then finding his eyes screamed louder and louder still, "Christ, Niles! Shit! What the hell! What is all this? Jesus! What the fuck is going on?"

Love is this. With Niles and Jeana, the conversation at the campus bookstore led to coffee and later a movie. They fell into dating, took a summer class together—a seminar on Parmenides—and found jobs working within a block of one another downtown, Niles at Ebertine Books and Jeana at the Hungry Heart Café. When told his son had a girlfriend, P. Kelly assumed nothing more serious than a bit of hand-holding in the balcony of the Main Theater. Still, he was curious and summoned Niles to his office where he asked about the relationship. Niles' answer was more than his father expected as he confessed then to being in love.

"At your age?" P. Kelly could not decide whether to laugh or lament his son's innocence, yet thinking perhaps the girl might get Niles to see that a man seriously smitten could not fritter away his education at the expense of a career, he reacted to the news with instruction to bring the girl around.

A dinner was arranged for Saturday. P. Kelly sat at the head of the table in his enormous dining room where his son and girlfriend were served swordfish and pasta by two young women in tight black dresses and shiny white shoes. Forewarned of the elder Kelly's tendency to be confrontational, Jeana remained composed and fielded all questions deftly as Niles' father pried her for information about herself, challenged her views on politics and business while dismissing her interest in philosophy as a "hobby at best." He assumed an imperious and irrepressible tone, was dissenting when their conversation turned to the writings of Jeremy Bentham who, as a social empiricist, championed a utilitarian ethic P. Kelly refused to countenance. "Cries for the common good are the lament of the weak," he said. "The vanguard of those who haven't the grit to prosper in a free-market system. I for one am convinced the concept of every man for himself is the single most significant factor in making America great. Why should I entertain utilitarian ideals when history shows it's always the work of the few which contributes most to the social fabric? Why shouldn't the greatest achievers draw the largest benefit?"

Jeana smiled in that offsetting way of hers, and extending her arms slowly in order to take in the size of the room, allowed her gaze to fall back on P. Kelly as she said, "And what is the largest benefit? This?"

Ahh, yes then. ("This!") The father shot his son a look, incredulous and disappointed, peering out with firm denouncement as if to say, "So this is the girl I'm supposed to approve of?" (Niles, in turn, was well pleased by the accuracy of Jeana's retort, and lifting his chin to his father's glare, answered in his own way, "But, of course!" What a disappointment! If such nonsense had to happen—and P. Kelly was not so old as to forget the indelicate ways of the heart—he had hoped Niles would fall for a sensible coed with her studies in business, premed or pre-law, a girl who'd speak to Niles in concrete terms about the future, exorcising all ridiculous notions while opening his eyes to the necessity of securing a legitimate career. But this girl? She with her faded jeans and tousled hair, her own concentration in philosophy and papers written on George Santayana's "animal faith" and Voltaire's liberal mores, her ears pierced several times—and God knows what else!—this creature gave a boy like Niles courage to cling to impractical pursuits while complicating the process of eventually getting him to Kelly & Kline. What was a father to do then when his son fell hard for someone who dressed like a refugee, who parroted such ludicrous prattle regarding happiness and the journey toward contentment, who performed yoga by moonlight, went braless and barefoot, ate vegetable stir-fry in plum sauce from a white Styrofoam cup, and possessed no more insight into the real world than a six-year-old child?

The summer before their junior year, Jeana and Niles rented an apartment together on the north side. Excited by the raw amazement of their commitment, they bought a futon and two chairs secondhand, mixed their prints and books together in the front room, hung their clothes in the closet, and set their shoes side by side at the front door. Niles phoned his father in order to pass on his new address, and while he intended nothing more than an innocent chat, their conversation quickly dissolved into dissidence as he mentioned his plan to apply for the master's program in philosophy with the hope of teaching one day.

"So you want to spend your life regurgitating useless blather?" P. Kelly scoffed. "You're building a house of cards." He was by this point convinced his son's decision had everything to do with "that girl," and requested again the boy come to his office where he offered his opinion unabated. "Your friend is doing you a disservice. Your affair is inappropriate and foolhardy. What exactly do you see in her? She's not the sort of person who's going to help you in any way. A man must be with a woman who knows her place, how to dress and smile, who understands the essence of a man's potential and encourages him to go forward and prosper, not obstruct his vision as she is obviously doing to you."

The office in which P. Kelly conducted his affairs was filled with antique furnishings, a mahogany desk and matching shelves, sea-blue Persian rug, plaques and pictures hung on expensive maple paneling. Niles shifted back on his heels, feeling ambushed, yet realizing how absurd it was for his father to try and lecture him about love, he clasped his hands behind his back, wondering which of the old man's wives succeeded best in fulfilling his needs, which of the eye candy he surrounded himself with these last twenty years, the trophy figures in hip-tight dresses and makeup applied by the pound, interchangeable girls who drained off the fluids in his cock-a-doodle-do and sated his ego when propped up beside him at restaurants and parties, and somewhat nervously, he asked, "With all due respect, Father, but who's waiting at home for you now?"

The old man drew himself up in his chair, all mercy vanished from his face, and speaking through his teeth, he set his tone with rigid regard. "Good for you, Niles. Let's get down to it then. I find the way you choose to live unacceptable. I had hoped you'd come to your senses by now and meet your responsibilities as a man who's been afforded every opportunity to prosper, but I was mistaken and can no longer wait for you to see your way clear. As far as I'm concerned, a degree in philosophy is a selfish indulgence. You go on and on about munificence and philanthropy, yet you tie your hands and limit your potential by refusing to earn real money. What can you expect to do on a teacher's salary? Don't you see spurning me this way for no reason other than to be with a girl is itself uncharitable? Think of all those likely to be hurt by your decision."

"I don't want to talk about this."

"Of course you don't. It's easy to feign austerity when you assume you'll be rich soon enough either way."

"That's unfair."

"Maybe so. What say we find out, shall we?"

Ten minutes later, Niles was walking home. The afternoon was warm and bright as he made his way to the metro and then across campus. He was eager to see Jeana, to be with her and confirm physically and forever the nonsense of his father's commination. He planned to say nothing, was prepared to let the entire incident pass, but the moment he walked in the door Jeana knew something was wrong, and when she asked he couldn't help but tell her.

His father's terms were cruel, and in listening to the conditions set forth, it occurred to him that only a person truly absent love could come up with such a caveat. "You are to sever your relationship with that girl, move out of the apartment, and have nothing more to do with her," P. Kelly said. "Upon finishing your undergraduate degree, you are to come work for me. Failure to do so will result in a complete disinheritance," the old man leaned back in his chair, his hands placed palms down in front of him. "You'll thank me one day. You've had your fling, now let it go. All this crazy indulgence."

At first Niles wanted to snap and tell his father exactly how depraved his threat was, to jump and shout "No!" and "Love!" but in the end he failed to do anything more than shake his head slightly once from side to side and back out of the office.

That night in bed, exhausted from the hours already spent going over the day's events, unable to sleep or give their minds any kind of rest, Jeana was first to wonder aloud how serious a hit their relationship had taken. Her concern did not involve asking why P. Kelly resented her so—the answer was irrelevant—but focused instead on the more pertinent issue, the potential problems which lay ahead in light of the sacrifice Niles was being asked to make. What sort of pressure would this put on the natural arc of their affair, and irrespective of their best intentions, was it love now or defiance that kept them together?

"Love." she said.

"Mmm?"

"Are you awake?"

"Yes."

Despite her desire not to give P. Kelly the satisfaction of taking his threat seriously, she couldn't help but ask, "What if your father's right? Suppose we're being selfish? Suppose you'll never be able to do as much with your life without the advantages he has to offer?"

Niles rolled onto his side. He regretted telling Jeana about his father's threat, realized he'd fallen prey to P. Kelly's plan of playing two sides against the middle, and still such was not the sort of news he could possibly keep secret, and in response to her concern, he said, "In order to do anything with my life I need to be happy, and I could never be happy without you." The words had to them a perfect pitch, a soft whisper delivered with certitude and even more convincing as he didn't try to touch her then or offer any further reassurance but allowed his declaration to gain momentum completely on its own. Such sentiment gave Jeana hope, and while it was easy to be overwhelmed by the magnitude of P. Kelly's menace, Niles' tone assured her there was greater risk in being made to part. The contentment she felt caused her to reach, secure enough to offer her own conviction against the unknown, and sliding over, she inspired a sweet and fluent unity, a merger wanting and silent in a warm and otherwise darkened landscape.

Early the next morning she showered as Niles lay in bed, and without telling him where she was going, caught the metro west to the Reedum & Wepe Building, where she hoped to speak with P. Kelly. She wasn't so much interested in getting him to change his mind, but wished to convey, as best she could, that in refusing to understand love, the father had only pushed himself further away from the son. She repeated Niles' name in her head, said as much out loud, ignoring the suitcase left unattended behind her, sliding up through the silver shaft until suddenly all words fell away, replaced by a virulent sound, thunderous and savage, a flash of light so bright its radiance extinguished everything in the whir which followed; walls of brick and grey, grey steel crumbling down, so strange and cold and unremitting as everything that was exploded into the belly of the storm.

The foot traffic along State Street was moderate in the late afternoon. Niles reached the Hungry Heart just after five and slid into a rear table where he ordered a tuna sandwich. His hip hurt from the fresh wound cut deep the other night, and adjusting his pants so they wouldn't rub against the gauze, he pulled the envelope Massinissa Alilouche had given him from his bag and sat for a time in review of the material.

He tugged at his right shirtsleeve, sliding the fabric over the heel of his hand, then surreptitiously raised his cuff in order to view the first sign of scar. Two weeks after the explosion at the Reedum & Wepe, with both Jeana and his father gone and his sense of reality effectively shattered, exhausted and falling into bed, he woke the next morning with a bloody welt just beneath his elbow. The contusion appeared out of nowhere, a freak occurrence Niles assumed, for somehow he must have banged his arm while sleeping and had no immediate explanation for the marble bookend in the center of the floor. He iced his arm and tried to give the matter no further thought. What a shock to discover another lesion four days later, a large blister on his stomach and a box of kitchen matches discarded in the hall.

Twice again in the next three weeks: a cut between his ribs made by the point of a corkscrew and a raw scrape on his shoulder where a metal file had rubbed in search of bone. Unwilling yet to confide his condition, he conducted his own research, found less than a handful of similar cases reported in the United States each year; young adults victimized by physical or psychological abuse who reenacted their trauma as a confused sort of catharsis. Articles by physicians, behavioral scientists, and psychologists offered no cure beyond intense analysis and prophylactic intervention. Niles accepted the findings for what they were worth, but otherwise believed the cause of his affliction was something altogether different from anyone else.

But what? He glanced again at his hands, the meek measure of his fingers confusing him, the incongruity of their capability between sleepfulness and waking. Back from Chicago, Bailey insisted Niles move into his building on Jefferson, so they could monitor his nights together. The flat below was vacant, the previous tenants relocating after spring exams, and following a period of trial and error—placing bells around the bed, locking away all potentially dangerous objects—Bailey thought to drill a hole in the floor and sleep with a rope tied between them. "This way, if you get up, I'll feel the tug and be able to stop you."

Their plan met with some initial success. Three and four and five times in those first weeks Bailey was summoned and rushed to Niles' apartment where he got him back to bed before any harm was done. Just as they reached a point where it seemed

Niles' troubles were well managed however, the world saw fit to remind them there were forces at play not to be fucked with and all the more resourceful symptoms of Niles' condition returned. He began untying the rope in his sleep and woke the next morning with fresh carnage. Even as they learned to fasten a better knot and took to using handcuffs and attached a lock and chain, Niles was still able to slip through by greasing the closed metal with spit, his determination never ending.

He finished his sandwich, reached for his wallet, and paid for his meal. For most of the last three years he had lived off his earnings from Ebertine Books and a minor account he established after receiving his inheritance; the codicil regarding Jeana rendered moot by the circumstance of P. Kelly's premature death. Once his father's will cleared probate, Niles chose to divest the bulk of his bequest and distributed cashier's checks to domestic violence shelters, inner-city clinics, libraries, and halfway houses for recovering addicts. He gave to the Sierra Club, Greenpeace, Affirmative Action, Amnesty International, and other organizations favoring gun control, solar energy, and free choice. Money orders were mailed to scientists and writers, philosophers and independent filmmakers, musicians and dancers, essayists, social theorists and teachers, along with funds distributed to families who lost loved ones in the devastation of the Reedum & Wepe. He established a permanent trust and had money mailed out year-round, sold off or otherwise donated the majority of his father's real estate holdings, and to those who asked said simply, "It's easier this way," which most everyone did not understand.

The café wasn't crowded, and sitting with the contents from Massinissa Alilouche's envelope spread out before him, Niles studied the information provided: a small map and a single name and address in Algiers, a second sheet of paper with a more detailed compilation of notes concerning the recent whereabouts and activities of the man Massinissa Alilouche believed Niles should locate. ("Forgiveness, my friend? Perhaps, yes. And yet, who is to say until one manages to confront his demons?") Niles considered tossing the pages in the trash, but instead sat for several more minutes, tracing the whole of the name with the tip of his right index finger, following each letter as they spelled out Osmah Said Almend, friend and roommate of Tyler Finne here before the blast.

# CHAPTER 5

# MEETINGS
# AND DEPARTURES

Emmitt shifts his pad around in order to resume writing, while I wait and watch, wondering how exactly the things I said are being interpreted. After a minute, I can't help but grow uncomfortable being so altogether exposed to Emmitt's analysis, and seeing the pen move across the page and darken the surface line by line with its own sense of permanence, I call out only half in jest, "Hold on, hold on. Don't get carried away. Hell, Emmitt, even I don't know that much."

I remained sitting on the bench outside the School of Art, the bookmark Niles gave me slipped back inside my pack, and checking the time I thought again about blowing off my committee and looking for Liz. Her leaving caused me to struggle more than I ever had at the end of a relationship, the glorious confusion we shared, the sweet din and clamor I could never quite turn into music replaced now by an irrepressible sort of alarm. Given what I saw happen to my father, I should have been more cautious when it came to falling in love, and for the longest time I was; my avoidance simplified by living in a uni-

versity town such as Renton where meeting women came easy.
Our streets were like the shelves of a handsome shop forever
replenished by the constant coming and going of graduate students, associate and full professors, guest lecturers, musicians,
painters and writers, researchers and retail workers, secretaries
and girls at loose ends just looking for some fun. Events on campus were scheduled day and night: readings and concerts, rallies
and parties, football games, carnivals and plays. My last affair
before Elizabeth was with a woman named Shannon Kaye, a student in Eastern Religions who taught Hindu meditation at the
community center where I enrolled on a whim.

Shannon had a lithe, athletic build, a sort of sinewy *Danae* by
Klimt, with sweet round breasts and thick, dark hair worn
loose and long. Her teaching included theories of Eastern philosophy combined with a series of introductory exercises in
Iyengar yoga. In class students were educated on the proper tech-
niques for breathing, how to sit and stand and hold their hands
in order to "suppress the activities of the body, mind, and will in
order that the self may realize its distinction from them and
attain liberation." Shannon lifted the definition from Merriam-
Webster and used it frequently in her instruction.

I enjoyed these Tuesday and Thursday sessions, and while I
failed to take Shannon's tutelage to heart and never once practiced the meditative exercises she assigned, I was aroused
nonetheless when she stood in front of the class and demonstrated the half-dozen drills which involved closing her eyes and
placing her fingers together beneath her chin, her body moving
like the flicker of a flame as she shimmied up and down. Two
weeks into the semester, I invited Shannon for a drink. She was
easy to talk with, the sort of person who enjoyed asking questions, was intrigued to learn I was pursuing a doctorate in Art
History, and mentioned her own favorite painters as Richard

Diebenkorn and Milton Avery. I described the poster of Avery's *Seated Blonde* which hung in my room and told her about my unfinished dissertation. At some point I got her phone number and called the next afternoon. We had dinner that night and saw one another frequently throughout the next several weeks.

At our twelfth class, every student received their mantra. Shannon explained how the mantra was our personal password into nirvana, that it was mystical and hypnotic and we should never share our word with anyone else. There were fourteen other students in the class and we all sat on the tiled floor, in a circle, our shoes off and legs crossed. Shannon had everyone close their eyes as she walked from one person to the next. I cheated and watched as she passed among us, her hair thrown back over her right shoulder, her legs stretched out smoothly, long and supple as she glided barefoot around the room, leaning down at each student in order to supply their selected word. When it came time to receive my mantra, Shannon bent even closer so that her lips brushed against my cheek. "Doomee," she said.

The heat from her mouth entered my head and rushed directly up to my brain, the combination of her proximity, the erotic smell of her skin and warmth of her breath overwhelming me as she repeated, "Doomee. Doomeedoomeedoomeedoome."

Startled, I nearly toppled over, then turned my head in order to follow Shannon around the circle. I peeked at the others who'd already received their mantra, saw them with their eyes closed, softly chanting, working their way toward some exalted plane of inner enlightenment, self-harmony, and meditated bliss while it was all I could do to remain where I was on the floor. ("Doomee!") At the end of class, I couldn't hurry Shannon along fast enough to my apartment where we undressed by the light of a candle and had a glass of wine sitting naked on the side of the bed. I played piano for her, Ellington's "Mood Indigo" and

"Creole Love Call." Our sex was exuberant, and afterward she fell asleep beside me and I pretended not to mind.

That December Shannon brought her books and prints, pillows and plants, lamp and clothes and two yellow blankets up the front steps of my building. (The surface was covered with ice and we had to be careful not to fall.) Despite Shannon's presumption, I did not so much invite her to live with me as I never openly objected, and her presence changed little in my life. I still spent my time sitting about reading, teaching a few classes, playing piano, practicing card tricks and sleight of hand. January passed without incident, though in February as members of my committee began leaving messages on my machine wanting to know why I was late again with my chapters and had failed to appear for prearranged meetings, Shannon grew concerned and began challenging my sloth.

She brought home books by Robert Goldwater and Franz Boas, had me discuss the theories of Primitivism and Dadaism, copied articles by Walter Friedlaender, Nikolaus Pevsner, and Francis Klingender, all names gleaned from my yellowing pile of notes. At night, hoping to provide sufficient inspiration, she crawled in bed as I lay smoking, having done nothing worth mentioning since dawn, and rubbing my shoulders, asked about Motherwell's *Elegy to the Spanish Republic,* de Kooning's *Woman and Bicycle,* and Pollock's *Number 2.* I answered all her questions with great enthusiasm while otherwise circumventing any specific discussion of my dissertation.

February became March and then it was April and still Shannon stayed on. She bought curtains for the window, colored soaps for the bathroom, and a doormat for the hall, organized my books and closet, proofread an old draft of my dissertation, and input changes onto my computer. Her endurance set new records, her determination to deal with the unproductiveness of my routine an increasing annoyance, how she insisted my torpor was just a phase and refused to understand. Unsure what I should do, I returned to my apartment one afternoon and sat in my chair reading the day's *Renton Bugle*. A feature article on the painter Richard Diebenkorn was printed across two pages, the artist having recently died in Healdsburg, California, at the age of seventy-one. I finished the article, then glanced for a time at Shannon's print of Diebenkorn's *Large Woman* hanging on the wall. The painting was of a tall female in a sleeveless black dress seated in a nondescript room, her left leg folded over her right knee, her left arm bent and angled out from her shoulder, her hand tucked in at the side of the chair with her right arm raised so that her head rested lazily inside her palm. The pose was provocative, while Diebenkorn's decision to leave his subject's face completely blank—everything ghost-white and featureless with but the faintest markings indicating the briefest thought of a nose and eyes—a unique inspiration.

Accompanying the article was a photograph of Diebenkorn seated in his studio, taken two years before his death, wearing an old long-sleeved shirt and jeans, his features weathered and gaunt. A tall man, his hair was brown and falling over one side of his forehead, his eyes shy, his smile warm beneath a white moustache. He had incredibly large hands, like my father, enormous grapples extending far out of the sleeves of his shirt. I pictured him in his younger days with brushes of varying dimension, wielding them mightily then delicately across the canvas. In the final eighteen months of his life, Diebenkorn suffered through two open-heart surgeries, pneumonia, and a bout of radiation therapy that left him bedridden; his ability to paint was reduced to small-scale sketches and canvases he created while sprawled out on a mattress laid flat on the floor. Looking at his photograph again, I imagined him connected to tubes, breathing through hoses, holding his brush in exhausted hands as he continued to paint daily, propped up and relying on his wife to arrange his supplies as he worked on, using what the article referred to as "soft, bleached colors nonetheless suggestive of a vast scale."

I studied the picture, puzzled by Diebenkorn's effort, wondering why he put himself to so much trouble this close to death. What was the point? As life remained ephemeral, with all things coming and going—love and ambition, achievement and joy, power and glory and the rest—how much better to want for nothing, to relax and not go clinging and grasping into that good night. I thought of Shannon then, and for the first time grew angry and went to the wall where I examined the Diebenkorn print more closely, exploring its consistency and subtext, its marriage of body and form. I ran my hands up and down the sides of Large Woman's remarkable blank white face, touching her surface, my fingers passing over her shoulders, tracing across her hips and onto her legs, and turning then, I glanced back across the room at a snapshot of Shannon framed and placed on the bookshelf. I said her name, waited for her to dissolve into an equally infinite abstraction, to vanish as all women did, leaving behind no more than a ghost, and in an effort to encourage the process, removed *Large Woman* from the wall, and retrieving Shannon's photograph from the shelf, set both on the floor beside the bed.

I went next to locate one of my magic books that I knew had a chapter on making objects disappear, and after scanning references to ancient magicians, sorcerers, and swamis, finally found what I was looking for in a section translated from a Hindu diary written in the thirteenth century. I did as the book instructed, covered the items with a sheet while concentrating my middle eye, raising my arms high overhead as I chanted the lyrical incantation, "In-wa-nee," on and on for several minutes, so absorbed in the process that I forgot the time and didn't hear Shannon unlock the door.

Confused, she glanced quickly between me and the empty space on the wall, then turned and saw her photo missing from the shelf, and flung back the sheet as I continued to chant, "In-wa-nee. In-wa-nee," my heart pounding as my trick was exposed and Shannon's face went pale. She gathered up her books, the Diebenkorn print, and a change of clothes and left the apartment without another word. I spent the night packing her belongings, moving all that wasn't mine into piles near the door, staying out as much as I could the next day so Shannon could pick up her things while I wasn't there. I didn't get home until very late, and once in bed dreamed of making love to a faceless woman, to someone who wasn't Shannon, and woke the next morning alone.

At five to three, I left the bench and walked inside the School of Art where I decided to try and catch Mel before going up to Dr. Freidrich's office. Melaine Haflestier was a well-respected scholar with three books published on Mordecai Ardon-Bronstein and the cross-hatched landscape of abstract art, Expressionism, and Cubism. At fifty, she was a plump version of John De Andrea's *Freckled Woman,* almost handsome with opaline skin and a thick raven mane of hair, her shoulders and hips somewhat large, her eyes emerald blue, her breasts heavy with the passage of time. Maternal and protective—our relationship dated back to my first days at the university when I took her survey class on European Art Post-1950 and impressed her with my paper on Georges Braque—she came to mentor my perceived ambitions. A woman of great resilience, Mel's ability to maintain a sense of sanity in situations otherwise rife with disaster a glorious thing to behold, she threw a party the day her divorce became final and danced a jig on a wooden sun deck flecked with children's play sand. Still, she often found herself at a loss when dealing with me and couldn't help joining the others now in condemning the delinquent approach I took toward my dissertation.

"Got a minute?" I caught her just as she was about to leave her office and tried backing her inside, but she cut me off with a quick "I do not," and stopping me from delivering an excuse for postponing our meeting, grabbed hold of my elbow. "You can't escape," she said, and turned me toward the stairs.

I assured her, "I'm not trying to skip out. I just want to gauge the climate."

"Have you brought your chapters?"

"Actually better," I replied, not yet sure what I meant by this, and when Mel exclaimed, "Don't tell me you've finished!" I felt almost guilty and could barely bring myself to disappoint her. "No, no. Not that. Something else."

Dr. Freidrich's office was on the fourth floor. Melaine's was on the third, while my small space was in the basement beside the room where the potters blast their works in the kiln. (During office hours I can feel the heat through the wall.) Mel tightened her grip on my arm and continued moving us along. "If this is another attempt on your part to stall," she said, but I promised her to the contrary, insisted I had news which would please everyone, and still unclear what I was talking about, added just the same, "Really, something."

Melaine frowned, her right shoulder bumping against me as we walked. "No one's in the mood for games."

"Shall I tell you?" I invited her to become a coconspirator in my fiction, the proposition giving Mel pause before she turned me down. "Surprise me," she said.

We arrived together at Dr. Freidrich's office, where Josh Needleman was already seated in front of Jim Freidrich's desk, and called out as I entered, "Well, well. Look who decided to show after all."

"Ye of little faith."

"Me? Not for a minute." I'd known Josh since he was still an adjunct, a plump figure in Brooks Brothers slacks and paisley shirts, a self-professed authority on post-painterly abstraction, his one publication remained a little-read volume printed at a cost covered by his grandfather and titled *The Hard Edge of Josef Albers in Abstract Form*. In his book, Josh claimed Albers, Barnett Newman, Ad Reinhardt, and Morris Louis all belonged in one homogeneous group despite their varied training, philosophy, and approach to Art, and whenever I pointed out their distinctions, referring to Albers's Bauhaus-influenced *Curious* (1963) and the inspiration Morris Louis took from Pollack and Frankenthaler, by way of Clement Greenberg, as in *Untitled* (1959) for example, Josh shook his fleshy jowls and bellowed at the insignificance of my interpretation.

I moved toward Dr. Freidrich's desk and greeted the head of our department with a wary, "Jim."

"Finne."

"I hope I haven't kept you waiting."

"You're kidding, right?" Although James Freidrich's specialty was High Renaissance and he'd written two seminal books on Raphael and the frescoes at Perugia, an abstract print of Sam Francis's *Blue on a Point* hung on the far wall. An unwilling inductee to late middle age, determined to put up the good fight, he'd replaced his framed copy of *Maddalena Doni* with newer art, divorced the first Mrs. F. and supplanted her, too, with a younger model, a postmodern nova who favored de Kooning to Da Vinci, Sting to Stravinsky, and Ecstasy to scotch. In order to demonstrate his youth to students and staff, he touched up the grey in his sideburns and let his hair grow slightly long, invited Stephen Westfall to speak at the graduation luncheon, added post-1990s art to the curriculum, and tofu to his diet. Despite these changes, he remained an old-school administrator, a strict adherent to specific rules of performance, loath to casual attitudes or methods in conflict with standard forms of review. He gave me a moment to settle my feet in front of the desk, then said, "You have something for me?"

Melaine took a seat in the one remaining chair while I stood front and center. From this point forward our meeting became a game of chess in which I was expected to play with only my pawns and a single horse, while Josh—in all his sycophantic glory—teamed with Jim Freidrich and brought extra bishops, rooks, and knights to their side of the board. The others waited for me to make the first move, and knowing it was in my best interest not to seem hesitant, I mounted a calculated offense. "I've got good news. If you recall, there are several references in my dissertation to L.C. Timbal."

"It's hard to remember anything from your dissertation, Finne, given how little we've seen of it," Josh grinned at Dr. Freidrich. I weathered the interruption, glanced toward Mel for support, still unsure where I was going, and surprised everyone—including myself—with the claim, "I've been in touch with Timbal."

"What's that?"

"You have?"

"Bullshit."

"Come on now, Finne."

"It's true. I wrote him a letter after his exhibit in London, and contacted him again when his wife died last year."

Josh shook his fat head while Jim Freidrich twirled the index finger of his right hand around several times in order to show he wanted me to get to the point. Proceeding then with an absence of caution, I said, "Timbal's invited me to visit him."

"Ha!"

"He's agreed to an interview."

"Come on, Finne." Incredulous, Josh snapped, "You and L.C. Timbal? I don't believe it. Timbal's dropped off the face of the earth. He hasn't given an interview in years."

"I know where he is."

"So what? Everyone knows more or less where he is. That's hardly news."

"But he's invited me to visit him," I said again, caught up in my own deception and Josh's rebuke. "In order to prepare," I continued then before Josh could say another word, "I've had to neglect my current chapters in order to concentrate on a full examination of Timbal's career. I want to write an extensive piece and explain what happened in London. I believe I can finish by the end of the summer and incorporate the article into my dissertation. Publishing the piece separately will be a coup for the university and our department, don't you think?" I expected Josh to burst out laughing any second and denounce my claim once more while demanding proof. (Under the circumstances, I couldn't blame him.) I no longer looked toward Melaine, certain she was disappointed, and while I assumed she wouldn't give me away and challenge my story in front of the others, I knew she must suspect I'd lost my mind. (L.C. Timbal after all!) I waited for Dr. Freidrich to reply, and answered when he asked, "When exactly is this visit supposed to take place?"

"In a few weeks."

"And how is it you came by his address in the first place?"

"I mailed a card to his New York address. It must have been forwarded because he wrote me back."

"And he is still overseas?"

"Yes."

"But this is ridiculous," Josh leaned closer to Dr. Freidrich's desk. "He wants us to believe he and Timbal are pen pals, that while Timbal's refused to speak with anyone since what happened in London, he's suddenly invited a graduate student with no credentials to visit him and write an article."

"As I said."

"It's absurd!"

"Not really," Melaine surprised everyone then by piping in. "When you stop and think about it, Timbal's problem is with established critics and the press. Why not Bailey under the circumstance, since he isn't one of them? If Timbal wants to discuss what happened now, it makes perfect sense he'd choose an unknown. Besides, I've seen the letters."

"You have?"

"Yes."

"From Timbal?"

"What did I just say, Josh?"

"All right," Dr. Freidrich shot a look toward Mel, no doubt debating whether to demand a review of the letters for himself, and deciding not to call my bluff—in deference to Melaine I was sure—he placed his hands behind his head and passed judgement. "OK, Finne, I'll give you until the end of the summer to produce this piece on Timbal. And if for some reason our famous friend fails to follow through on his invitation, I'll expect you to turn in the whole of your dissertation before the start of fall semester. Anything short of this and I'll assume you no longer wish to be part of our program and I'll find someone else to fill your slot. Do I make myself clear?"

I accepted the terms at once, satisfied to have scored a brief reprieve, and wishing everyone a good summer, left the office quickly. I got only a few feet into the hall however, before Melaine again caught hold of my arm and ushered me toward the stairs. The firmness of her grip remained intact as we descended to the third-floor landing where she stopped and turned me around. Her features were pinched, her lips squeezed together, the coloring in her cheeks accenting her choler. I wondered whether I should apologize but sensing she didn't want any sort of concession, I simply thanked her for helping out. "Don't worry," I said. "I'll get everything together by the end of the summer."

Her eyes were like my mother's, powerful and beautiful and sad. The comparison didn't surprise me, I had noticed the similarity before, but the timing was curious. If Melaine had become a mother figure, why did I go out of my way to disappoint and expose her to my nonsense, pushing her into corners and forcing her to come to my defense? ("Why, indeed, Bailey?" Emmitt posed the same question in turn.) At such moments I couldn't help wonder why I didn't simply finish my dissertation and be done with it, but each time I tried to answer I wound up ambushed by another riddle instead. As a follower of both abstemious and eudaemonistic principles, I assumed contentment came in the absence of ambition, that all joy flowed from narrow expectations, and if I sacrificed security and pension while neglecting traditional forms of progress and transporting myself from point A to point B and so on down the line, I gained in the exchange all my days to do as I pleased without heartache or disappointment, and wasn't this then the perfect way to get by?

Melaine dropped my arm, turned and slapped my shoulder before walking me again toward her office. The loose sweater she had on rode up and down as if small animals were trying to escape from beneath. "Why Timbal?" she wanted to know.

"Why not Picasso?"

"Picasso's dead."

"So? Would your story be any more implausible?" she refused to indulge me, her voice exasperated, resentful of the position I had once again put her in. She looked at me then as if the world had never known a bigger fool, and hoping just the same to produce something positive from this latest mess I created, she insisted, "You have to know Freidrich would like nothing better than to see you produce a firsthand piece on Timbal. He's not the enemy. He's actually rooting for you to complete your dissertation."

"And put me on tenure track, I'm sure."

"That isn't the point. That hasn't even come up. Since when are you interested in a full professorship anyway?"

"Bingo," I gave a nod of my head and reminded her that once my dissertation was done my adjunct position was over.

Again, Mel chimed, "But that isn't the point. One thing at a time. You have to finish what you start and move on from there." She opened the door to her office, turned back around and barred me from coming in, wanting me to consider her words without distilling them in further debate. I granted her this and remained in the hall, adjusting my backpack as it hung off my shoulder. Melaine tried to keep her expression severe, but her overall concern outweighed her anger, her face full and fat and warm. I watched her features soften, saw her make an effort to show that her worry transcended the crisis of my dissertation, and adjusting the neck of her sweater, she asked about Elizabeth.

The reference caught me unprepared and I answered on reflex, "She's great."

"When does she leave on her tour?"

"Soon."

"And you?"

"Me?"

"I thought you were going with her."

"But I have Timbal."

"Bailey."

"What? Now you don't believe me?" I continued to stall at giving her a straight answer, though in the end I was unable to resist, and added, "It seems we're in the same boat, old Timbal and me."

"What are you talking about?"

"Our predicament."

"Which is?"

"The way we both lost our girls."

"Don't tell me!"

"His wife, remember?"

"Bailey!" Melaine stepped out of her office, her arms flailing like wings, her instinct to extend comfort though she was angry once more, and knowing me well enough she couldn't help but ask, "What have you done this time? Not Elizabeth. Not her. Jesus, Bailey! What did you do?"

I gave her a second to look me over, offering with my eyes whatever truth was there to find before backing away and walking toward the stairs where I called out as if insulted, shaking my head while sounding exactly like my father in all his huff and howling, "But I didn't do a thing. Nothing, really. It wasn't my fault. Why is everyone so quick to point the finger at me?"

# CHAPTER 6

# SEVERAL VIEWS
# FROM DIFFERENT PLACES

"All right, Bailey, let's try again. What's the last thing you remember?"

"That would be your asking me what's the last thing I remember."

"Can you be serious, please?"

"Sorry. The last thing before what?"

Emmitt takes a moment to write a few more lines down on his pad, then says, "I have a better idea. Let's do some free association."

"You're kidding."

"Humor me."

"Whatever you say, doctor."

"All right. Fear."

"And loathing."

"Life."

"And death."

"Mother."

"Teresa."

"Father."

"Time."

"Brother."

"Where art thou?"

"Is that the best you can do?"

"Am I supposed to answer?"

"Love."

"What's that?"

"I'm asking you to associate."

"I understand. If you could just repeat what you said."

"Love."

"What's that?"

"Enough, Bailey."

"But Emmitt, I'm only doing what you asked me."

Franklin Finne stands on the thirty-fourth floor of the Ryse & Fawl Building, looking down at the street from the window of an office he slipped into earlier that morning. After a while, a girl in a beige spring coat and brown leather bag slung over her shoulder appears below, looking much like Maria as she used to approach the Reedum & Wepe years before. Half drunk and with his head against the glass, hoping to fool himself however briefly, Franklin knows this is the reason he came downtown. He watches the girl move along and disappear inside the building.

The ritual of his return—once a year on their anniversary—follows a night of such extreme imbibing he wishes now he'd brought a bottle to help clear his head. At Finnigan's, he pulled three snapshots from his wallet and drank a toast to each. There was Tyler at fourteen, in black T-shirt, black boots, and jeans; Bailey at a similar age photographed by Germaine; and Maria in the garden beside a dogwood tree. He drank to his dead wife, "Dear love. Dear, dear, dear, dear, dear, dear, dear"; to his first born, "Tyler Finne not seen in ages"; and then to Bailey, "Babe of the brood and wastrel, too, in the family tradition." Whiskey helped drown all that cleaved. It also cost him his job at Kendrecke Construction. In recent years, he was employed as a general laborer, groundskeeper and mason, cab driver, factory worker, and for the past six months as a security guard assigned to Our Lady of the Sorrows Hospital, where he stood stolid for many long hours each day in his untailored blue uniform, rubber-soled shoes, and stiff-brimmed cap, like St. Camillus de Lellis guarding the halls of the healers, he remained otherwise solitary and unnoticed.

Staring at the street below, his memory like a sticky web that captured and constricted him absolutely, he recalls a time when he stood on girders naked to the wind as everything was under construction and he was then Ulysses tethered to the mast, taking in the promise of dreams cast into oceans filled with feasts of plenty, expecting to draw from the sea his fair share of bounty and never to tumble. "Myth," he says in response to what otherwise came his way, and gazing at the sights below, sets his eyes on shapes and visions so far removed as to be observed now only from a distance.


Tyler stretched out on his bed, a large man in T-shirt and undershorts, his weight pressing a curve in the mattress, his heels dangling off the front a few inches above the floor. A hot night. An evening not made for sleep, he listened for Oz as the ticking in his head grew worse and the hours fell away. Around 5:00 a.m. he got up and went into the kitchen where he sat at the table and sipped old coffee. Oz was moving about the front room, seeing to last-minute details, his suitcase and coat by the door, an overflow of papers and letters stuffed into three black plastic trash bags. Other items—clothes and toiletries, books, and linen and additional personal effects not going with him—had already been discarded.

Oz carried the trash bags into the hall, down the stairs, and into the alley. When he returned, he disappeared into the back of the apartment while Tyler remained in the kitchen, trying to organize his thoughts in a manageable chronology, curious to see how he got here, working his way up from the time Turk first took him in, gave him a room to sleep in, and put money in his pocket. Encouraged to learn a new profession ("You want to stay in the lumberyard forever or what?"), he was taught the rudiments of shakedowns, running numbers, and collecting debts. He learned how to strip cars parked in public lots, which trucks to hijack, and how to break a man's nose with the heel of his hand. As he grew beyond his father's size and added serious strength to his mass, his value to Turk increased, and when arrested, as happened now and then, Turk was always there to pull a few strings and bail him out.

In his early twenties, Tyler almost beat a man to death in a protection scheme gone bad, and charged with aggravated assault, Turk did what he could to get the sentence suspended. Given Tyler's record however, the conditions of his release were tied to his enlisting in the service. ("We want this pecker-fuck out of the city" was how the offer was extended.) Tyler refused, considered the consequence of going to jail or simply running off, and only as the agreement was about to be rescinded did he accept the terms.

He was shipped to Berlin a week after boot camp, where he became part of a peacekeeping force conducting regular tours of Bosnia, Somalia, and the Balkans. For much of the next eight years he also spent time in Africa and the Middle East, Grenada, the Falklands, and Yugoslavia, where he witnessed the carnage in battles he secretly came to question. Although his own past was filled with aggressive acts directed at things he couldn't control or easily understand, he'd reached an age where factiousness seemed outmoded, and eventually, as a consequence of his experience in the service, he began rethinking his life in general. During the final months of his enlistment, with the rank of sergeant and military benefits including financial assistance for school, he enrolled in engineering classes at the University of Berlin. For someone who struggled to complete twelfth grade, such studies seemed extreme, yet concerned with what he would do once he was discharged and already past the age of thirty, his ambition took hold and acquired momentum.

The curriculum was difficult, the books and projects assigned demanding the sort of concentration he wasn't used to, and still he threw himself into each task completely. He favored electrical engineering and studied the theories behind BTUs, coulombs, joules, and ohms. He read his assigned texts and bought used copies of *Ugly's Electrical References*, *The Art of Electronics*, *American Electrical Handbook*, *KC's Problems and Solutions for Microelectronic Circuits*, and *The Complete Guide to Home Wiring*. After a year he considered returning to the States and enrolling in whatever school would have him, but instead he landed a job at Berchup Brothers—a small electronics firm in Hamburg—and transferred his remaining studies to Hamburg Technical University.

One of his first classes at HTU was taught by a graduate instructor named Osmah Said Almend, a small man in neatly ironed shirts and slacks, a few years younger than Tyler, his skin the color of ginger, with piercing black eyes and thin fingers sprouting from the tiniest of hands. His beard was short and scraggly, and speaking in a reluctant English and halting German only a bit better than Tyler's, he saved his least flattering comments for the three women and two Americans in his class. "It makes perfect sense you're confused," he would say to Tyler, and answering again some such question on MATLAB and micro-electronic circuits, would remark, "There are special books for this you know, Mr. Finne."

"Books that improve on your teaching, no doubt," Tyler learned to respond in kind, and as a way of goading his instructor further, wore his old uniform to class one day and from that point on Oz referred to him testily as Sergeant.

That spring, Tyler was sent from work to rewire a small office whose electrical circuitry was damaged by a water main leak. The job was easy—for all the studying he put himself through, much of the labor he did for Berchup Brothers presented little challenge—and coming up from the basement, he was surprised to find Oz sitting behind the front desk. "So you're who they've sent," Osmah's tone was as always mocking. "Do I need to check your work, Sergeant? If I turn on the lights are the toilets going to flush?"

"I'm afraid we haven't covered that chapter yet in class, Professor," he handed Oz the work order to sign, the name, The Band of Forbearance, printed above the address. The office was the size of a small market with several metal desks, a series of file cabinets and maps, dull white walls, and brown tiles crisscrossing the floor. A dozen people were talking on phones unaffected by the flood. Oz examined the bill, produced a folder from the bottom drawer of his desk, filled out and assigned payment to Berchup Brothers, and slid the check toward Tyler, who clipped it to the work order. "What is this place?" he asked.

"The Band of Forbearance is a Muslim charity," Oz explained. "I am an officer."

"So you're what, moonlighting?"

"*Minfadluk!* Teaching you is what I do on the side."

"And the rest of the time?"

"But I just told you."

At a tavern around the corner, Tyler stopped and had a beer. Since leaving the service his evenings varied between studies, work, and recreation. He knew a few places he could gamble, drink cheaply, and buy a bit of hash. He hit the gym and lifted weights a few nights a week, but in the mood for something different, he found a pay phone and invited a girl from Düsseldorf to keep him company. (Leta was a secretary at HTU with dinosaurian hips, equally large breasts, and the sort of endless ass designed to take a pounding. "What I like about American men," she said to Tyler beforehand as if an explanation was required, "is their ability to be beastly without the abuse, something German men inherently lack.") Tyler covered two jobs for Berchup Brothers the next day, and with no classes to attend, returned downtown just after 5:00 p.m. where he decided to stop again at the Band of Forbearance.

He found Oz sitting as yesterday behind the front desk. *"Ahwiz ayh?* Back again, Sergeant?"

"I thought I'd check my work."

*"Mahlesh.* Everything is fine."

Tyler dropped into the chair beside the desk and folded his arms across his chest. Curious, though he couldn't quite say for certain why, knowing he and Oz never got along yet in the mood to chat, he asked, "So what is all this?"

Oz hesitated before answering, suspicious of the American's interest, thinking then of his father and the inscrutable way Amir Emam Almend had of turning the most innocent conversation on its head. As a Saudi, born the only son in a house with three sisters and a doting mother, Oz remained close to his father. Amir Almend was an engineer working for the government, a nationalist schooled in the capital city, an intelligent and ambitious man, a devout adherent to religious tradition who accepted nonetheless the benefits of a full education, he instructed his son on the laws of Islam, repeating over and over again, "As a Muslim, you must abide by all that is holy and requiring of you in terms of obedience, sacrifice, and honor." He educated the boy on the Qur'an and the prophet Muhammad, insisting he read— along with the curriculum assigned at school with its emphasis on science and mathematics—books by Fazlur Rahman, Ignaz Goldziher, Al-Ghazzali, and Majid Fakhry.

Eager to learn, a bright student with a quick, inquisitive mind, Oz accepted his father's challenge as his sisters had before him. (All three girls went to college, earned graduate degrees, and secured professional careers, embracing a Westernized curriculum also fully endorsed by their father.) Over time, as Oz passed from adolescence into his teens, he tried to resolve the inconsistencies in his father's convictions: how willing Amir Almend was to rail against the U.S. and complain of Western influences on the Saudi government which was more than passively supporting the transformation of a Muslim state into a consumer republic, and yet how he stopped short of dismissing capitalism and consumerism in total. Amir condemned secular values and imperialistic views, yet preached to his children the significance of Western vision and prudence when focusing on their education and individual goals. It was Western dogma the father espoused when demanding a disciplined career from his son, American dollars Amir Almend earned as he oversaw the construction of office buildings, pipelines and airports, roads and apartments to house all the many government workers, and how was Oz to reconcile his father insisting Western influence was ruining Islam and reducing the will of Saudis to maintain strict adherence to the prescribed laws of diet and prayer when he otherwise championed moving forward in a modern world?

As his father had some twenty years earlier, Oz studied engineering at the city's main university. He had great plans for using his education to better the living conditions of his countrymen, but before earning his degree the economic landscape in the country changed, the business relationship between Saudis and America cooled, and political complications affected the internal growth of the entire region. Government workers were left unemployed, communities that once benefited from what seemed endless development fell into disrepair. "You see," Amir Almend ranted at his son. "This is what comes of such dependence. It's one thing to learn the ways of the West and educate one's self accordingly as a means of improving Muslim communities through business and a network of capital investments, and quite another to crawl into bed with these people and adopt their selfish views at the cost of our culture and all we hold dear."

Unable to find work in the field for which he was specifically trained, Oz was encouraged to get an even higher degree. "The more qualified you are, the less they will be able to refuse you," Amir insisted. (It was hard enough at the time for Amir Almend to keep his own engineering position and quite a mark of shame that he could not secure a job for his son.) Osmah spent the summer and much of the following fall working for an urban planning firm in the capital, taking to the job with serious ambition, relishing the idea of bringing refurbishment to Saudi cities no longer prospering and at risk of ruin—a fault he blamed on the West and the unreliable influence the United States imposed throughout the Middle East—impressing his employers with his drafting skills and dedication. He decided to get a dual graduate degree in Urban Planning and Engineering and—again at his father's suggestion—elected to study abroad. He received a scholarship from Hamburg Technical University and flew to Germany the following spring.

Three things happened before he left that set the tone for his Hamburg years. Fearing a loss of connection to his Muslim roots and determined not to lose sight of who he was when he moved abroad, Oz decided to dedicate himself more completely to Islamic tradition. He embraced anew the precepts of fate and faith, destiny, and purity without compromise, redoubled his efforts on diet and prayer, rejected all forms of alcohol and pork, going so far as to scrape the frosting from cake on the off chance it contained lard. In the course of further commitment, he threw himself into the project he'd spent much of the summer working on, the refurbishing of government apartments in the capital and surrounding cities run down as a consequence of a stalled economy and lost jobs. The plan was to create schools and specially subsidized shops, and Oz was devastated to learn at the last minute the venture was terminated, that instead the buildings were to be razed and replaced with a Holiday Hilton, Pizza Hut, and Chili's restaurant—all with new American financing—and that the surrounding neighborhoods would be torn down as well in order to improve the area for tourists.

"It's a crime against us!" Osmah raged as his father once did, cursing his own government and its complicity with the West. "Are we a Muslim nation or a playground for the United States?" To his surprise, his father remained subdued in his response, and when Oz eventually learned that Amir Almend was employed as the supervising engineer on the Holiday Hilton site, the son left for Germany with no immediate plan to return.

He came forward in his chair, his small hands placed in front of him on the desk, and staring at the American seated nearby said, "All of this is Allah," in answer to Tyler's question. Before saying more however, he stopped and asked something of his own. "Exactly what sort of soldier are you, Sgt. Finne?"

"I'm out of the service," Tyler corrected him. "Discharged two years ago this spring."

"When you were in then. Were you an active participant?"

"I saw action, if that's what you mean."

"Where?"

"Here and there."

"So you participated in implementing America's imperialistic policies and are a supporter now of what is taking place in Iraq?"

"Hold on there, Professor," Tyler felt himself being backed into a corner, and refusing to be pigeonholed, said of his time in the service, "I was part of a peacekeeping force. There was nothing imperialistic going on. Any action I took part in was a calculated response to serious aggression."

"Aggression the United States had no legitimate reason being involved in to begin with."

"Maybe so. But I saw innocent people die on both sides. How many more would have died, Kurds, Muslims, Arabs, Serbs, if America wasn't there in the first place?"

"So you were in Bosnia?" Oz shifted forward once more. "As part of a peacekeeping force you say, and now you want to know how many more would have died without the Americans?" He shook his head and described the American effort in Yugoslavia as, "Worse than incompetent. While you GI Joes were marching aimlessly through the hillsides, setting up random roadblocks and sniffing out one in a million land mines, your placement in the country shut down supply routes and drove innocent people directly into the line of fire where armed Serbs lay in wait. I was there, too," Oz explained how the Band of Forbearance had ties to a dozen countries hoping to provide aid to Muslims in need. "I was in Bosnia for a month my first summer in Hamburg as part of a group from the Band working with displaced Muslims in the Croatian port of Split. I heard their stories and saw first-hand the effect of rape and torture and murder upon Bosnian refugees. I learned how the Serbs referred to themselves as Orthodox Christians on a crusade against Islam and a mission of ethnic cleansing to kill us all.

"What good did America's intervention do?" he spoke as if the collapse of Yugoslavia was somehow the fault of the West, and what took place between the Serbs and Muslims and Croats was a domino toppled by an American plan gone horribly wrong and otherwise not part of a thousand years of internal unrest. He recounted his work in aiding fellow Muslims through efforts organized by the Band, and did not mention the additional enterprise he'd recently undertaken separate from his charity work; how he prayed regularly now at the Al-Tauhid mosque—a black-walled room in the back of a butcher shop—where the imam, Ahmed Emam, preached bitterly against the West, referred to America as the enemy of Islam, and insisted under the edicts of the Qur'an that every part of American influence be purged from Muslim lands.

Tyler sat back in the small metal chair, listening to Oz while looking around the room again at the Muslim men—there were no women, no Americans or Germans—and in response to Oz's diatribe on America, decided to say only, "This Band of For-bearance sounds like a huge undertaking."

Osmah in his halting English, though in a tongue no longer completely foreign, replied in kind, "A good deal of undertak-ing, yes."

# CHAPTER 7

# CHURNING THE WATERS

"How do you feel, Bailey?"

"Good."

"Convince me."

"Can't we just get on with it?"

"Soon. For now, I want you to tell me."

"What?"

"That's up to you."

"But I don't want to say any more. I'm here because you said you could help me."

"Before you can forget, you need to remember."

"Mumbo jumbo."

"You have doubts?"

"I have fears."

"An honest answer. Good for you. All right then, let's try something different. Suppose you tell me what you do believe."

"I believe in the eternal connective, the answer to Why forever linked to Then."

"Go on."

"I believe in the effect of history, the weight of a world that can't be changed, What Is governed by What Was, incidents and accidents, the way my mother bathed and fed me when I was a child, the heat of my father's angry howl and his heavy hand upon my head, images returning in and out of sequence, a flash of color, of light and sound."

"That's all very poetic."

"It's bullshit. It's crap. I want it to stop."

"And you want me to get rid of it for you?"

"Yes."

"Not to worry," Emmitt gives the paper on his desk a bit of a shuffle, and smiling smugly says, "Bailey, Bailey, I am the cure."

Walking from the School of Art, I thought about my committee and the fiction I concocted regarding L.C. Timbal. Although I was relieved by my cleverness and how I escaped relatively unscathed—with almost three months to dig myself out of trouble—I couldn't quite explain what came over me and how such nonsense found its way into my head.

Ebertine Books was a five-minute hike from the west side of campus, near the Hungry Heart Café and the Nectarine Ballroom. A fixture in Renton since 1958, with oak-stained shelves creating separate sections for Literature and History, Social Commentary, Poetry, Philosophy, Children and Music, Criticism and Art, Ebertine offered a pleasant alternative to the monolithic chain stores that multiplied across the landscape at an alarming rate. A handful of customers was inside as I arrived and found Niles in back. I made my way around a center display of books set out on a long wooden table, the latest works of David Lodge, Kazuo Ishiguro, Zadie Smith, and Claire Messud among others all neatly arranged. Niles put a check mark on the order list he was reviewing, and looking up, asked, "So, how did it go?"

"Great," I told him the story of L.C. Timbal, watched Niles shake his head and wonder, "Where do you come up with this stuff?"

"I've no idea. It's a gift. Really, I'm blessed," I reached into my pack and fished out a cigarette and lighter. "What time do you get off? Can you take a break?"

Niles buzzed up front then led the way into the alley where he found a red plastic crate and sat down. "So now what?"

"Now? Nothing. I have the whole summer."

"And after that?"

"You mean when I don't produce the piece on Timbal? Hell," I blew smoke. "It's probably a good thing. It's about time I let Freidrich kick me out."

"Enough is enough."

"Exactly."

"Procrastination can be exhausting."

"I have been feeling overextended lately."

"You are looking worn."

"Around the edges, I know," I stared across the alley, away from Ebertine and toward the graffiti painted on the opposite wall. (A green and gold fish with a silver hook in its mouth and the phrase Bite Me! spelled out in bold block letters covered the upper third of the brick.) Niles stretched his legs out in front of him, and shaking his head once more said, "L. C. Timbal. Isn't he the painter who disappeared a few years ago?"

"After his wife died. And it isn't so much that he disappeared. People know where he is, it's that he refuses to speak with anyone or to say if he's even painting anymore."

"Where exactly is he?"

"The last time anyone reported he was in Algiers."

I saw Niles' expression change, his hands clutching hold of the crate as his legs bent in, his face queer and much as I also noticed last night—though he refused to talk about it—and puzzled, I asked, "Are you OK?"

"Me? Sure."

"You look weird."

"Do I?"

"No troubles?"

"None," he shuffled the soles of his shoes back and forth across the alley's blacktop. "So you aren't planning to go see this Timbal?"

"What? Fly to Algiers and hunt him down? Why would I do that?"

Niles changed the subject, asked then about Liz, wondering if I'd seen her.

"No."

"Called?"

"She asked me not to. I'm trying to do what she wants," the irony of my claim wasn't lost on Niles, who raised his eyebrows in such a way as to make me frown. "Let's not go there," I crushed my cigarette beneath my heel. Despite my objection, discussing Elizabeth was exactly what I wanted to do, and I waited then for Niles to say more. Instead, he stood and pulled at his sleeves, turned his hips slowly and moved back toward the store. "I should get to work." The sun overhead fell between the buildings, warming the dark tar of the alley which was thick and soft. Niles stopped for a moment and shaded his eyes in order to look at me. "Are you playing tonight?"

"Yes."

"Maybe I'll come by. Sometime after ten."

"Good," I told him, and seeing Niles face appear odd again, I asked once more, "Are you sure you're OK?"

"Definitely, yes."

"Nothing you want to tell me?"

He stared for a moment off into the far side of the alley, then glanced back at me and said, "We can talk about it tonight, all right? I'll see you then."

I slipped my backpack over my shoulder and headed out of the alley, walking downtown, across Liberty and toward McClarne Avenue. The sun sat a few degrees below its crest, the late afternoon drawing it down. My shadow floated along the cement, chased after me as I passed Union Center where the old train station was recently converted into a state-of-the-art shopping mall. The air remained warm, the heat transformed into a sort of cloying dampness that settled over my face and arms and crawled up under my shirt as I circled around Renton Plaza and Ninth Avenue where the Reedum & Wepe once stood—the crater cleaned of debris and left like a wound now tended fenced as a memorial. Afterward, I returned to Seventh and made my way back toward campus.

Hungry, I debated going straight to Dungee's and having a free burger, then changed my mind and headed to the Hardy Bistro, where I sat at a small table and ordered a fried egg sandwich while glancing out the window on the off chance Elizabeth might pass by. Halfway through my meal, a second chair was pulled out and Harry Fenton sat down. "Guess then," Harry said. "Go on and guess." One of the advantages of living several years in the same neighborhood was how familiarity between the locals created a camaraderie and such was true with Harry and me. At fifty-four, Harry was round-shaped, balding with strands of brown-grey hair near his ears, a gap between his eyeteeth and rear molars that gave him an offset smile. The Director of News at radio station WRQB, 91.7 on the FM dial, a 50,000-watt local outlet that catered to a tame mix of evening jazz and homogenized white pop performed by flavor-of-the-month boy bands, Harry's face was full like a balloon given too much air. He sported a square pair of black-framed glasses, the center bar perched on the bridge of his nose wrapped with a narrow piece of flesh-toned tape. In baggy slacks and short-sleeved button-down shirt, the briefcase Harry carried was a weathered black satchel filled with countless strips of papers on which he scribbled notes, messages, quotes, and phone numbers. "The Canary Islands," Harry answered his own question for me.

I closed my book and glanced across the table. "And the category is?"

"The money trail."

"Clabund?"

"And Garmore."

"Are what?"

"Falsifying accounts, using dummy corporations to launder the skimmed funds overseas."

I shrugged and reminded Harry, "This is an old theory."

"It's not just bar nuts anymore."

"Says?"

"Sources."

"Not another waitress at the Redlight."

"Scoff if you must, Bailey boy." For three years Harry had looked into Mayor Julian Clabund's plan to refurbish Union Center while awarding the bidding for construction to Garmore Builders. Six months after completion, with the demographics of Renton never favoring the mall's success, business at Union Center was already off. Two members of the city council resigned in protest against the project, which experienced several cost overruns and led to whisperings of fiscal impropriety. To date however, only Harry had conducted any sort of serious review, with dozens of large files locked in a portable safe kept in his bedroom and a plan to publish a book once his research bore fruit.

He finished his water and ordered a burger to go. I sipped at my coffee, ate my sandwich, glanced outside and back at Harry who sat with his right arm hanging down toward his briefcase, his left hand resting against the side of his empty glass. "So what's up with you?" he asked. "How are tricks at the academy? Are you teaching or taking the summer off?"

"I'm off for the most part."

"Good for you," Harry had the waitress refill his water, and pushing his black spectacles up his nose said, "I ran into your friend the other day. The little guy at the bookstore."

"Niles."

"That's it. We were at Revco. Did he tell you? Funny kid. He was in there buying a bunch of gauze and antibiotic creams and when I asked what was up with all the supplies, he just kind of pulled everything in against his chest and said better safe than sorry."

"He's a Boy Scout. He likes to be prepared."

"Yeah, well, he's a funny kid."

After Harry left, I sat for a while and tried reading more from my book. (I was at the part in Hamsun's *Hunger* where the hero found himself outside late one night, broke again, with only his keys in his pocket, tired and, of course, hungry.) At the end of each page I looked up and thought about Liz. I went back and forth this way, reading and stopping, thinking and reading and looking out the window, until sometime after seven, when I got up and walked the six blocks from the Hardy Bistro to Dungee's Bar and Grill.

Inside the bar were college kids who traveled in packs like hounds still learning to hunt, a few couples eating at the side tables with plans to catch a movie, four women at the bar, salesgirl types with roomy hips and hair a bit too large for their heads, three waitresses, and Jake Telly mixing drinks. Built just after the Second World War by Blake Dungee and passed down in time from son Earl to grandson Jon, Dungee's was something of an institution in south Renton. (Old Blake was over ninety now, with two artificial knees—one graphite, the other plastic— a nearly transparent skin, and amaurotic milky blue eyes, though he came and sat beside the piano every now and then, picking away with surprising skill on his old mandolin, which he once played with the Ballyhoo Glory Band—circa 1947—and had a 78-recording of "Izzu Baby" to prove it.) I got a beer and my tip jar and made my way to the piano, which was stationed some six feet back from the front window.

I put my beer beneath the bench, the jar in front of me, and settled in to play a bit of Ellington's "'A' Train." After this, I switched over to a jazzed-up variation of Chopin's concerti—one of Elizabeth's favorites—then on to Brubeck and Gershwin, again turning the melody inside out, filling the notes with altered meter and tones, up and down, largo, legato or adagio, all in an aggressive sort of conversion. Later, depending on the mood of the crowd, I would perform various combinations of jazz and pop, big band and rock, cabaret and torch songs, taking requests until the bar closed after midnight. In the middle of "Symphony for New York," thinking about Niles and how strange he looked when I left him earlier, I glanced up just as Josh Needleman was coming inside.

A visit from Josh was unprecedented, though something about tonight was almost predictable, the topic of Timbal too much for him to resist. Josh was accompanied by his girlfriend, Leslie Stone, all hipless and hard edged, a sylphlike woman, dark haired and androgynous, a mechanical engineer at one of Renton's new robotics firms. I switched from what I was playing to something more fitting—a bit of Prokofiev's "Peter and the Wolf"—as Leslie disappeared down the bar and left us to talk. "Some crowd, Finne," Josh pulled a chair over from the nearest table and sat with the puffy knobs of his knees creasing his pants.

"It's early."

"Maybe," he smoothed his pastel shirt over the swell of his belly, and interlocking his fingers, dove right in. "I thought you'd be out buying your ticket."

"Not yet."

"Saving your pennies?"

"The best I can."

"So you talked to your friend lately?"

"You mean Timbal?"

"I suppose you have his phone number."

"As a matter of fact," I answered by banging out a spirited rendition of Dizzy Gillespie's "A Night in Tunisia."

"You think this is funny?"

"Not at all."

"Finne."

"Good."

"All right."

"What am I supposed to think, Josh?"

"Can you stop playing for a minute?"

"Do you mean the piano?"

"Christ," he snapped his fat fingers in front of my face, his voice a nasal pitch which registered high and shot upward like sparks drawn from metal, and leaning back said, "What the fuck are you doing, Finne?"

"Right now? Gillespie."

"Freidrich is going to kick you out of the department."

"And that worries you?"

"I just don't want you trying to blame me or Mel for it. All this Timbal bullshit."

"What bullshit, Needlebrain?"

Josh tossed up his hands, and leaning forward again fumed, "You're a real piece of work, aren't you, Finne? You get off thinking everyone's against you, and those of us who aren't amused just don't get it, right? You waste my time, Melaine's time, Jim Freidrich's time over some goddamn dissertation you never plan to finish. You string us along and when we give you the benefit of the doubt you laugh at us for being fooled."

"I don't think Mel or Freidrich are fools, Josh," I stopped playing for a moment, weighed the accuracy of Needleman's claim, and uncomfortable with his conclusion, resumed performing a few seconds later, offering up Hammerstein and Kern's "All the Things You Are." Leslie returned to the piano and Josh draped a stout arm over her shoulder. "Have it your way then, Finne."

I smiled, determined to say nothing and let Josh make his exit, but just as suddenly I found myself calling out, "I'm going to see Timbal." Immediately I regretted as much as Josh chimed back, "Sure you are. And I hope you do. Truly," and reaching into his pocket he pulled out a quarter which he tossed into my jar. "Maybe that will get you started," and with the quarter still spinning, his grin self-congratulatory—he had wide, indelicate features which were particularly menacing whenever his intent was to convey a specific harm—and drawing Leslie closer to him said, "I suppose Elizabeth will be going with you? How is she by the way?"

I spent the next two hours playing nonstop while trying to clear my head. I knocked off a furious version of Todd Rundgren's "Be

Nice to Me," followed by arrangements of Max Roach and Thelonious Monk, Count Basie and Michael Stipe, the music merging as a series of separate waters thrown together. The crowd picked up, was better than average for a Thursday night, students and young professionals, boys in jeans and women in shorts and bright cotton dresses who drank and ate and dragged their dates up to dance. When I finally stopped playing, I took a second beer from the bar and went out back. A minute later Marthe Raynal, one of the waitresses just finishing her shift, came into the alley and joined me.

Marthe was a dark-haired girl in her early twenties, a native of Tipasa studying biological psychology at the university. ("Don't get me started on lithium," she cracked the first time we met, her laugh contagious.) She had a large Roman nose and full lips, her figure soft and nicely curved, with bracelets on her wrists and two rings in each ear, though her fingers remained vestal and unadorned. "Full moon," she motioned with a rattle of her silver bangles, then reached inside her large straw bag of a purse and pulled out a pack of Lucky Strikes.

"Almost," I offered her a light.

"It's there. Look hard," she waited for me to search the sky above Dungee's, and as I did so, she asked, "Who was that you were arguing with before?"

"You mean Needlehead?"

"That's his name?"

"Josh Needleman. He's on my dissertation committee."

"He seemed upset with you."

"Let's just say Josh isn't my biggest fan."

"You all right?"

"Definitely."

"The way you played after he left, I was sure something was wrong."

"Needlemind's annoying, that's all."

"Then you're OK?" she asked again.

"I'm great," I blew smoke, and changing the subject, mentioned Niles. "He's supposed to come by later. You should stick around."

Marthe smiled and kicked at my boot. "And why would I do that?"

"Because you want to."

"How do you know?"

"Because you told me." A year ago, just after Marthe started working at Dungee's, she asked me to introduce her to Niles— "He looks like a sweetheart"—and hoping something might come of their meeting, I watched and waited. Nothing evolved however, and so when Marthe touched my arm and mentioned Jeana, I was confused. "It's all right," she said, and informed me that she and Niles had, in fact, gotten together recently.

"You and Niles?"

"That's right."

"Really? When? Where?"

"So many questions."

"I haven't heard a thing. You and Niles?"

"We're friendly," she crushed her cigarette against the wall and stored the remains in a clear plastic vial kept in her purse. I waited for her to say more, anticipating details, wondering and hopeful, though for the moment Marthe wanted only to discuss Jeana. "You knew her?"

"Yes."

"He was very much in love with her?"

"They lived together. And yes, he loved her."

"How terrible. To lose someone like that, I mean."

I didn't reply. Marthe in the moonlight noticed my silence, and surprised me again by saying, "'I don't believe in suffering, in severe grief or regret. I don't even believe in memory. In time, everything is forgotten, even old loves. Our despairs should be vague and we should bear them with one deep sigh and move on.'" I looked over, amused and intrigued. "So Niles has you reading Camus?"

"We exchanged a short list of our favorites."

"And what did you give him?"

She smiled a bit differently than before, and in response to my question answered, "Pablo Neruda. A bit of poetry," she said.

I returned to the bar and waded through a pile of requests written across napkins left on the piano bench, choosing Kate Bush's "Watching You Without Me," which required a few alterations to the techno-pop melody to make the piece work as a solo. It didn't take long before I was running one arrangement into the next, playing "Shame on Us," "The Big Sky," "Hot House," and "Break Your Heart" by Barenaked Ladies, hoping to lose myself again in the music, though I'd even less success this time than before.

Niles arrived just after eleven and went to the bar where he waited for me to finish my final set. He ordered a beer, listened to me play a bluesy send-up of "Madman Across the Water," before I picked up my tip jar and joined him. "So," I couldn't resist and immediately asked, "what's this I hear about you having a girlfriend?"

"My what?"

"Come on, tell me."

"If you mean Marthe."

"So it's true."

"We're friends, that's all."

"She says you're friendly."

"We have coffee. She comes by the bookstore now and then."

"And?"

"We talk."

"And?"

"It's not what you think."

"Why not?"

Niles took a drink from his beer while I went around and poured myself a whiskey. The bar began to empty just after midnight and busboys anxious to finish their work and get home began clearing the plates and glasses. I waited a moment to see if Niles would say something more about Marthe, and was caught off guard when he mentioned instead L.C. Timbal. "I've been thinking you should go and find him."

"What?"

"I think you should try."

"You must be kidding."

"And," he said, adding a new twist, "I want to go with you. I want to see Algiers."

I could tell he was serious and this confused me all the more. "Where is this coming from?"

"I have my passport and you have yours," he continued. "You were going to be with Liz all summer, now you can travel with me," his face was set in the same odd expression he had that afternoon, only there was a measure of anxious anticipation in his eyes, a confessing of resolutions made for reasons I didn't yet understand. I sipped from my drink, laughed a bit if only to encourage Niles to tell me he was joking, but he insisted, "I want to do this. I want to get away for a while. I speak the language well enough and there's no real risk in travel despite what you read about the region's civil unrest. I'm not going to put us in the wrong place. You'll see, we'll be fine."

"What about your condition? Your nocturnal two-step, the somnambulistic shuffle?"

"You'll be with me," Niles gave this as his answer, then qualified his response with, "I'm going to go with or without you. It'll do me good to get away."

I shook my head, pictured the series of old scars and bruises beneath Niles' clothes: the purple and yellow contusion on his left shoulder, a swollen knot in the center of his chest, cuts and carvings down his legs and an egg-shaped lump on his left elbow. His right thigh had the aftereffect of a gash, the butterfly stitches used to close the wound leaving the flesh a pasty pink, and unsettled I asked him to tell me, "Why do you really want to go?"

"I want you to find Timbal."

"And?"

"I'd like to see where Camus was born. I'd like to explore the same streets Mersault walked in *A Happy Death*."

"Jesus, Niles."

"And Dr. Rieux and *The Stranger*'s faceless man."

"All uplifting works."

"I think if I go, maybe I can reach some sort of peace," he admitted this much to me, and to further support his claim recited from memory a quote from André Gide: "Anyone wishing to discover new lands must be willing to first lose sight of familiar shores." This he followed with a line from the essay "Death in the Soul," and what Camus wrote about travel: "Inside unfamiliar cities, the curtain of habits, the comfortable loom of words and gestures in which the heart drowses, slowly rises, finally to reveal anxiety's pallid visage."

I listened closely, doing what I could to pull everything together, interpreting the quotes Niles offered enough to say,

"So that's it? You think flying to North Africa is going to help resolve your condition?"

"I want to go, yes."

"And do what? Await an epiphany?"

"Something like that."

"In Algiers?"

"I can't explain it any more than it feels right."

"And going doesn't seem a bit desperate to you?"

"Compared to what? Staying here and tying myself into bed at night?"

I rolled my eyes and set my hands down flat atop the bar. "You realize you're not suffering from anxiety's pallid visage," I said. "Your affliction's a bit more serious than that. You slice yourself up in the middle of your sleep for Christ's sake."

"All the more reason to go."

"But you haven't even tried to get help here."

"That's because what I need isn't in Renton."

"You're talking in riddles."

"I'm answering you the best I can."

I raised my voice while revisiting old arguments, insisted Niles go see a doctor or try some specific form of treatment beyond the rope run between our two rooms if he really wanted to be healed, but such pleading was in vain. "Algiers is different," he said. "You'll just have to trust me. I bought two tickets this evening. I'm leaving two days after you give your final exam. With or without you."

I got up and returned to the piano where I banged out an up-tempo rendition of Cole Porter's "All Through the Night." The bar was empty then. Mark "Bozo" Farell, the manager at Dungee's, stepped out of his office with the day's deposit tucked inside a blue zippered bag and headed toward the door. (Bozo's nickname came from his huge mop of orange hair, the whole of his head looking as if the fibrous entrails of a pumpkin exploded.) "Lock up when you leave OK, Professor?" Bozo made sure I had my keys. Niles moved to a table as I got up from the piano and joined him. "What if you go and things don't work out?" I began pressing the issue anew. "What if nothing improves? What if there's an incident and you can't get anyone to help you? Think about the hospitals there, Niles. Shit. What if I try and can't find Timbal? What if he isn't even there? What if the trip turns out to be an unmitigated disaster?"

"What if? What if? What if?" Niles smiled in a way which reminded me all too much of Elizabeth, and frustrated, I squirmed in my chair.

"Come with me," Niles said.

"No."

"I'm going. If you're concerned about me, come along. Besides," he mentioned Elizabeth traveling so near to Algiers, how her itinerary put her in Spain, near Vasqueze and the beaches of Zahara de los Atunes, "a person could easily cross the Strait of Gibraltar and find her there if he wanted."

"Liz has nothing to do with any of this," I reached for my whiskey and finished it off.

"All the same. Come with me."

"Forget it."

"Come on."

"You're chasing ghosts."

"Maybe," he tugged on the cuff of his sweater.

"I'm not going," I repeated.

"Find your Timbal."

"He's not mine."

"Surprise everyone."

"Why should I?"

"I'm leaving."

"Fuck, Niles."

"It's your call. Stay or go."

"I can't. Shit."

"One or the other, Bailey. It's up to you."

BOOK II

# ALONG THE WAY

# CHAPTER 8

# IN PREPARATION

"All right then," Emmitt adjusts his glasses. "Let's move on. Tell me whatever you like."

I've been trying to keep things in order, to follow a certain progression, but it's not always easy to avoid skipping around. "Not that it matters," I say to Emmitt. "There's no order to memory after all, is there? I mean, once something happens, it's there in your head with all the rest."

Emmitt raises his eyes, letting me know he's intrigued by my statement. "If you'd like to keep some sort of chronology, Bailey, that's fine," he says. "However you're comfortable. If you prefer going straight on through until the end."

"But that's impossible," I don't know if I'm being purposely difficult or have somehow hit upon an unexpected truth. "Nothing ends," I insist. "It's why I'm here. If things simply came to an end, I wouldn't have to talk with you now."

"But they do end, don't they?" he counters. "It's the conflict between what ends and our need to continue that causes trauma."

"What continues, it's true," I hear only this, and remind Emmitt, "That's what I'm saying. Everything goes on and on forever, even what's buried and dead."

———

Tyler stood by the window as the day's first light appeared. He expected the morning to be a flurry of activity, of time passing quickly with no chance to think, but here he was confronted by gaps inside of which time ran on forever, thick and eternal with anticipation, like gazing after a stone as it sank deeper and deeper into the sea.

Oz came in after removing several more plastic bags from the apartment and walked back to his bedroom, surveying the space for any forgotten items he didn't want to leave behind. (The bed was stripped and the sheets disposed of, the mattress sprayed with Lysol to mask any sweat or other traceable fluids that might have seeped into the surface.) He went from the bedroom into the kitchen and scanned the counter, unplugged the coffeemaker and tossed it into yet another plastic bag. From there he returned to the front room where he knelt in order to offer the morning's prayer.

Tyler watched in the reflection of the window as Oz rolled out his prayer rug and began his ritualistic hum. Any other morning and the drone would not have bothered him, but today such prayer seemed absurd. He went to the kitchen where he stood staring up at the space where Oz had removed the clock from the wall. The queer history of their alliance—what brought them from Hamburg to Renton and now to this—seemed a mystery, though the chronology was easy enough to trace. A mix of restiveness, uncertainty, and curiosity, all contributed to Tyler's coming to the Band of Forbearance night after night. In time he began volunteering his services, offering the use of the Berchup Brothers' truck to deliver food and other staples, making repairs at the Band's office, at Muslim homes and businesses in and around town.

"If you're after leniency on your grades," Osmah challenged the American's motivation, was wary in his acceptance and stingy with his thanks. In class, he did not let on that the American sergeant was now a regular downtown and how they often spent long hours together. Twice that winter, and twice again the following summer, during breaks from school and work, Tyler volunteered to accompany members of the Band to Bosnia and Pakistan, Saudi Arabia and Afghanistan, and subsequently to a half dozen other Muslim states where his brawn was a welcome addition to the many physical demands. Oz went as the coordinating officer—it amused Tyler how even a charity such as the Band of Forbearance used military titles and procedures—and in the course of these trips Oz tried to educate Tyler further on the history of Islam and its conflict with the West. He encouraged the sergeant to read in translation editorials in the *Al Ahram* by Ibrahim Nafie, who denounced America's policies throughout the Middle East. "Desert Storm. Desert Shield and now once more Iraq. The attempt to westernize every Islamic nation. The very fact your country exists is a threat to us."

American sanctions were a particular bone of contention for Oz, who was quick to quote the number of Pakistani and Afghan, Iraqi and Iranian children who died as a consequence of the West's invisible assault. ("You Americans have a great capacity for living with ignorance and exonerating yourselves from all sense of blame, but your hands are bloody and your souls are weak.") Tyler tried to argue in turn, citing the Lebanese civil war, the tribal battles in Afghanistan and Pakistan, and the eighty-year conflict between Iraq and Iran as proof that America was not entirely to blame for the region's discord. He recited what information he remembered from the little reading he'd done, and noted, "America isn't the one blowing up hotels in Yemen or embassies in Kenya. Hell, America gave stinger missiles to the mujahedeen and sent millions of dollars to Pakistan, and what did those fuckers do but funnel the cash through Kabul to anti-Western extremists."

All of which caused Oz to shrug indifferently, and rejecting Tyler's assertion that much of the medicines and foods, equipment and gas, clothes and supplies brought to the Band of Forbearance came from America—"It's political posturing at best"—he waved a crooked finger, and snapped, "So what's your point?"

That spring, Oz took a leave from his position as an instructor at the Hamburg Technical University and disappeared from Germany for nine months. He told Tyler he was traveling to raise funds for the Band of Forbearance, that he'd be in London for a time, and then stop in Saudi Arabia to see his family, but his morning flight took him straight to Afghanistan where he carried a letter from his imam, Ahmed Emam, to Shayh Said.

Tyler finished the semester before deciding to leave school as well. (There seemed no point in clogging his head with further material when the work he did for Berchup Brothers required little more than what he already knew.) He continued volunteering at the Band of Forbearance, delivering food, taking on electrical projects, providing drywall and carpentry, and whatever other handiwork had to be done. In July he met the sister of Mustafa Al-Bar, one of the other volunteers, and they began to date. Shari Al-Bar was a salesclerk at a ladies dress shop on the east side of Hamburg, an attractive girl with long black hair and deep Mediterranean skin, the daughter of Egyptian parents both educated in the States and owners of a consulting firm in Cairo. Shari came to Germany with her brother as he studied politics at the university, and joked to Tyler the first time they met, "My, my, but are all Americans so big?"

Sleeping with Shari was a welcome experience for Tyler. Though she was hardly virginal and no more a Muslim really than any of the other Westernized girls in Hamburg, he found himself behaving with a certain caution, as if he was a guest in a house he was surprised to be invited. Their relationship wasn't serious, yet people on the street seemed compelled to treat their involvement as something more than a harmless curiosity. Looks of judgement were extended, cruel and telling glances. American soldiers found Tyler's keeping company with a Muslim girl offensive—they pronounced the word "Musss-liimm" like a hissing snake—while local teens were equally vocal, following after them as they came from a restaurant or went to a club, shouting, "Hey, American! What are you doing with the darkie? Muslim mamma, you want a piece of white meat, do ya? Third-world cunt!" Twice there were scuffles and once a well-muscled boy with a rock found out firsthand that lunging at Tyler was a mistake.

Mustafa stepped in and presented his concern. "Germany isn't America, my friend. It is not even London. Please, enough is enough." Shari agreed and said, "It isn't worth the trouble. Just forget it. I'm sorry," and did not return his calls.

Two weeks later, Tyler learned the office space the Band of Forbearance had leased for the last ten years was being bought by an American conglomerate and a GAP was set to open on the spot. "You see?" Oz said upon his return. "Here's what happens, inch by inch and brick by brick." He was standing in the bathroom of his apartment, having invited Tyler over with some news he had to share. In his time away he'd grown his beard quite long, the hairs jutting out dark and unruly from his otherwise sunken cheeks, and picking up a pair of scissors, he began clipping back his whiskers in preparation to shave. When asked, he provided only scant detail about his trip, saying he met with some success in the raising of funds, that he traveled "here and there" and "back and forth," though in mentioning his journey home to see his family, he became annoyed describing the changes and how the entire city was annexed by the West. "I may as well have been visiting New York for all the American restaurants and hotels, bars and banks my own father helped build."

He finished with his shave, and stepping into the front room, surprised Tyler with, "I feel as if I'm howling into the wind. Nothing's going to change this way. I'm trying to get the attention of a people who don't even know I exist and here I am waving my hands a million miles offshore. I need to go to America, to open an office for the Band of Forbearance and raise opposition to America's interference with Muslim nations from within the eye of the storm. America needs to know it isn't impervious to protest and this can only be done in their backyard. I've obtained a visa and made arrangements through the help of Ziad Shehhi, an old friend of one of my professors who says he can find work for me in Renton."

"Did you say?"

Osmah pointed the razor still in his hand. "If you're ready to return, I think you should come with me. Having an American on my side will be of great benefit. I will be the foreigner then and you can help me should certain situations arise that might otherwise—what is the expression?—blow up in my face."


I walked home from Dungee's with Niles sometime after 1:00 a.m. and dropped into bed, running the rope around my ankle before stretching out to stare at the ceiling and consider what I should do. ("Stay or go, Bailey.") At some point I drifted off without having made up my mind, and woke late the following morning. I was scheduled to teach in just over two hours, and rolling over, I reached toward Liz's side of the bed, where her absence registered severely as I stroked and grabbed and strained to feel her there. ("A person could easily cross the Strait of Gibraltar and find her if he wanted.") I pictured her on stage, dressed in a black velvet gown, her feet in a thin pair of soft leather slippers as she lectured the audience on Beethoven's influence over Schubert, the way Schubert's "Sonata in C Minor (D. 958)" relied heavily upon gestures found in Beethoven's "Pathetique" for example. I saw her sitting at the piano playing her own compositions, and performing with guest pianists, sharing a bench with Radu Lupu and Murray Perahia, Evgeny Kissin, Garrick Ohlsson, Boris Berezovsky, and Marc Hamelin no less. The image made me uneasy, and undoing the rope, I got up and went to my piano where I played Chopin's "Ballade No. 1 in G Minor, Op. 23" which, rather than soothe, only exacerbated my raw state of disrepair.

Liz's leaving had me muddled and dysphoric, and even as I switched my focus and concentrated again on Niles, I couldn't hold my train of thought and wound up reflecting once more on the vagaries of love. I saw the wounds beneath Niles' clothes, pictured him with Jeana while Marthe ran around the windows outside looking for a way in. If here was the root of Niles' nocturnal dementia—the madness of love taken as a whole—then it seemed in terms of Liz the only distinction between Niles' carnage and my own was the advent of physical harm.

I went to shower, and wrapping a towel around my waist, came out of the bathroom and sat in my chair, flipping through the pile of books I pulled from my shelf in the days since Liz's leaving. I reread passages marked in Kafka's "Blumfield, an Elderly Bachelor," and "A Little Woman": "This little woman, then, is very ill-pleased with me. . . . If a life could be cut into the smallest of small pieces and every scrap of it could be separately assessed, every scrap of my life would certainly be an offence to her." I set the book down and picked up another, a novel by Max

Frisch that contained a paragraph where the protagonist's inability to sustain a relationship was described as "an incapability to be loved as the person he was . . . and therefore he involuntarily neglects every woman who truly loves him, for if he took her love really seriously, he would be compelled as a result to accept himself—and this was the last thing he wanted."

Disturbed, I got up again and went back to my piano where I played a rousing piece by Don Pollen, using my elbows, forearms, and fists to flail away, filling the air with splash clusters and two-handed chords. After a while I moved to the window, where I leaned against the glass and stared outside. A heavyset woman in a paisley summer dress and black walking shoes came around a corner and collided with a man in a grey T-shirt and white slacks. The man stumbled and the woman reached to hold him up, both posting awkward grins and quick apologies before parting. I observed their crash as yet another example of how shit happened—the consistency of consequence, how the fat woman climbed from bed a minute early while the man rose a minute late and their intersection was set in motion from that point forward no matter what they planned or otherwise wanted.

What an uncompromising system, and infallible counterclaim to Chaos, the foundation of Universal Order, which upset rather than comforted me as I recalled my mother slipping on her coat and carrying my father's shovel from the garage. The chill on her flesh as the winds rose and howled, and the autocracy of Order not shielding her in any way, the absence of abatement and temporary interruption deliberately cruel, for what could be more vulgar than a universe that adhered to such an impervious sense of Law and mechanical indifference when in a less austere world the winds would have warmed, the snow subsided, and my mother not have died.

I came from the window and sat again in my chair, where I

thought further about the Order of Things and what connection such had to Niles' determination to fly to Algiers. "I need," he said, and immediately then I considered my own desires, the consequence of What Was and the resistance I created for myself these past several years, all my need to want for nothing, and how the two forces clashed until, with Liz, the latter willed out and I fell foolish and fitful back to earth.

CHAPTER 9

# ELIZABETH

The summer after Shannon left, I went to Dungee's on a night I wasn't scheduled to play, thinking I could earn a few extra dollars in tips nonetheless. I performed for an hour or so, knocking out a melody of "Cry Baby," "Satin Doll," and "Wheatleigh Hall," and around 11:30 p.m. collected the few bucks I made and went to the bar for something to drink. I had a deck of cards with me and practiced a trick while sipping my whiskey. At last call, I put the deck in my pocket and went off to the bathroom where a woman in a pale blue cotton dress and light leather sandals was talking on one of the pay phones in the hall. Her hair was a thick orange brown hanging just above her shoulders, her cheeks fine and sharply drawn. She stood with her right arm tucked beneath her left, her head tipped to one side. I heard her laugh in response to something said on the other end of the phone and watched her full lips as they parted.

As I came from the bathroom she was just getting off the phone, and wanting to speak with her, I removed the deck of cards from my pocket, turned and showed her the ace of hearts. I then placed the card back in the deck, shuffled and fanned the deck in front of me, and asked her to pick one. She reached with her left hand and pulled out the ace of hearts. "Magic," I said and introduced myself. She had a long neck, like one of the models painted by Klimt, and extending her right arm toward me the feel of her fingers caught me by surprise. I could see she was waiting for my reaction, and not wanting to disappoint her, I said, "Hands down, your trick is better than mine."

"It's an icebreaker."

I laughed. "Yes, I'm sure it is."

She settled her right arm back beneath her left, turned and began walking off when I asked if she'd like to have a drink. "Are you alone? Am I keeping you from someone?" She didn't answer at first, but when I told her that I'd just finished playing piano and was hoping to have a drink, she said, "I know."

"What?"

"That you were playing," the green of her eyes caught the light as if she might be teasing me, though I couldn't quite figure how by what she said, and standing there, unsure what to say next, it was Elizabeth who reminded me, "About that drink."

We went and sat at a side table near the piano where I got another whiskey and brought Elizabeth a glass of wine. The bar was ready to close though I told her, "If you're in no hurry, we can stay as long as you like." She held her wine in her false hand, everything from the creases in the knuckles to the shades of vein in the plastic designed with anatomical exactness. I posed a series of casual questions, curious to know how long she'd been in Renton and if she ever stopped by Dungee's before. After ten minutes or so, she asked about my piano playing, identified the song I was performing when she came in as Ellington's "Pie Eye's Blues" in E and wondered, "Where do you study?"

"I teach Art History at the university."

"No, I mean your music."

"I don't study."

"I see," she took a sip from her drink. "You just play?"

"More or less." I told her about the lessons with my mother and how, "Basically, that's it. Why?"

"You play like someone self-taught," she said.

Again I didn't quite know whether or not she was teasing me, but decided to give her the benefit of the doubt. "You can tell from hearing me play one time?"

"Actually, I've heard you play before," she took another sip from her drink. "Enough to recognize the absence of instruction. Your mechanics are erratic. There's no consistency in how you perform. Your tone and tempo tend to drift in and out, as if you're restless and feel a need to tinker with the music," she mentioned again Ellington's "Pie Eye's Blues," and how I interpreted the twelve-beat formula perfectly at first, only to gravitate toward something ancillary by the start of the second refrain. "You don't do any exercises either, do you? You're all gusto and wild performance."

I was stunned. What was this? What did she mean my mechanics were erratic? I wanted to get up and play "C Jam Blues," or "In a Mellotone," or Rachmaninoff's "Prelude, Op. 23, No. 6 in E-Flat," and let her tell me then what was wrong with my music. "If there's a rawness to my playing, it's because it's supposed to be there."

"Ahh."

"It's true."

She removed the stem of her wine glass from the space between her right thumb and index finger and set her drink down on the table. The stiffness of her hand made moving the glass look surreal and when she lifted her chin my image appeared in her eyes. I wasn't used to being criticized this way, and lighting a cigarette, asked, "How is it you think to know so much about my playing?"

"Does it matter?"

"If I'm to take you seriously."

"So I need credentials to critique you but you don't need the slightest bit of training to play."

I couldn't help but smile at this, and Liz in turn told me, "I teach Performance, Theory, and Composition at the university. Those who can't," she tapped the surface of the table with her false hand and went on to explain, "I was at the Peabody Conservatory in Baltimore through last year and came to Renton because there are other projects I'm working on and I was promised a certain flexibility. Listen," she said suddenly, "you shouldn't be offended by my comments. Your playing is actually quite good." She brushed her hair back behind her ears, her attractiveness unconventional, her features edged sensually, and as I sat and tried to decipher her compliment, she laughed at my apparent confusion and wondered, "What would you have me say? Do women usually tell you that you're brilliant? Is that what you want to hear?"

I blew smoke high into the air. "I don't usually talk about my playing."

"Why?"

"I just don't," I said. "I play, that's all. I don't even think about it."

"Bullshit," it was somehow exciting to hear her swear. "You should think," she insisted. "Having a love for music doesn't mean being out of control."

"So now I'm out of control?"

"You're too talented to ignore your responsibility."

"And talented, too?"

"I never said you weren't."

"And if I prefer using my talent to play as I like?"

"I'd say that's fine but rather a waste."

"Well, then," I blew more smoke and sipped off the remaining whiskey from my glass while letting Liz know, "as far as I'm concerned, there's a huge distinction between academic assessment and the actual joy I take from sitting down to perform. You have to realize, I like the way I play. Changing my mechanics won't improve how I feel and why should I try and fulfill someone else's expectation of what the music should be? Learning to interpret Liszt's "Liebestraum" or Beethoven's "Für Elise" doesn't make anyone a great musician. There's much more to it than that, and besides," I foolishly continued and dared Liz to find anyone in Renton who played better than I.

Three things happened then in quick succession. First, Elizabeth got up from the table and went to the piano where she played a remarkably beautiful piece using only her left hand. I would not have thought it possible had I not been there. The music was transporting. Beginning adagio, the arrangement built its way through an intoxicating lyric, into something bluesy and classical and slightly jazzed. The melody was simple, yet filled with such intricate harmonies and rifts, with hints of arabesques, trills, and tremolos, that no one would have guessed a single hand could produce such a spectacular sound. Elizabeth did not sit down but played while standing and looking out into the empty bar. Her expression made it seem she was doing nothing more than demonstrating scales, yet the corners of her mouth showed the most private start of a smile.

No sooner did she finish then someone knocked on the locked door and a man I didn't know, older than I with short cropped hair brushed forward, a round head, and wire-framed glasses pushed high up on his nose, stepped inside as Elizabeth undid the lock and greeted him by name. In the next moment she thanked me for the wine and ended our night by inviting me to come see her at the music school sometime. "If you like," she turned away and disappeared outside.

———

I waited almost a week before accepting Elizabeth's invitation, sitting at my piano in the time between, practicing chords and scales and the mind-numbing mechanics of finger exercises. I was determined to impress her and spent hours searching through countless recordings, stacks of sheet music and books, racking my brain for just the right arrangement to perform. I considered hundreds of compositions, from baroque to ragtime to jazz, a dozen obscure masterworks by Dizzy Gillespie, Cootie Williams, and Erroll Garner, torch songs and show tunes, pop hits and classic rock and roll, everything from Clapton's "Badge" to Debussy's "Reverie" and Chopin's "Fantaisie-Impromptu, Op. 66." I'd a very clear sense of what I wanted and still it took forever to find.

Such enterprise was new to me, the motivation behind my industry hard to explain. My affinity for jazz notwithstanding, I decided on Rachmaninoff's "Prelude, Op. 32, No. 5" in G, convinced this was the music Elizabeth preferred. The composition was not as overpowering as some of Rachmaninoff's other scores, not as explosive as "Op. 3, No. 2," nor rousing like "Op. 23, No. 7," and in this way depended more upon the pianist's skills to reproduce the inherent awe of the arrangement. Just short of three and a half minutes long, "Op. 32, No. 5" was built upon a lyrical conversation exchanged between the right and left hand. While the right hand was buoyant, flowing from slow to fast and back again, swooping in and out like a clever bird, the left hand provided ballast, was sotto voce, more tempered and exacting in its rhythm. Overlapping, the two voices created a harmony which, if played by a less skilled musician, risked cacophony and disorder.

I practiced the score over and over again, until each note had its own identity and every phrase was worked out, and just after noon that Friday I walked to the music school where a woman in the main office suggested I look for Elizabeth downstairs. I found her in a rehearsal room and slipped inside as one of her students finished Liszt's "Hungarian Rhapsody No. 2." (A boy of maybe twenty, his straight black hair clipped in bangs above the dark frame of his glasses and his crisp short-sleeved dress shirt buttoned all the way up to his neck, he performed while concentrating less on the music than on not making a mistake.) After Liszt, Elizabeth conferred with her student, who left the room with a great sigh of relief.

"Good morning, Mr. Finne," she spoke formally once we were alone and in such a way that I couldn't be sure if she was happy to see me. She appeared to know that I was there to play however, and pretending she was my instructor and I'd come for a lesson, she asked if I was ready to begin. I sat at the piano while Elizabeth stood off to the side, and eager to dazzle her, I couldn't otherwise keep from performing with the same physical animation as my father, squirming about on the bench, hovering in tight above the keys then swaying side to side before leaning far back in order to let the music dance down my arms. When I finished, I folded my hands in my lap and watched Elizabeth stand silent for several seconds before walking back toward the piano.

"Your mechanics are hopeless," she said. "What is it you're doing? Your elbows seem to be fighting with your wrists and your wrists with your fingers. As for the music," this caused a second silence that lasted even longer than the first. I tried to free my mind of all expectation and was rewarded in this way when Elizabeth said, "You are a bastard, aren't you, Mr. Finne?"

"It's a beautiful piece," I told her.

"There's potential in your playing."

"There's always potential, Ms. Rieunne."

At this she smiled. "I guessed you might choose Rachmani-noff."

"Does that mean you've been thinking of me?"

She pressed her knees against the front of the piano. Her shirt was sleeveless, dark blue with small white threads outlining the shoulders and collar. She had on shorts and no shoes, her sandals tossed to one side of the room, and resting her false arm atop the piano, she said with assurance, "No more it seems than you've been thinking of me."

"It's true, I have. All week, I confess."

"And what am I to do with this information?"

"Have dinner with me."

"All right."

"Are you free tonight?"

"No."

"Then?"

"Pick me up at seven."

Elizabeth's apartment was on the west side of campus. I don't drive much in the summer and wound up spending an hour that afternoon cleaning last winter's trash from the floor of my old car. I showered and put on a blue shirt and sport coat, clean slacks and dark shoes. Elizabeth wore a white dress which hung loosely from her shoulders and was tied at the waist with an orange sash. Her hair was pulled back and set inside Chinese sticks. We went to Lutrane's and drank wine before dinner. Elizabeth asked about my studies at the university, about my interest in Art History, the subject of my dissertation, and the classes I taught. She wanted to know how long I'd lived in Renton and what precipitated my playing at Dungee's. We talked about the time she spent teaching in Baltimore, about the trip she took to Italy last year, and the project she was finishing now, an article on Louise Talma, the neoclassical composer and first American to teach at

Fontainbleau. We had a second glass of wine at the end of our meal and I asked her then about her hand.

"An accident," she said.

"I'm sorry."

"Me, too," she looked up and smiled. The story she told began at the Bristeen Academy of Music. "I had shown an early aptitude for piano and my parents were generous in having me trained." At fifteen she won a national competition, and at twenty was living full-time in France, in a small apartment on the grounds of an old estate donated to the French Academy of the Arts. "I was studying very hard and working with some of the best teachers in the world, including Philipe DarChmonde. Philipe was brilliant," Elizabeth said, "but we were poorly suited for one another. I was reserved and somewhat timid at the time. I spent my childhood pursuing music, and as a consequence my identity became tangled up in my playing so when I wasn't practicing or performing I'd no sense of who I was. Philipe on the other hand was all vanity and ego and wanted to instill the same sort of self-possession in me, convinced if I was ever to make the transition from child prodigy to a fully mature musician, I had to broaden my range of experience."

At forty, DarChmonde's own career as a solo performer had slowed after a promising beginning due to an onset of arthritis in his fingers that seemed to flair just as his own rehearsals were going well and his agent booked a series of recitals. "I don't know how he behaved with his other students," Liz said "but with me, after an hour or so, as I played and we discussed the nuances of one or two particular compositions, Philipe would alter his approach, begin exhorting me to up the ante and turn myself loose in order to get deeper into the score. Such abstract notions were initially little more than fodder for my imagination, but then Philipe began bringing me books with unusual philosophies and provocative themes. He said I had to open myself up fully to experience if my playing was ever to reach its potential. What he meant by this I wasn't sure, and still, I appreciated his tutelage and waited to see what would happen as he began taking me to parties and after-hours clubs, had me meet people whose attitudes and talents differed from anything I'd ever known.

"The grounds of the estate were bordered by woods and I used to walk before dinner along the path near a small ravine. From time to time a dog would meet up with me, a runaway I assumed from one of the nearby farms, large and dark brown, at least eighty pounds, with thick fur and a huge head dominated by a flat nose and square jaw. I began bringing him scraps of food and several times tried coaxing him from the woods but he never once agreed to leave. My practice sessions with Philipe continued through the summer as I was scheduled to perform in Vienna that August and was learning Chopin's "Piano Sonatas Nos. 2 and 3" and "Concerto No. 1." "Philipe's knowledge of Chopin was extraordinary," she said, "though his insistence that I continue focusing on personal abandonments in order to establish a true connection with my music was now an obsessive theme of our rehearsals. Once when I was playing he brought a woman to the studio, undressed her in front of me and made love to her right there on the floor, all the while barking at me to play on. I could have refused, I suppose, but I didn't, and while I noticed no immediate influence on my music, I stored the experience away as something Philipe said I could draw upon in the future.

"Two days later, Philipe suggested I practice for him in the nude. I refused and questioned why he assumed broadening my personal experiences was necessarily tied to sex, to which he said if I could think of another way in which to get my heart to race as fast, by all means, we would try it. I thought for a time, then stood and took off my clothes. We spent much of July this way, with me playing Chopin while Philipe watched and caressed me. We made love often before and after my performance, and while I didn't think I was falling in love with him, the sex confused me. I was still quite young and shocked when suddenly in early August Philipe came to my apartment for our session and ordered me to not undress and said there would be no more physical contact between us. The arthritis in his hands had returned and he hid them deep in his pockets. I asked if there was something I did to disappoint him, but he replied angrily and told me to just play and otherwise leave him alone. When I faltered over the first movement in Chopin's "Concerto No. 1," and surprised myself by weeping, Philipe chided me for being so naive and insisted he was doing me a favor, that the personal experience he alluded to for so long wasn't limited to our carnal antics—as he called it—but evolved from the ashes now that things between us were over and done.

"I took my walk as usual that night, mad at myself and feeling both confused and foolish, and entering the woods found the dog waiting for me. I was glad to find him, eager for company, but as I waved and walked toward him, he suddenly began to bark. This surprised me, for in all the months before he never made a sound. I assumed he was hungry and excited to see me, and it was only as I came nearer that I noticed blood on his coat, wounds across his neck and hindquarter and a tear in one of his ears. I hurried to him but his barking only grew worse, and as I knelt to set the food I brought down on the ground, I was knocked over and felt a wet explosive heat tear through my right arm. I lost consciousness and didn't wake until I was at the hospital where the doctors took me into surgery, removed what remained of my arm, cleaned the wound and sewed everything off. I was later told that my screams brought people from the estate into the woods but I can't remember any of it. A dog was found standing at my side and one of the caretakers came running with his gun and shot him dead. Sometime the next morning the body of a second dog was found in the woods."

Elizabeth stopped then and finished her wine. The details of her story were still spinning in my head as I stared across the table and tried to think of something appropriate to say. Rather than offer up some needless bit of sympathy, I hoped for a more intelligent reaction, but in the end the best I could think of was a somewhat banal, "Things do come at us from all sides, don't they?"

"It's true."

"Left and right."

"Very funny," she laughed, and passing her false hand through the smoke I created with my cigarette, swirled the air with gentle strokes.

We drove out Garber Road after dinner, past where the street lights stopped and the pavement became dirt and the night filled with the sound of my old car moving over ruts and stones. Around midnight we went to Dungee's for a drink, and later I parked my car near Elizabeth's apartment and we took a walk along West Washington, beyond the iron gates of the arboretum where Elizabeth spoke aphoristically of deciding to teach after her injury. She described enrolling at the New York Conservatory where she earned her doctorate in music theory and then accepted a professorship in Baltimore. "I miss playing as I once did, but the reality seems pointless to mention. We all miss things don't we?"

She asked questions of her own, wondering about my past, all of which I answered in a way I hadn't for a very long time. I told her about my mother, provided anecdotes about Tyler and my father, described all that happened at my aunt's and the Haptree

Theater and the night my father smashed his piano with an ax and danced beside the hissing flame. Elizabeth walked close to me, her left hand in my right, our hips in rhythm and occasionally touching. The strength of my reserve, inviolable and self-protecting for so many years, faltered as we walked back through campus and I briefly suffered a panic. When I tried to pull my hand away however, Elizabeth clung knowingly and refused to release me. The moon was ivory, large and white as Elizabeth stepped around in front and slipped her right hand beneath my left arm. Instead of kissing her lips, I fell gently against her neck while reaching to touch her perfect fingers nestled then against my sleeve.

I called her the next day and invited her to meet me at Dungee's that evening. She came in the middle of my second set and sat at one of the side tables. I finished playing around eleven-thirty and went to join her, ending the night with "Blue Rondo à la Turk." (Even the kitchen staff who'd heard me play a thousand times before stopped what they were doing and came out to listen.) On the chance of Elizabeth coming back to my room, I spent the better part of the day reshelving my books, folding my laundry, sweeping the floor, and rehanging the Milton Avery print leaning against the wall. I dusted and carried empty glasses from beneath my chair to the kitchen sink, picked up loose papers, washed dirty dishes, made my bed, set out clean towels in the bathroom, and wiped the grime from around the toilet and bathtub drain.

At six o'clock, I showered and dressed and stood in front of my window examining my handiwork. Everything was absolutely spotless and yet something wasn't right. The transformation of my room was startling, with even the doorknobs polished and the nicks in the wood floor waxed over twice. Leaving Dungee's, Elizabeth suggested we go somewhere else. We discussed stopping in at one of the after-hours clubs, walking over to Liberty for coffee, or catching part of the midnight movie at the Main Theater. None of these ideas appealed to us however, and when I suggested going to my place where Liz could see my old piano, she laughed and said, "So you want me to see your instrument, is that it, Professor Finne?"

Upstairs, I watched her walk through my room, examining the space, stopping so we could kiss, my hands undoing the buttons of her shirt which she let slip down her arms. Instead of a bra, she wore a sleeveless white undershirt, the smooth sides of her breasts exposed. I knelt and helped take off her shoes. She peeled her pants down and stepped from them before we kissed again. A moment later she moved away and to my surprise looked back around my room, frowning now as she said, "This isn't how I pictured it."

She went to my bookshelf first where she removed a half dozen paperbacks and tossed them out across the floor. She then opened my closet and pulled laundry from a cardboard box, removed dishes from the cabinet in my kitchen and refilled the counter and sink. She scattered the stack of magazines and messed the neat lay of my bedsheet. Each time a part of her task was complete, she came and kissed me and helped me remove an item of clothes. When I was naked, she undid her prosthesis and set it on top of my piano. I moved toward her and cupped her half-arm against my face, kissing the knotted end with my lips, tasting her flesh from just below her elbow on up to her shoulder. Elizabeth stroked my head, stared into the disorder she'd created inside my room, and whispered, "There, Bailey. There. Isn't that better?"

———

We spent the rest of the summer together, and when fall semester began, adapted our schedules according to the needs of our affair. We took long walks late at night and went with friends to concerts and movies and parties around town. While I maintained my usual sloth, Elizabeth always had several projects going—teaching and tutorials, composing original arrangements, and writing articles for magazines and journals—her latest on William Schuman, winner of music's first Pulitzer prize. She read countless books, went to meetings and exercise class, attended conferences and recitals, all in endlessly ambitious waves. Many times I woke in the night to find her up and laboring over one of her new compositions and had all I could do to bring her back to bed.

As for my own less inspired routine, Elizabeth took no note of it and never made my conduct an issue. Despite all she said the first night we met when she challenged me to take responsibility for my music, she spoke little now about my playing, about my dissertation and the prospect of my teaching position being lost, and insisted only, "If you're happy living as you do, that's what's important." If I stood for hours in front of a painting by Ad Reinhardt or Marc Chagall, or sat home all day rereading essays by Clement Greenberg or Edward Lucie-Smith, Elizabeth would smile and say, "How wonderful for you, Bailey," as if nothing in the world pleased her more.

Here then was something unexpected, for while my contentment typically came as a consequence of subtraction and learning how to jettison with no appreciable residue everything which drew too near, Liz had me suddenly wanting for more. Our lovemaking was performed with rapture and high spirit as we moved in a fluid tangle of limbs spread out wherever the moment took us and leaving me at times to feel like a man on a highwire who, after years of successfully mastering the feat, inexplicably chose to attempt as much while staring into the sun.

For Liz, believing the universe operated under principles of a delicate confusion did not keep her from finding purpose in the madness, and unable to change what happened to her arm, she reinvented herself by treating the incident as little more than a nuisance best ignored. Initially, I couldn't imagine how she felt composing music she'd never be able to perform on her own, but as we played her works together I came to appreciate the implication of her effort and how no one in this world was ever more than half of some greater whole. One piece in particular moved me, arranged as both a separate score for the left hand and right, each beautiful on its own yet intended to be played as one, interwoven as it were, transforming the music into a spectacularly imbricated duet; her accomplishment as beautiful as the concertos of William Bolcom and the overlapping quartets of Milhaud, her scores conjoining like two glorious sides of a painting by Duccio, like shadow melting into light.

Early that fall, I went in the middle of an otherwise uneventful afternoon to stand outside Elizabeth's classroom window, listening as she lectured on Beethoven's "33 Variations on a Waltz by Diabelli." The composition was universally regarded as Beethoven's most difficult piece. Elizabeth encouraged her students to "Think of the music as a revelry for all that has ever astounded you in life. Concentrate on the division and unison between each variation, and how change occurs unexpectedly and suddenly from one movement to the next." She described the many intricacies of the composition, how the transformations in tone were rapid and put the pianist at constant risk of destroying the fragile center of the piece. She said the inherent brilliance of the score was that it grew out of a very simple theme and evolved into something enormously complex. "No one has ever actually mastered it," she said. "Not Emanuel Ax or Horowitz, nor any of the rest, although some have come closer than others. The key is not to think of failing or worrying about going too far wrong. As performers, the trick is just to play," and then she pressed a button and a recording of "33 Variations" came through the window, as spectacular as any performance I'd ever heard and one which Elizabeth didn't tell her class was her at twenty, the year before Philipe and the dogs in the woods.

In October, Elizabeth attended a conference in New York. She left on a Thursday and didn't return until the following Monday night. I played Friday and Saturday at Dungee's, sleeping both nights alone in my room where I had the same peculiar dream. I was outside in a cold and icy rain, following after a woman who looked a good deal like Elizabeth. I knew it couldn't be her and yet I continued running after her as she stepped around a corner and disappeared. A gust of icy wind kicked up and I felt a sudden stabbing in my right arm. My heart began to race, and when I awoke Sunday morning my arm was quite numb and remained that way until Monday evening when I went to pick Elizabeth up at the airport. No sooner did she arrive in the terminal, hurrying toward me with a wave of her left hand, than the deadness in my dangling limb gave way and I felt completely fine. I tried not to give the incident too much thought, but the reality made it difficult to ignore the course I was on.

Early that November, Elizabeth's father flew into town for a day's visit. Sharply tailored with a patchy head of reddish-white hair, pink cheeks, and coal-dark eyes, Charles Rieunne was a senior vice president for Caldwell Securities, passing through Renton on his way to New York for business. Liz and I took him to dinner and just before ten went back to her apartment for a nightcap where I was persuaded to play a bit of Bellini on Liz's baby grand and then she joined me for a duet. The conversations between Charles and myself were genial, and as Liz had already told her father much about me, he asked informal questions regarding my teaching, music and art, and only as Liz went to the kitchen for more coffee and to call down for her father's cab did our exchange become something different.

"About your dissertation," Charles guided me to the far side of the living room where he inquired in earnest, "When can I expect to see it in print?" He wondered what articles I'd published, where I planned to teach once I finished my doctorate, and if I'd any thoughts of doing more with my music.

I answered as he wanted to hear. I said my dissertation was coming along well and would be finished in the next few weeks. I explained that the University of Renton intended to put me on tenure track once I completed my Ph.D. and mentioned a series of articles published. As for my music, I confided a plan to record Chopin that summer for a small label and that there was the possibility of a short tour. All of this delighted Charles very much. He was eager to approve of me, and before he left in his cab I was given a warm squeeze on the arm and a cheery "So long for now then, son."

I regretted my dishonesty as I lay in bed that night, confused and afraid Elizabeth would find out, and getting up I went to stand by the window. The streetlight on the curb glowed brightly, and leaning against the cool glass I wondered again what motivated my deception. ("What the fuck, Bailey?") I remained troubled in the days following Charles's visit, dissecting again and again the source of my deceit, questioning what exactly I was calling into play, what alterations my prevarication seemed to be suggesting, and why. More and more I felt there was something I should be doing but feared admitting exactly what.

In January Elizabeth began spending a good deal of time preparing for her summer tour. There was a large amount of research and rehearsing to do—she not only planned to play original and traditional arrangements in duet, but to provide a series of lectures on a number of influential composers and musicians—and she was assisted in the process by Eric Stiles, a pianist and graduate instructor at the Music School. The aspiring Mr. Stiles, though a second-rate pianist as high standards went, had studied extensively, spent time in Vienna, and published articles on Mendelssohn, Carl Orff, and Leonard Bernstein. Elizabeth turned to Eric for help gathering material on Beethoven and Schubert as part of her first lecture. She had him play the right hand to her left on "Pathetique" and "Sonata in C Minor," and grateful for his effort, trumpeted to me each night just how invaluable his service had become.

Notwithstanding the fact that Eric was a dowdy figure with a protuberant chin and round belly, an unkempt mop of black wiry hair, globular nose, and pasty skin, I felt a certain jealousy toward him and couldn't help but notice Elizabeth's smile each time she described Eric's enterprise, how her voice rose and held a note of exhilaration as she rattled off his skills and achievements. Perturbed in this way, convinced I could do everything the efficacious Mr. Stiles was hired for—and better—I suggested to Liz, "Why not let me help you?"

"You?" I fully expected her to appreciate and accept my offer, but was rebuffed instead with kind thanks and firm assurances that my assistance wasn't needed. "You have your things and I have Eric."

Annoyed by the insinuation that I somehow couldn't be trusted with the task, I wondered if this was how Elizabeth felt about me when it came to her work, what did it say of our affair? I imagined what Charles Rieunne would tell me if he knew the truth, how he'd laugh at my ignorance, and in terms of my care-free aesthetic say, "If you prefer to be irresponsible, why should you expect my daughter to take you at all seriously?"

I slept little that night, struggling for answers, and reaching what seemed the best-laid plan, got up early the next morning and began pulling together the existing pages of my dissertation. I went to the library and conducted additional research on Josef Albers and the influence Gestalt psychology had on his art, incorporated the new material into current chapters, and typed everything into my computer. The process was productive, the whole of my effort performed exclusively for Liz's favor, though I failed to enjoy a single moment of my labor. I cursed through-out, my mood dissolving from idle and calm to temperamental and distant, abrupt and even harsh. The change in my demeanor was obvious the moment I crawled from bed each morning, grousing and grumbling on my way to gathering up all my nec-essary notes and books before skulking off to campus. Liz and I quarreled over what was wrong, and when she questioned what I was doing, I snapped, "I'm just trying to finish. I want to get done, that's all."

"Since when?"

"Now."

Who could blame her for being startled by the sudden shift, and yet somehow sensing what I was up to, she stroked the side of my cheek with her false hand and said only, "All right, Bailey, if that will make you happy."

Clever girl. How I delighted in her company! How much I wanted then to kiss her thighs, to sniff her neck, and lick her face and the back of her knees. The depth of her generosity moved me, her words alone making me glad. After another day of much the same, I put down my book, my pad and pen, and quit my effort with an exhausted "That's enough for now."

Elizabeth sat across the room at my piano, working out a new score, and turning to look at me again, she replied, "You will when you want to." I spent the next four days sitting in my room, reading Chekhov and Richard Ford. Saturday night I played at Dungee's. Elizabeth came downtown with me, and as I ran through a medley of Brubeck and Bud Powell, she applauded the energy of my performance and smiled at the pleasure I exhibited. We made love that night, and relieved, my dark spirits lifted and I was restored.


Returning to old habits was a comfort, and so inspired, I tried not to dwell on the irony of sustaining love this way.

As reward for coming to my senses—and not that Liz didn't wish I'd eventually finish my dissertation or one day choose to do something more with my music, but knew such had to happen on my own terms—we entered a period of renewed jubilation. Our affair seemed sweeter after clearing this first awkward hurdle and we enjoyed a time of rediscovery and confirmation. Eager to celebrate our happiness, we decided to consummate the moment by getting a pet. "Something we can share together" we agreed, and went the next day to Chapperman's Pet Emporium, where we settled on a yellow-green parakeet in a silver cage.

Elizabeth immediately disposed of the cage, allowing Clarence—as she named our bird—to fly about my apartment as he chose. "We need to respect Clarence's freedom and not confine him against his will," she said, a view I accepted in theory, though I wondered in secret how Clarence would ever know he was being restrained if we never let him out.

A bird in open flight is a glorious spectacle, graceful in its glide and stretch of wings, but a parakeet darting about in cramped quarters is an altogether different thing. Despite our best intentions, Clarence could not adjust to flying inside, and no sooner did he get going in one direction than he was forced to quickly draw up, his tiny feet thrust in front of him, his wings pumping frantically in a desperate countermotion, straining not to smash into the walls at high speed. After several days of bruising his beak and exhausting his spirit, he abandoned flying altogether and took to walking back and forth across the floor.

I voted for returning the bird to his cage, but Elizabeth said we should learn to be accommodating. This meant keeping a constant eye out as Clarence pranced about the apartment, forcing me to monitor my steps, checking the cushion in the chair before sitting, and watching where I kicked off my shoes or dropped my books. All sudden turns, sideways strides, and backward actions were discontinued as a matter of course. Where Elizabeth had no problem adapting and easily maneuvered about the room with Clarence beneath her feet, I was less disciplined, nervous and uncoordinated. So convinced my own clumsiness would eventually reduce Clarence to a feathery goo, I had no choice but to work with him in an effort to incorporate his habits into mine.

Such enterprise was difficult for me, and still I managed to conduct myself with diligence in arranging drills and practices until bit by bit Clarence and I got used to one another, my once stuttering stride giving way to a more fluid sense of movement about the apartment. My effort thrilled Elizabeth, my ability to develop an awareness of where the bird was at all times. "You see what you can do when you put your mind to it?" she cheered, her smile a mix of gratitude and great relief. I was delighted to please her and have her look at me with such happiness, though in the process I came again to wonder if such ambition was a part of love I was somehow supposed to sustain.

Toward the end of February, Elizabeth invited a group of people to her apartment. (Although we spent most nights together, we still maintained separate addresses, and for the evening we agreed it would be best if Clarence remained at my place.) On hand were Eric Stiles and his date, a willowy clarinetist named Amber Tilman; Dr. Willum Kabermill, the dean of the Music School, and his wife Eunice; a few more of Liz's colleagues; and Niles for me. Our guest of honor for the evening was the pianist André-Seve Harflec, who came with his girlfriend, Janet Minot. Andy—as Harflec insisted everyone call him—was an old friend of Liz's, a musician on the verge of real fame and due in four days to perform a recital at the Miller Theater in New York.

I played host, took coats and helped set out the hors d'oeuvres, made drinks, and engaged in conversations while Liz saw to Andy. (Harflec was a slender man with dark brown hair cut about the edges of his pretty face and arms forever bent and reaching forward.) Liz wore a sweater dress that fit her figure snugly, her own hair done in a way I'd not seen before, a single thick tail made on the right side extending in an orange arch. I watched her standing near the piano, Harflec beside her, shoulder to shoulder as others in the room came and spoke with them. They smiled at one another with a familiarity composed of history, and noting the ease with which they carried on, I continued observing them even as I was involved in my own conversations.

I was talking at one point with Eric and Niles when Andy's girlfriend came over and held her empty glass out in front of me. "Drink," she said. Dressed in black, with bare shoulders and smooth, creamy-white skin, her body slightly fuller than Liz's, a provocative face, her attractiveness wielded with aggression,

Janet was obviously a girl used to turning heads. Instead of taking her glass I pointed her toward the bar. When she came
back a minute later she said dryly, "You might at least have asked
what I was drinking before you sent me away."

"I had a feeling you'd find what you want."

"I usually do," she held her glass with two fingers. "Your girlfriend's lovely. André's been talking about her all day."

"You mean Andy."

"Whatever," there was dissmissiveness in her tone, a worn
sound which seemed to arrive from a great distance. I glanced
across the room again, at Liz and Andy laughing together over
some such thing Dr. Kabermill told them, and looking back at
Janet—she'd made herself a whiskey with a single cube of ice—
I could imagine without much trouble the whole of our affair;
the banter between us performed in prurient waves without
future complication, no entanglement or emotional wondering
as we enjoyed our sex with ease and a like understanding. Such
an uncomplicated arrangement made me laugh to think how fast
I would have pounced as recently as last summer. (Janet in her
tight-fitted dress and golden hair so thick and long I could
imagine clinging to it like reins.) The issue then was not temp-
tation but the reality of its absence, how steadily in the last few
months my need for Liz had reached a point beyond anything
before. Laying in bed at night, I'd try and pretend she wasn't
there, and occasionally when she was off teaching or working on
some other project, I'd tell myself she didn't exist and that the
emotions I felt were a deliberate fiction. The exercise always
alarmed me however, and I'd quickly quit the test, though not
before the experience took its toll.

I was just about to excuse myself from Janet when Andy
and Liz came to join us. Elizabeth slid in next to me and
wrapped her left arm around my back as Harflec stood close to

her right. "Bailey," he said my name as if it was for him something of a curiosity. "I was just telling Lizzie that Evgeny Kissin is coming to hear me in New York and she is so jealous. Do you know Kissin?"

"Not personally, André."

"No, of course not. And Andy, please," he gave a shameless sort of smile, and after confiding in some detail his friendship with Kissin, looked me up and down and asked about my teaching. "Lizzie tells me you're an instructor at the university."

"Art History. I'm an adjunct."

"Yes, well, I must say it seems quite a coup for your Renton to have landed Elizabeth." He said no more about me, and touching Liz on the shoulder, went on to say, "When I heard she was leaving Peabody and coming here, of all places, well, frankly, I wasn't sure what to think. Don't get me wrong," he had a way of sublimating his insults behind a wink, "your university has a fine reputation."

"But it's not the Peabody."

"Exactly," he nodded, satisfied I understood, while Elizabeth spoke in defense of Renton, referring to the excellent faculty Dr. Kabermill had put together and how the autonomy she had here to conduct her work and develop her own curriculum had many advantages over the more established institutions. I appreciated her statement, but the university was not the focal point of Andy's comments, a truth not lost on Janet who rolled her eyes when our guest of honor said, "Yes, of course, but Renton is so saturnine, is it not? An odd place for music."

"I would guess Gershwin and Copland would argue otherwise."

"Ahh, American composers, of course. You do call them composers, don't you?"

I was once more watching Liz, waiting to see what part of

Andy's criticism registered and which I could ignore as trite party banter, when Andy told a story about a time Liz and he were in France. "The music, my God! Do you remember?" The purpose was as before, to make me understand that Liz's presence in Renton was an aberration, the insinuation impossible to miss, Harflec driving the point home every chance he could.

"Why don't we talk about something else," Janet yawned and André quickly replied, "But sure. Janet hates when I get to rambling about music and I'm certain it must be taxing for you as well, Bailey."

Again Liz rallied to my defense, mentioned my piano playing, my knowledge and talent which I interrupted to say, "I dabble is all."

"Yes, well, it must be pleasant for you. Sometimes I wish I could simply—what is the word?—dabble, to relax a bit and enjoy the lighter fare."

"Oh, for Christ's sake, André," Janet waved her whiskey glass in front of his face and frowned. Andy's own expression filled with surprise as if to intimate—quite falsely, of course—that he truly didn't understand. "What did I say? I meant only there's something to relish in the ability to enjoy a simple tune and play such as a lark. A serious musician doesn't have that luxury," he puffed out his narrow chest for Liz's benefit. "A hobbyist can enjoy whatever he fancies while a real pianist can never be satisfied banging out such a rudimentary repertoire as Beethoven's 'Appassionate' or Mussorgsky's 'Pictures at an Exhibition,' for example. There is for us always the issue of challenging one's talent."

To his credit, André Harflec had, in fact, made his reputation performing the world's most difficult compositions, works by brilliant yet obscure figures such as Godowsky, Alkan, Medtner, Henselt, Catoire, and Kaputsin, which other musicians avoided as a matter of course. Critics regarded Andy as a technical wizard, whose hands the reviewer Alex Ross referred to as "a wonder and a marvel," the mastery of his interpretive performance exceeded only by the voodoo of his dispatch. All this aside, I found the man an ass, and when he goaded me further with, "Music is music, don't you think, Bailey? It's good to be able to appreciate both the simple tunes and the classics and play each the same way," I felt Liz's fingers on my waist go tense and draw me in tighter.

"What I mean," Andy said while moving toward the piano, "is that all music has a fundamental center. Even the more difficult arrangements I play can be dissected and reduced to where someone such as yourself can figure out their essence and knock them off in a modest fashion. For example," he sat then and played an elementary send-up of "Mary Had a Little Lamb," which he soon transformed into ragtime, classical, and jazz. "You see, it's all there," he smiled as everyone in the room turned and listened to what was going on. "As for the more sophisticated works, someone such as yourself needs merely find what notes he's comfortable with and tease them within your limitations."

He performed then Nikolai Roslavets's "Etude No. 1." The piece was nothing less than a fundamental marvel which no one—save Harflec—dared play anymore. While Roslavets invented his own harmonic system based on altered scales, his "Etude" infused with double sharps and flats creating a glorious white elephant of a knuckle buster, Andy seized control of each note, stared at Elizabeth then glanced at me in order to make sure I understood the depth of his inspiration. So completely mesmerized was Eric Stiles by Andy's playing that he drifted back and appeared to hide behind his date. Liz was awed as well and the corners of her mouth rose as André turned the air electric. I was envious, worse than before when I tried to impress Liz by finishing my dissertation, and with the manifold of my happiness now forever diverted, removed from the days when sloth and leisure were able to sustain me, I conceded the stakes were infinitely higher and required something more.

I waited for Andy to finish and as he stepped forward to bow while the room burst into applause and cheered his name, I slipped behind and took my seat at the piano. I was out of my league, for sure—but what purpose heaven then?—and sneaking a final peek at Liz, uncertain what I could pull off, I closed my eyes and was back again at my father's piano, laying down the notes as they came into my head, guiding them through the tips of my fingers like a hot current passing through ten separate wires. Where Andy performed with his upper body stationary and in faultless display of his command, I rocked and swayed as madly as ever, producing grand accompanimental refrains while knocking out Roslavets's "Etude No. 1" with my own mastery and verve.

Although I never heard the piece before, the notes formed in my head with the unmistakable preciseness of an echo. At some point during my playing, oblivious to everyone but Liz, whom I couldn't quite bring myself to look at, and with my eyes still closed, I grew frightened by what I was doing and nearly thought to stop, but by then I couldn't and finished with a flourish. Opening my eyes, I turned first to Liz whose face was fixed in absolute amazement, and then through the silence of the room with everyone in shock and no one quite sure what they just witnessed, I grinned at our astonished guest of honor, and said, "Something like that then, Andy?"


A fluke? Most definitely and not to be repeated. (What did I know about love after all and how to yield what was required?) Liz glowed and brought me a fresh drink. She kissed my cheek and stood close by while everyone congratulated me on my performance. Even Andy gave a begrudging "Good show," only to leave soon after, excusing himself with the mention of an early flight out in the morning. I acknowledged the response with a diffident shrug of my shoulders, my interest only in Liz, elated to have made her smile the way she did—the expression on her face a mix of revelry, shock, and wonder—and was otherwise clueless at the time about the can of worms I'd opened.

Later that night, after everyone was gone and we'd cleaned up from the party, rinsed the plates, and put away the remaining food, we took a walk across town and wound up back at my apartment. Liz's mood remained sanguine, and when I asked if she was worried about André who was clearly upset by my performance, she smiled and insisted Andy was a big boy and could take as much as he dished out. "Besides, your playing was remarkable."

"The others seemed to like it well enough."

"You think?" she kicked off her shoes. We were upstairs by then, Liz undressing near the closet before disappearing into the bathroom then slipping into bed. I sat on the floor with Clarence, joining Liz after a minute, eager to be praised and even rewarded for my playing, kissing her neck and lower onto her shoulders and the first soft knoll of breast. "What about you?" I asked. "Did you like what you heard?"

"You know I did," she positioned her left hand beneath my chin, preventing me from exploring further down, drawing my head back from under the sheet and causing me to look at her then. The anticipation in her face, the expectation and hopefulness were different from the gladness I found there earlier as I knocked off Roslavets's "Etude," and when she asked, "What about you? What did you think of your playing?" I answered cautiously with, "I was good enough, I suppose." I tried to resume kissing her then, turning my head so I could get at her fingers still holding my chin, but Liz drew away, sat up on the bed, smoothing her T-shirt down and scolding me slightly. "I'm serious. What happened tonight is significant."

"For whom?"

"You don't think it's worth discussing?"

"There's nothing to discuss."

"You're kidding, right?" Liz's expression filled with disbelief, her good humor lapsing, and when I shook my head, she raised her half-arm like a broken marker and demurred. "So what are you telling me, that you thought you'd sit down in front of André-Seve Harflec, before Eric and Dr. Kabermill and a half dozen other world-class musicians and bang out Roslavets for them and call it a night?"

"Something like that," I tried to laugh off the aggravation in Liz's tone and went so far as to remind her that we had this conversation months ago and she agreed that I was right to do whatever I chose with my music.

"I said the ultimate decision for handling your talent is your responsibility."

"All right then."

"And that's what you did tonight. You accepted the responsibility," she tried to amend her position, said her support was predicated on the assumption that I was happy playing in relative anonymity while pounding out rock and jazz at Dungee's, only "You and I both know that's not true anymore."

"Do we?" I tried again to throw her off, insisted what happened tonight was no big deal, but my comment only added fuel to Liz's fire. "Sure, Bailey. Anyone could have sat and played the way you did. Why should your success with Roslavets convince you it's time to start taking your music seriously?"

"It shouldn't," I answered as a matter of fact, and reminded her again, "I was only trying to put your friend in his place when I played tonight."

"Meaning what? That you think so little of your music now that you're content using it as a party trick?"

"I didn't say that. It's just that Andy pissed me off."

"So it bothered you that Andy assumed you were a second-rate musician?"

"Sure."

"Because you know you have talent."

"It bothers me because André's an ass."

"Because you don't like anyone talking down to you when it comes to music."

"Because I don't like anyone who's a smug son of a bitch."

"Because you have talent," she said again, her half-arm atop the sheet, her prosthesis laid out inside its velvet case across the room. She continued to argue, insisting, "You never would have sat down to play if you didn't think you had something to prove. You know you're good and you wanted Andy to hear. What you did tonight made everyone sit up and take notice. You can't just ignore all that now," her face had gone red with annoyance, and when she said, "They won't let you ignore it," the phone rang as if on cue and I went to answer it.

"Mr. Finne? Bailey?" the voice was vaguely familiar, a somewhat formal yet eagerly pitched sound. "Willum Kabermill," the man said, "Dr. Kabermill from the Music School."

I looked over at Liz, then turned myself sideways, keeping my face from her though she already seemed to know the nature of the call.

"I hope it isn't too late. It is late, isn't it, but I just couldn't quite wait until morning."

"It's all right. We weren't sleeping."

"Good. Excellent. About your playing this evening, Mr.

Finne," he went on to compliment my performance saying, "I was most impressed. We all were. The consensus, Bailey—may I call you Bailey?—is that we'd witnessed something extraordinary. A discovery of this kind happens most infrequently." He asked then about my training, where I might have studied and played professionally, and with each answer I gave he sounded all the more surprised and excited. "I have some people I'd like to hear you perform. A showcase if you're at all interested, a few colleagues and agents who know how to manage these sort of things. Assuming, of course," he paused briefly before his own exhilaration got the best of him and he started in again. "A chance like this. A talent like yours. I'd like to help in any way I can," he spoke in sound bites, in enthusiastic bursts, alternating between further praise and additional questions regarding my playing, stopping only after I promised to call him the next day with my decision.

Liz remained on the bed, listening and watching for my reaction. "The others will call, too," she said as I shrugged my shoulders and returned to sit beside her. I wasn't worried about any of the others—"Let them call." I could only think of how to answer Liz as she asked, "So, now what?"

"Now nothing," I was unprepared for any of this and told her, "Let's sleep on it."

"What's to sleep on?" she was unwilling to let the matter drop, afraid my ambivalence would only increase by morning. "You should at least be curious."

"Of what?"

"Where this might lead."

"I don't need it," I scooted back so that I was now across from her on the mattress. "I like things just the way they are," I smiled tentatively and made an effort to reach for her but she pushed my hands away. "Do you?" she asked. "Really?"

"Yes."

"Then why bother showing Andy you could play?"

"I already told you."

"And I think it's more than that."

"More than what?"

"I think you want something different. I think all these years of avoidance have caught up with you. I think you need more."

"I do or you?" the question came out before I could stop myself and I wished I could take it back. Liz gave my statement just enough pause to let me know my claim had registered, then said as if I hadn't spoken at all, "Playing Roslavets. Playing Shostakovich, George Crumb, and Thomas Tallis, it makes you happy. I know it's true. Playing with the big boys no matter how much you deny it. Living as you have is all well and fine if it's still what you want, but how can it be now, Bailey? Jesus, what are you so afraid of?"

I crossed my legs and faced Liz who sat with her back against the pillow while Clarence on her shoulder bobbed his tiny head. ("What, Bailey?") Her question suggested a patience worn thin, and while I wanted to answer with reassurance, I had nothing new to say. I sat in silence looking at her on the bed, the red of her hair in the lamplight, the shape of her cheeks and green of her eyes. After a few seconds I reached out again, my hand falling inside the empty space of her right arm where her fingers should have been. I curled my hand around the void and clung to the absence, and thinking of my mother then and the way love inspired her to sing for my father even as she was otherwise reluctant to perform, I found myself anxious to experience exactly what my mother felt in the time before love seduced her and brought her outside and dropped her into the cold white snow. Inching my fingers up, I said her name, said, "Liz," and gave her what she wanted.

———

In the days that followed, as the aftereffect of my playing at Elizabeth's party acquired a life of its own, we became singularly disciplined in our ambition. Liz was eager to help me pick out the three arrangements I was to perform at my recital. (I had phoned Dr. Kabermill the next day and agreed to play for a select audience, a date was scheduled for late April—I said I needed the time to prepare—and one of the small auditoriums at the Music School was chosen as the site.) Roslavets was a unanimous choice, but while Liz was of the opinion I should keep with the classics, Ornstein's "Danse Sauvage" or Scriabin's "Sixth and Seventh Sonatas" for example, in order to give my performance cohesiveness, I was of the opinion that a work of jazz would better exhibit my range and skill and selected an obscure composition by Clark Terry. As for the third and final score, I gave in and settled on Pierre Boulez's "Second Sonata."

I undertook a rigid schedule of practice, conducted my rehearsals in secret, thanked Liz for offering to help whip me into shape but said, "I prefer if you were surprised." The weeks passed more swiftly than I expected, my commitment unprecedented, and while on occasion my mood fell off and I questioned what exactly I was doing, my sense of incertitude never reached the point it did with my dissertation. Here was what Liz wanted, and here in turn was what I needed to give her. If I exhibited anxiousness, if now and again my spirits darkened and I worried about the effect of surrendering myself so completely to anything and the risk my desire created for possible disaster, Liz took my ambivalence in stride, restored my faith while assuring me, "It's all only natural, Bailey. Don't worry, I'm here. Nothing bad is going to happen."

On the evening of my recital, I arrived at the Music School

just after seven, decked out in my usual jeans and light cotton shirt, determined to be comfortable. Dr. Kabermill greeted me at the door, reached to shake my hand, then changed his mind— unsure if I was one of those self-absorbed performers resistant to having his fingers touched—and settled for resting his palm beneath my elbow and walking me into the room. (Dr. Kabermill was a short man with thick brown glasses, a puffy pile of dark grey hair, and a mouth somewhat too large for his chin so when he spoke—as he did that evening with great anticipation— the bottom half of his face opened up comically like that of a puppet.) The hall he chose was more intimate than the larger auditorium, with six rows of chairs for an audience of thirty. I was introduced to a group of writers and agents along with a few professors I knew from Liz's party. Eric Stiles was there, standing with Liz as I entered the room. After chatting with people who'd traveled from as far away as Boston to hear me perform, I settled onto the piano bench while Dr. Kabermill delivered his opening remarks.

Liz smiled at me expectantly from her seat in the front row. (How lovely she looked!) I was not the least bit nervous, my recent rehearsals having gone quite well and whether it was the lighting then, or how the room felt suddenly heated—as if a great vent was sucking out all the air—or if it was fear waiting until the last possible moment to take hold, or the image of my father which came to me as he danced in the yard just after my mother's death, I'd no idea. Perhaps it was worry for winding up as deranged as he if I exposed my love through this sort of pledge and something unforeseen still happened, but as I began to play and started with the first notes of Roslavets's "Etude," the cooperation from my hands turned erratic, the music channeled down intercepted so what came out was an unruly din and clamor.

At first those in the audience were sure I must be joking, but when I didn't stop and continued with a sway and bounce which made my father's convulsions look tame, a murmur began to pass through the room, a questioning of whether I realized the dreadfulness of my performance. After a short while, as the notes I struck descended faster and faster into chaos, everyone in the hall turned their heads, dumbstruck and wondering if the person next to them was experiencing the same appalling exhibition. I went on for two minutes or more, banging through the "Etude" before switching gears, plummeting further while breaking into a spastic rendering of "Mary Had a Little Lamb," and then "Bad Luck," and while I can't be sure when I realized the awfulness of my playing, at some point I got up on my own and walked out the door.

I went directly back to my apartment, where Clarence followed me to the bed as I sat with my head in my hands and tried to make sense of what just happened. I stared out the window, toward my bookshelf, and across the room where a silver-framed print of a painting by Francis Bacon, a Christmas gift from Elizabeth, was displayed exactly where Shannon's poster of Diebenkorn's *Large Woman* once hung. The picture was entitled *Self-Portrait* and showed the face of a middle-aged man whose features were greatly exaggerated and oddly contorted. An exhausted, day-laborer's face, both comical and frightening with hair thick and black combed off his forehead, clipped short above an enormous brow, a single strand dangling down between Bacon's deep-set eyes. A crooked and beastly nose centered the face, created with broad, aggressive strokes, the mouth pulled violently up and sideways across a chin that was split and drooped to the left like a dab of wet putty.

I came from the bed, and standing before the print, recalled how during the early part of his career, Bacon was highly regarded by contemporaries and critics, but attacked in the middle years for using the same narrow group of images and inventions, abstract portraits of distressed and tormented souls, twisted and bent in deliberately shocking ways. Bacon, in turn, insisted that using only a handful of subjects did not restrict the substantive evolution of his art, but rather helped improve his eye and refine his craft. (Of painting, Bacon said such was a way to "challenge the boundaries of my perceptions and conquer my recognition of the world as a meaningless cluster of stars. I am an optimist," he said, "but about nothing.") After much debate, in the time before his death, nearly all detractors agreed Bacon's later works had evolved appreciably, his painting demonstrating a lyrical and incorporeal conceptualization despite the familiarity of themes.

I took two steps closer and compared Bacon's approach in handling his art to the narrow net I cast over my own life, and despite surface similarities, found our inspiration entirely different. Where Bacon was absorbed in a single-mindedness aimed at an altogether visionary sort of evolution, I was confining as a matter of avoidance, undisciplined and erratic in my projects, drawn to episodes of sloth while refusing to commit to anything long enough to demonstrate actual regard. Even now, when I tried to please Liz, my focus splintered like cold light passing through a cloud. The reality unsettled me, everything that had happened that evening, and struggling to come up with a way I might explain myself to Liz, I wound up unable to think, all paralyzed and addlepated.

Clarence left the bed and hopped onto the piano where he sang, "Twee-twee!," whistling louder when I failed to respond, bobbing rhythmically, hitting the wood with his tiny beak then jumping onto the keys. He strutted across the ivory, his talonlike feet dancing back and forth as he encouraged me to play.

I shook my head. "You don't understand."

"Tweeee!"

"Clarence."

He glared at me then, as only a bird can do, leaped from the piano and pecked at my leg. I moved away from him, went to sit back on the bed, but he followed after me and resumed gnawing at my ankle. I endured his supplication as best I could, trying once more to explain, saying "I'm sorry, but I can't," over and over until finally he seemed to grow tired of me and walked across the floor. The closet was open and he disappeared inside, returning a few seconds later, pulling the miniature bike Liz bought for him several weeks ago. (Purchased as a joke, the bike was of no interest to Clarence until now.) I wasn't sure at first what he was up to, and watched as he dragged the bike into the center of the room, his yellow and green tail feathers jutting straight up in the air before he stopped and released the cycle, stared at me and gave a commanding whistle.

The bike was six inches high, red with a thin yellow corkscrew stripe painted around the center post and frame. The tires were real rubber, the pedals designed for a birdlike motion and a special handlebar Clarence could operate when perched on the seat. He whistled again and I got down on my knees and balanced the bike while he climbed aboard. The process of learning to ride was difficult and Clarence had trouble with the pedals, with keeping the bike upright and gaining enough momentum to travel in a straight line. He spent ten minutes falling and climbing back on, though eventually he got the hang of it and managed to ride from one wall to the next, pedaling better and better still, his balance improving, becoming secure and unwavering.

After establishing his expertise, he hopped off the bike and walked back to the piano, whistling for me to follow. I hesitated much as I had earlier, unwilling to be inspired by the machinations of a bird. "You don't understand," I said again, all of which caused Clarence to shake his head and whistle harshly "Twee-twee!" I grew angry, and scooping up the bike, held it out in front of him. "You think it's so easy? What do you know about it? Why don't you try a real trick."

I went to the closet then and retrieved a stretch of twine that I attached between the bookshelf and the chair, a distance of some six feet and a good thirty-six inches off the floor. Undaunted, Clarence leaped up and stood on the string. I lifted the bike and placed it on the stretch of twine, gripping the rear wheel while Clarence climbed on board. It took a while for him to grasp the difficulty of this new trick, such a fine measure of balance and how the slightest error sent everything crashing. Soon however, I began reducing my assistance and he learned to open his wings just enough to feel steady, monitoring his own momentum, understanding how much speed was required to keep the bike upright, churning the pedals inside his claws and flapping his wings at the end of each ride.

No sooner did he master the stunt than he stopped again and jumped from the bike, went back to the piano where he stood atop the sounding board. I ignored him as best I could, even as his whistle became a screech and he dove toward the keys. Despite his limited weight, he managed to pound hard enough to produce a clear middle C. I turned to face him and told him sternly, "Forget it. I won't. I can't," to which he responded by flying from the piano and crashing hard against my chest.

The force of his velocity jolted me, his trajectory intentional. I couldn't remember the last time he tried to fly, but as I bent down to make sure he was all right he scooted away and avoided my hand. "Come on, Clarence," I called after him, imploring him to see things from my perspective, saying, "I get what you're doing, but it's more than simple application. If that's all it was, well, hell. But it isn't. It's complicated. Fuck, Clarence. You're a bird! What do you know about anything?" I almost had him cornered, was about to pick him up and start my excuse all over when Elizabeth set her key in the lock and opened the door.

There's a point in every piece of music when the melody completes itself and what's left is a final refrain. Occasionally an aria will vary its rhythms just enough to reinterpret the music through a less predictable finish, and other times an arrangement ends so suddenly the audience isn't quite sure the music's over until the last echoing notes have faded and the room falls eerily still. Either way, the song is done. Elizabeth stood just inside the door, staring at the tiny bike and stretch of twine. Her face was wan, more tired than I could ever remember seeing her before, cast over with sobering shades of resignation, and sizing up the situation in the aftermath of what happened at the Music School, she said, "Bird tricks, Bailey?"

"I can explain."

"That's all right."

"About what happened," I got up from my knees, stood a few feet away on the opposite side of the twine. I wanted to apologize and make sense of what went wrong, but unsure what I could say, I held out the bike like a sacrificial offering, my hands trembling as Liz shook her head and I tossed the toy into the chair. Clarence moved toward Elizabeth, who reached down and scooped him up, setting him on her shoulder. A car honked on the street. A set of tires squealed. I stood in the center of the floor, the space between us only a few feet yet we seemed to be communicating across a broad chasm. "Quite a show," Liz said.

"I'm truly sorry."

"For what?"

"Elizabeth."

"You played exactly as you wanted. Like always."

"But I didn't. What happened was a fluke."

"I don't think so."

"It was stage fright, nothing more," I tried to think of something clever to say, was prepared to go to the piano and perform whatever she wanted to hear, but she was already cutting me off, raising her hand and saying, "Enough."

"You don't understand."

"But that's just it, I do. I should have paid attention before when you were trying to finish your dissertation. I should have known then what you were telling me."

"I wasn't trying to tell you anything."

"Yes, you were."

"Liz."

"And you have. It's obvious you're not happy, Bailey."

"What are you talking about? Of course, I'm happy."

"No."

"I'm trying."

"You shouldn't have to try so hard."

"Playing, I mean. It just isn't coming as easily as I hoped."

"No, it isn't," her tone was barbed. She glanced at her false hand, then back up. "I shouldn't have put you in a position to disappoint me," a curious confession. "As for the rest," she spoke as if she'd thought everything through well in advance, "it's a self-fulfilling prophecy."

"What is? This? But that's not true. I didn't want any of it. That's crazy."

"You're making yourself crazy."

"But I'm trying to change."

"Why, if you're so happy?"

"Wait. You're confusing what I'm saying," I paced through the space where the string hung, struggling to make myself clear, only Liz cut me off and said again, "Tonight's exactly what you wanted. All those people, Bailey. Dr. Kabermill came off looking like an ass. You forced yourself to fail without a thought of what it meant to his reputation, and why? Because you can't trust yourself to want anything. You chose playing Roslavets because you knew, more than your dissertation, more than anything else, promising to take your music seriously was the surest way to get to me. You knew screwing up would be the perfect way to show me how miserable you are."

"Elizabeth, no. That's not it at all," I argued as best I could, challenged the accuracy of her contention by insisting, "You have it all wrong. I admit I messed up. I know I've been driving us both crazy these last few weeks. It's all my fault but everything's been such an aberration."

"What has? How you played? The way you've been acting? But there's no such thing, Bailey. How can anything you do be aberrant? Everything's real, don't you get it?"

I watched her walk to the window where the moon outside was silver white, and scared, I whispered, "This isn't what I want."

Elizabeth heard and turned around. There was a moment then where I might have salvaged a brief reprieve, a half second when opportunity offered me a way to make amends if I could only answer what Liz asked next. "Tell me then, what do you want?"

How to explain? (I still can't.) For despite the chance, I failed to say a word.

Elizabeth reacted to my aphonia by taking hold of her right arm with her left, just below the elbow where her prosthesis fit over her stump, and removing her arm she placed it on the floor. Not finished, she pulled off her shirt, framing in full view the absence of her limb. I stared at her nakedness, at her shoulders and belly and breasts, her arms in their eternal state of non-symmetry like two sides of a Picasso painting where the difference in shapes composed a unique harmony of interdependence. Viewing her half arm alone, I felt the insult of her amputation exactly as she intended, the violence of her injury a raw spectacle, her right arm hanging partway down her side, the end rounded off with a patchwork of flesh covering truncated bone, her condition infinite and without cure. By exposing her fractured form to me, the sight of her said, "There, you see, Bailey? Look at me and still I'm able to choose. I still know what I want!" Here then was the difference between us.

I picked up her prosthesis from the floor, went to the bed, and set it on the pillow. Next I knelt and handed Liz back her shirt. I ached with the need to tell her more, but the moment had passed. Clarence returned to Liz's shoulder and together they moved to the window where Liz pried away the screen, and cupping the bird against her cheek, she whispered something in his ear. Clarence strutted to the end of her arm which Liz extended out over the street. When she whistled, he took off. I rushed to the window where I looked overhead and up into the trees. Elizabeth whistled again, and from out of nowhere Clarence instantly reappeared. I was astonished. (How was such a thing possible?) Elizabeth stared at me mournfully. "Even a bird knows to do what it wants," she said, and with her arm still extended outside, she had Clarence perform the trick twice more.

The first cool breeze of night blew against my neck and I trembled as I came from the window. The air in my apartment chilled as Clarence flew to my piano while Liz gathered up her things and walked into the hall. I left the screen out of the window and soon Clarence disappeared as well. After a time, I stumbled back and sat in my chair.

# CHAPTER 10

# DISTANT SHORES

Emmitt isn't writing now, is staring at me with a rather pitiful look. "What did you think would happen with Elizabeth?" he asks. "Did you expect she wouldn't leave?"

"But I didn't think anything," I made clear. "Obviously, I didn't think at all."

"So you never planned to play the way you did?"

"I already told you. You don't honestly think I did it on purpose?"

Emmitt lifts his head, his gaze clinical, and by way of answering says, "I read the book you loaned me. Not all of it. Not yet. It's not a text to read straight through, but most of it. What do you think of the line: 'Man is the only creature who refuses to be what he is.' Do you agree with that?"

I consider the query, not surprised that out of the entire book, with all its historical and philosophical significance, Emmitt has singled out this one passage.

"The quote is a puzzle," Emmitt continues. "As a syllogism, it doesn't work. How can Man ever simultaneously be the very thing he denies? Man can only be what he is and not what he isn't, and yet, as Man is a cognitive rather than instinctive creature, he has the freedom to choose a course of conduct he might otherwise object to. If a person refuses to act as they know is best, if they compromise and sacrifice their convictions for fear or folly or worse, have they become what they are or are they still someone else?"

Before I reply, I stare down at my hands and think of my last night with Liz, and as a consequence of what I remember, I answer as honestly as possible, and say to Emmitt, "Yes. Without a doubt."

That Monday, Niles took his one final exam—a graduate seminar examining the principles of Parmenides in which the class was asked to explore the issue of time and space being illusions of the senses, and "What then is real?" Professor Lucy Tius posed. He handed in the first draft of his master's thesis for review, his paper entitled "The Subjectivity of Truth: Kierkegaard's Unhappiest Man and Memory as Avoidance and Ruse," and went home to pack, filling his duffle with jeans and shorts, underwear, shirts and socks, toiletries and bandages, a copy each of Camus' *The Rebel* and *A Happy Death* tucked beside the file from Massinissa Alilouche.

I monitored my students' exams on Tuesday, asking them as part of 100 multiple-choice questions to distinguish between the significance of Clyfford Still and the comparatively lesser works of Sam Francis, to identify Jean Fautrier's *Hostage,* to trace connective links from Bauhaus and surrealism to post-painterly and abstract expressionism, and whether *North America* (1966) was produced by Jack Tworkov, Morris Louis, or Barnett Newman. At four o'clock I invited my class to Dungee's, where I provided the first pitchers of beer and played a soulful rendition of Freddie Hubbard's "Little Sunflower," Victor Young's "Street of Dreams," and Albert Brumley's "I'll Fly Away." Time passed and people danced.

Elizabeth flew to Europe the following afternoon. I graded my students' exams and left the next night with Niles. We were scheduled to land in London at ten, depart Heathrow into Bechar and head for Algiers later that evening, where Niles arranged for us to travel by train across the High Plateaux and western edge of the Saharan Atlas, up through Oran and northeast for a distance of some five hundred miles, "To get a feel for where we are," he said.

Our flight into London arrived on time, but our plane to Bechar departed an hour late, and reaching North Africa we went immediately by bus to catch our train. Niles struggled beneath the weight of his duffle and the video camera he brought as we raced from the terminal into the hot street. Our bus was almost full, nearly every inch of space occupied, including the overhead rack and the aisle where more than a dozen people paid to stand with their possessions stored between their feet. We jockeyed for position while stumbling against one another like stones tossed together in a sack, tipped and bounced until we arrived thirty minutes later at the train station which was but an outpost made up of three sand-colored walls and several short wooden benches.

A thin man in a long cotton shirt and dark trousers, flecks of white and grey whiskers on his dark cheeks and a dense mustache swooping down from his upper lip like a scythe stood behind a counter where it was possible to buy pieces of flat bread, a roasted meat called mishwi, and rice. Niles ordered our food— he also asked the man to wrap two meat sandwiches for the train—and we ate our meal standing inside. Afterward, we stretched our legs along the gravel path to the left of the station. Another busload of people arrived and took up space on the platform, groups of families and men traveling alone, their belongings packed in many different sorts of luggage, from ancient leather bags to quilts tied up and knotted with twine. A small boy lay sleeping on one such bundle when the train pulled in—an hour late—the noise startling him and immediately he began to cry. Two men on the near side of the platform looked over and laughed while three women came at once and comforted the child.

Niles bought tickets for a private compartment but the idea of being left in peace was impossible to enforce as the door had no lock and people routinely invaded our space: travelers wishing to escape the public cars, others hoping to sell trinkets of jewelry, sunglasses, and wine, an old man with a metal box chained around his waist offering to exchange our American currency at a rate of 9DA to the dollar though we were already required to exchange 125 American dollars for 1,000DA as we arrived in Bechar. After an hour or so, another man in a green shirt, black slacks, and brown shoes came in and dropped beside me on the seat. His breathing was raspy and there was the odor of fever about him. He begged our forgiveness, but asked if he might just sit a moment. "I don't travel well," he said in Arabic which Niles translated for my benefit.

Our compartment was small, no more than five feet square, and the addition of a third body drove what little fresh air there was back out through the door. The train itself was old and rattled along the iron tracks, causing the man to bump his elbow against my side and press against me hip to hip on the seat. "Possibly, it's all in my head," the man referred to his trouble with travel and coughed into a white piece of cloth. "I don't know. I am otherwise a very active person. I have a beautiful wife and many friends. I own a small business selling and repairing furniture and musical instruments. If not for things beyond my control I would move to the city and be done with these trips, but for now I have no choice."

Aside from his current affliction, the man did not seem to be suffering from any real illness. He had the sinewy musculature of a runner, the appearance of someone whose energy rarely betrayed him. His dark eyes were quick and alert even through his fever, while his voice, if a bit raspy, did not sound altogether weak. "Twice a month I'm forced to travel," the man continued. "Four days out of every thirty I spend this way. As to why it bothers me so, I can't say. I've been to many doctors who insist there's nothing wrong with me. I've taken pills to alleviate motion sickness and similar traumas, but even when I'm drugged near the point of passing out, nothing helps."

Niles asked the man a series of questions in Arabic, wondering about his business, about his family, and the history of his aversion to travel. He translated for me, restated the man's confusion about his condition. "Anah mish ahrif layh (I do not know why)." After several minutes of listening to the man's complaint, I still did not understand and asked Niles to translate, "I don't get it. If traveling is so hard for you and no one can find a cure, why not move closer to Algiers? Or hire someone to go for you? Why put yourself through such torture?"

"But I told you," the man repeated. "Certain things are beyond my control. I have no choice," and getting up from his seat, he thanked us again for allowing him to sit inside our compartment, bowed twice, and turning away from me then, he reached inside the small valise he had with him and produced a jeweled dagger, the stones were actually glass but shined beautifully nonetheless in the light through the window. "A gift," he held the knife out to Niles, "for your kindness." Niles tried to refuse but the man insisted, and turning on his heels, made his exit.

The train ascended a steep hill and the motion of our car shook in protest to the climb. Niles put the dagger inside the bag with his video camera and shrugged his shoulders as if there was nothing more to be said about the man. I considered drawing attention to the coincidence of the man's condition and Niles' own peculiar affliction, but not quite sure what to make of it, I decided to let the subject drop.

Niles reached into his duffel for a tube of ointment and fresh gauze, stood and lifted his shirt in order to apply a new dressing to the wound on his stomach. He discarded the old bandage inside a small paper bag that he then buried back in his duffel. As he finished with the salve, he sat down and searched for his dog-eared copy of *A Happy Death*. Although it was well after midnight—and later still in Renton—he seemed not yet ready for sleep, and finding a favorite part in the novel where Camus' protagonist first goes for a dip in the sea, he read aloud how Mersault "lost himself in order to find himself again, swimming in that warm moonlight in order to silence what remained of the past, to bring to birth the deep song of his happiness."

I untied my boots and stuck them under my seat, listening to Niles while shifting closer to the window. I stared outside at the endless expanse of purple black sky dotted by pearl bright stars, and pressing my nose against the glass, felt the motion of the train while experiencing the reality of moving farther and farther from home. I thought again of Liz and tried to make sense of what happened, considered the quickness of my mistake and speed of my own departure, how I went from a state of absolute dormancy to hurtling along in a blind kinetic whirl.

"We travel with such velocity these days that the most we can do is to remember a few places names. The freight of metaphysical speculation will have to catch up with us by slow train, if it catches up with us at all." The quote appeared in a story I read on the plane, a cautionary tale in *The Collected Stories of John Cheever*, and staring outside again, I thought how true this was in terms of Liz and Niles and all the rest, the speculation I felt over what I was doing in relation to each, the velocity of my trip such that even my most intimate impressions were slow to reach me.

I dozed then and woke with the sun just starting to rise outside the window. Niles was asleep with his legs spread out and his head tipped back against the top of his seat as I got up quietly, slipped on my shoes, and went off in search of a bathroom. After this, I stood outside on the small platform connecting our car to the one in front and smoked a Turkish cigarette from the pack bought the night before. The sun stirred from behind a dense range of mountains, the morning air dry and warm, filled with the smell of esparto grass and the unexpected scent of salt and ash. In the High Plateaux, several pastures of blue green alfa waved lazily in coordinated rows, though for the most part sand was dominant, blowing across the tracks and scratching against the underside of the train.

We cut through a canyon of stone, followed shortly by an orchard of palm trees. I leaned into the metal rail as the train ascended and descended and saw fit to take me, the wheels below making a steady grinding sound that vibrated up through the floor. I gripped tight and looked out toward the horizon where two men suddenly appeared shepherding some twenty goats. Surprised—for I had no idea where they came from nor where they were headed—I watched until the train angled around yet another curve in the track, passing through morning shadows that stretched out elliptically and changed my view altogether.

I crushed my cigarette against the rail, and gauging the speed of the train, wondered if it was possible to lower myself over the side and land safely on the ground without too much damage. The idea of being completely lost this way, so many thousands of miles from home and just one thin metal barrier removed from being utterly abandoned, appealed to me briefly, though in the end I came to my senses and chose to stay on board. My decision caused me to think back to last night and how the man with the fever insisted, "I have no choice," when asked about his own course of travel. The claim seemed so preposterous at first, given how easily the man might have otherwise resisted boarding the train, that I couldn't bring myself to show compassion. What troubled me most was the way it seemed that, if a person had no choice, they had no reason to feel tortured by what they were doing. A person became fevered, melancholy and remorseful not because of circumstances beyond their control but when choices made—or not made—turned out to be in error. This was why I regret what happened with Liz, because I sensed I didn't choose to behave the way I wanted.

And yet, standing there I couldn't help but wonder what if, in some crude way, the man was right? What if there were times we had no choice and what did this say then about my recent blunders? Perhaps I had no choice but to play Roslavets as I did, and as such mangle my affair with Liz. I thought about this for a while, and feeling no better from the possibility of such complete surrender, stared further out in the desert where I spotted three dunes rolling end to end, their curves in an erotic sort of undulation. I pictured Elizabeth laid out in the sands, propped up on her hip and shoulder, imagined her asleep in Spain, in her hotel room, naked atop the smooth white sheets while first the moon and then the sun glowed over her. I watched her sleep, anticipated her every breath and slightest movement until all at once I remembered Niles dozing in our compartment and dashed inside.

The train chose that moment to pitch left and I lost my balance in the aisle, falling against the arm of a snoozing man who woke up cursing. I ran on, already envisioning Niles with the point of a pen jabbed into his neck and the blood everywhere mocking me for being so careless. Terrified, I tossed open the door, relieved to find Niles sitting with his camera filming the desert through the window. "Fuck," I panted. "I'm sorry. I wasn't thinking."

Niles switched his camera off and put it back in its case, the light from the early morning sky white and gleaming. "It's OK," he said. "I'm fine." The train ran on. I sank down in my seat. We were now a half mile up the track from where I first rushed inside, the dunes that reminded me of Elizabeth out of view. Niles reached for the bag with our meat sandwiches, and offering me half, repeated a bit too enthusiastically, "I'm great, really."

Eight hours later we arrived in Algiers. The main railway station was located at the port near the Gare Martime. At mid-afternoon the buildings seemed a fortress set against the dark green water of the bay. On one side, by the El Djazair islets and the Ilot de la Marine, was a lighthouse, the glow from its beacon extinguished, the road leading away from the marina dividing the old Turkish harbor and the Darse de l'Amiraute where, despite the poverty of the region, a handful of lavish yachts were moored to the docks. Niles reserved a room at the Sahel on the Rue Drouillet, and we took a cab across the Admiralty Causeway into the heart of the city, where the streets were crowded with pedestrians and small Italian- and Spanish-made cars. (In contrast to the urban tangle, a few miles farther south at Ouargla and Touchourt people still lived as their ancestors did a thousand years before, in goat-hair tents, nomadic in their movement, shifting as easily as sand.) The desk clerk at the Sahel was indifferent to our arrival, the tourist trade in Algiers having declined so far in recent years the city no longer felt a need to cater to travelers.

Niles paid for three nights stay in advance. (As the one most determined to travel, and as his resources far exceeded mine, Niles most generously offered to cover all expenses of our trip in total.) Our room was moderately sized, with two beds, a wooden chair covered by a flat blue cushion, a tall beige dresser whose open drawers emitted a scent of cedar. A large fan turned overhead, doing little to cool the air. A fly soared several times from wall to wall before landing upside down on the ceiling. The bathroom had a half-sized tub, emerald green tiles, and polished silver piping. After we showered and washed the sand and sweat from our trip down the drain, we went to a small restaurant a few blocks from the hotel where we sat outside and had dinner.

Naive to the customs, I asked for whiskey then settled for juice. Niles was quiet, his coloring off and eyes narrowed as if pinching back an ache. He spoke only to answer questions I put to him about his plans to take his camera and explore the city in the morning, and later as he asked about my strategy for finding Timbal. I had no idea really, had thought of contacting the American consulate and local wire service, had the name of a café Timbal allegedly liked to frequent—the information provided from an article now two years old—but other than that I'd not given the matter any thought.

We finished our meal and before returning to the Sahel wandered across the boulevards, past apartments and darkened shops, grey and white high-rises and squat adobe houses, handsome mosques columned with horseshoe arches and crowning minarets jutting up toward heaven. It was almost midnight by the time we went back to our room and dropped into bed exhausted, a rope attached between our ankles, the overhead fan gyrating like a slowly falling star. "So here we are then," I said to Niles, hoping he'd answer and provide additional insight into what we were really doing and could expect tomorrow. In the dark, Niles was too tired to say anything however, and after a few minutes I closed my eyes. I lay very still, focusing on images where Liz sat with me at a long table shared by my father, brother, and mother, and despite the confusion that came from these half dreams, I soon managed to relax and drift off to sleep.

# CHAPTER 11

# THE ROAD TAKEN

Between his hands, in the glare as he continued to stand at the window on the thirty-fourth floor of the Ryse & Fawl Building, squinting through the sun toward shadows created by the Reedum & Wepe, Franklin Finne sees a blue Ford Escort slide up to the curb and a man in a long coat tug a heavy case from the back just before the car drives off. Shortly after this, a young woman in faded jeans and orange sweater comes from the metro and also goes inside. Then the blue car returns, almost crashing against the curb as it rolls to a stop and another man gets out from the driver's side this time, Franklin watching confused as the figure appears as a haunting.

Returning to Renton, Tyler shared an apartment with Oz on the east side of the city. ("Just until we have some money," they both agreed.) The move from Hamburg went without incident, though finding work in the States proved more difficult than expected. Local 457 of the electrician's union wanted $300 up front on top of dues then said, "Two months wait, so long as you're paid up each month and someone pulls your name." Tyler was charged $150 to take a test to prove his knowledge, then told—despite his high score—his best bet was to join the local for general labor and see if that didn't get things started. (It didn't.) He put in applications all around town, at handyman services, heating and cooling specialists, with contractors and subcontractors who consistently turned him down. "Tough times," he was informed, patted on the back and sent away.

Frustrated, he decided to finish his degree, convinced this would help, only trying to transfer credits from HTU to the University of Renton meant dealing with bureaucratic fuckups and resistance on the part of Admissions to accept his transcript. (A smug provost suggested credits toward an electrical engineering degree from a German institution were of no value in the States as, "America runs on an altogether different current.") Further complications arose as the V.A. was slow to authorize money from the GI Bill Tyler had coming, waiting they said on forms from Hamburg, on paperwork and additional information lost somewhere in the system. In time they stopped answering his letters and refused to return his calls.

"Some homecoming," Osmah goaded. "Your country is quick to stick its nose into the affairs of others, yet what does it do for its own? Where is your country now, Sergeant Finne, to share its wealth and abundance?"

Tyler said nothing. He did not have a ready argument, was thinking the same himself—"All my years in the army and what is this shit?"—though he kept quiet and continued to search the papers for potential positions, paid his dues at the union but was quickly running out of cash and rarely called for a job. Two months went by, and then another, and with his prospects no better and his money situation worse, he decided Oz was right. Relying on a system that never cared a rat's ass about people like him was foolish, all hope and promise propaganda, and resorting to a different strategy he caught a bus across town.

"Sure, I got something for you," Turk said, his wisp of a moustache no different than ten years before, his narrow face aged not disagreeably though he looked still much like a harvest mouse. "Two hundred dollars and it'll take you ten minutes. For you, Ty, it'll be no sweat."

And so it was he went back to work.

Oz spent a great deal of time with Ziad Shehhi, prayed daily at a mosque on the west end of town, spoke vaguely to Tyler about opening an office for the Band of Forbearance while paying his share of the rent and other expenses in cash. He told Tyler he found a job doing research for one of the professors at the university and was in line for a teaching fellowship in the fall, and when Tyler assumed such a job would lead Oz to think differently about the States, he was met with derision. "You are wrong. They hire me to teach because I am good and they can get me cheap. It is exploitation, nothing less." What Osmah Said Almend saw of America—what he spoke of constantly and refused to be dissuaded—was a country of excess, as backward in its spirit as a camel trying to drink water through its ass. "Such arrogance is mind-numbing. Yours is a culture driven by consumption. The effects of worshiping capitalism—which Americans confuse for democracy—is everywhere," Oz said. "The rich here are all like spoiled children while the lowest worker is no better, aspiring for nothing more than a larger paycheck so he might acquire goods he doesn't need and still can't afford.

"And the women—Sweet Allah!—worse than the Germans by far. Here they're without shame," Oz insisted. "Salesclerks in whores' dresses, acting as if they're doing you a favor when you come into their shop, looking you square in the eye, and sizing you up like a fish in the market." One in particular, an American-born Moroccan girl named Isha had gotten Oz's attention. Isha worked as a seamstress in a tailor shop where Oz took a pair of slacks to be repaired. She had bright red streaks dyed to the ends of her otherwise jet black hair, wore a sleeveless yellow T-shirt with a leather necklace dangling in front, her skin a cool caramel brown while her long fingernails curved and were dotted with fake jewels. She examined the area Oz needed mending—a separation in the crotch due to poor stitching and a suspect sort of thread—and chewing her gum far back on her molars, Isha joked, "You must be carrying some extra weight down here."

Osmah blushed, the reaction a puzzle for he would have expected himself to respond with anger toward such audacity. "It is," he heard himself quip instead, "a cross I bear."

The next afternoon, when picking up his slacks, he dropped off a shirt with the underside of the right sleeve pulled almost completely from the seam. ("An accident," was how Oz explained.) He returned the following day, pleased by the smile Isha extended as he approached the counter, and when she asked if he liked reggae—he wasn't sure—and would he like to go to a club later that night and check out the scene, he agreed at once then hurried off to pray.

The music was loud with large drums and electric instruments and a singer who made it altogether impossible to understand the words, but Oz, who didn't know how to dance and was startled by these American women convulsing among a crowd like snakes shimmying in the heat, found himself jumping into the center of Isha's motion as she swayed about with sinewy arms above her head. Back at her apartment, with a different sort of music playing on the stereo, Isha stripped and mounted Oz on the living room floor, continuing her dance until his body groaned and shivered in its own release.

All the next day, in his meetings with Ziad Shehhi and at prayer, he was distracted by thoughts of Isha, confused and wondering now that he had a woman how his priorities might change.

These thoughts were new, terrifying and exciting, and continued on until that evening when he went to Isha's apartment and sought to embrace her the moment she opened the door.

"Ozzie, Ozzie," she held him off with arms extended, the snakelike fluidity of her limbs from yesterday turning hard now and pushing him back. "Hold on there, Tiger. What are you doing here?" The red tips of her hair flashed across the center of her face like candle flames. Osmah stood bewildered, wondering at first if she might not simply be teasing, and realizing at last she wasn't, managing to stammer, "But last night? Isha, dear?"

She could only laugh, half with pity, as she continued to block the entrance to her apartment. "Last night was fun," she sounded bored. "I'm sure I'll see you around."

"But?"

"What?"

"We?"

"That? Jeez. Come on now, Oz. Really, I'm busy. I have a date."

"But, but?"

"You were wonderful, Ozzie," she tried to say what she thought might work, then grew annoyed as Osmah insisted on arguing with her. (What was it with these foreign men who moved to America yet refused to accept the liberties of their new culture?) "You didn't really think that was anything?" she laughed again, more cruelly this time. "I mean, what? We didn't have that much fun. And your dancing. And your weenie. For a change of pace I suppose it was fine, but really, I have to go."

In midnight prayer Osmah wept for the generosity of Allah to have bestowed on him a test, and beat his face with fisted hands for having failed his master so. The mistake, he swore, would not happen again. The mistake only proved that America was a land never to be trusted.

In February, Tyler took a job as a bouncer in a club where Turk controlled the sale of drugs: opiates and Ecstasy, coke and heroin and weed. ("You're in charge," Turk said. "You keep things running and no one sells but people working for me, understand?") He quit the union, stopped sending letters to the V.A. and phoning the university, while Oz scoffed at Tyler's new career. "Your own country has made you a criminal," he mocked Tyler's enterprise and wanted to know, "What sort of people so mistreat their own? On every corner, in every face I see blasphemy. You are a mongrel nation that looks upon my country with condescension and greed, and yet you are all infidels! A man would be providing a great service to the world if he could rattle America's confidence and let everyone know its foundation is false."

The rantings Oz subjected him to grew more wrathful and extreme, talk of anarchy and rebellion, and only the cash in Tyler's pocket allowed him to ignore Oz's howl. If he otherwise felt himself living on the precipice, he denied his concern until late March, when the club was raided and finding himself arrested, he called Turk to bail him out. The response he received was not like years' past however, Turk more cautious now and protective of self-interest, and instead of help he was met with "Who's this? Ty Finne? I don't know you. You can't be calling me here." Eventually, he got word to Oz who came with the necessary cash. "You see?" Oz railed the whole ride home. "Not even your American criminal friends can be trusted. Even honor among thieves is a foreign concept in your homeland."

"Fuck!" and "Fuck!" and "Fuck!" again. Tyler in his rage sounded much like his father wagging an enormous fist at the heavens while cursing forces he couldn't defeat. "What a crock of shit!" Every direction he turned another dead end. When Oz approached him then with an offer of several thousand dollars' profit to help secure a list of special materials, when he said, "Here is opportunity, the only good chance coming your way in America," when he spoke not in terms of anarchy, nihilism, and rebellion but more cleverly of profit and progress and personal gain, Tyler saw no reason to turn his back. "Write 'em down," he avoided asking questions, said simply, "I can get whatever you need."

Occupied in this way, it took less than three weeks to obtain all the supplies Oz asked for, and when Oz told him what he had planned, Tyler said, "You got me confused with someone who gives a damn." Sufficiently paid, he refused to concern himself with larger issues, and not until the night before did he admit to himself the misgivings he had. His clothes, along with the rest of his few possessions, were packed in an army-issued duffle, all his money converted to cash and a map marked to get him out west. (As part of their deal, Oz provided additional money to buy a used car.) The drive across town took twenty minutes, and once he had dropped Oz at the curb Tyler sped off.

He stopped three blocks up and pulled into the parking lot of a Gas-n-Go, where he bought a fifth of whiskey, sitting in the car and drinking in order to clear his head. He thought how little things had changed after so many years, the way Renton revealed herself, how she showed him still to be no more than a hustler and brawler—and worse—a half orphan who remained in Hamburg because he felt no great urge to come home. ("What did I think would be different when I got back to the States?") His time in the army, studying electrical engineering, working for Berchup Brothers, and the charity performed at the Band of Forbearance were all bullshit now, and even if he wanted, how could he possibly reclaim that which had already fallen away?

"Shit," he said. "Shit and shit," again. "Here I am. I am nothing but this." The revelation came spontaneously, making everything else that followed a matter of reflex, and shifting into reverse he produced but a brief grinding of the gears.

Franklin raises his hand in an imaginary toast, "To shit that is and can't be changed." Just as he believes no truer words have ever been said, he sees the blue Ford return and a large man climb out. The figure runs around the front of the car on his way inside the Reedum & Wepe, glancing quickly over his shoulder and up at the sky as if spotting Franklin there on the thirty-fourth floor of the Ryse & Fawl, so that even from a distance the father knows and cries out, "God!" Such a thing and on this anniversary day no less! Here was Chance singing out in perfect pitch. Franklin jumps and waves and screams for his son, while in the blink of an eye all things change again, hope and refor-mation passing as a flash of light so bright it blinds. A crash of thunder rings out, the rattling of windows and swaying of steel, while across the way the structure that was the Reedum & Wepe bursts from within and drops down, shattered and gone along with Tyler, leaving Franklin in the grey, grey smoke of the smoldering waste to stare outside and strain to see through what is once again nothing.

# CHAPTER 12

# IN ALGIERS

In darkness memory is all. There is nothing but what the mind remembers.

By the time I woke, Niles was already up and gone from our room. I looked about, confused at first, taking a moment to recall exactly where I was and wondering where Niles might be. I stared across the floor at his duffle, moved my legs slowly over the side of the bed, undoing the rope while searching for a note. Niles' camera was still in its case, his copy of Camus' *A Happy Death* where he left it last night on the table. I checked the time—just after 9:00 a.m.—and sure he'd be back any minute, I went into the bathroom, then dressed and sat down to wait.

"I couldn't sleep," he said as he came in, carrying a manila folder that he tucked back inside his duffle. "I went for a walk," and wiping sweat from his brow, he asked if I was hungry and suggested we get something to eat. We had coffee in another outdoor restaurant then spent the day—and much of the next—exploring the city. As a man in tow, I followed Niles wherever he led, walking through the markets (souqs) and qasbahs, where crafts and foods, clothes and carpets, jewelry and vegetables were sold. Niles used his camera to record the crowds, the interior of hotels, stores and movie theaters, the main post office, the fish market, and port. Later we went by hired car out into the country, and the following day drove from the Palais du Gouvernement and the National Library out along the skyline above Les Tagarins, down to the beaches and back up again to the Parc de la Liberté and the Museum of Antiquities.

One afternoon—and more to humor Niles than any ambition I had—we stopped at the American consulate and the local English press and asked after Timbal. The answers we received confirmed that he was still in the area, though interest in the old artist had waned and no one knew much about him or seemed to care. We were told only that he lived outside the city and came into Algiers now and then. I considered my effort in that regard complete, and concentrated otherwise on Niles. I asked frequently how he was doing, wondered if our trip had brought him any closer to the curative he was after, and how being here made him feel. Despite his claim of being in good spirits, I noticed in his face a guardedness layered beneath his pale complexion, his gaze at times distant and distracted. He did his best to divert my concern, explaining the history of a particular area of the city, educating me on the unrest in the region, the clashes between the government and rebel forces, the AIG and ISF, Muslim extremists opposed to a conservative Islamic state, the bombings and recent assassinations of Adbelbak Benhamouda and the AIG's leader Antar Zouabri. I showed an interest only because it seemed to make Niles happy, and still in secret I continued to wonder if something was wrong.

Our third morning in Algiers, I got up to the sun pouring through the blinds. Niles was gone again, his early walks now part of his private routine. I untied the rope from my right ankle and went into the bathroom to pee. After washing my face—the water came out cold and had a rusty odor—I dried my hands and returned to find Niles back in our room, sitting in the chair and staring toward the window. His complexion was paler than yesterday, with beads of perspiration in his hairline and beneath his nose. I didn't like the way he looked—a sense of the febrile had entered the equation—and finding my pants and pulling them on, I asked, "Are you all right?"

"Sure."

"You look sick."

"It's hot."

"It's more than that."

"I'm fine."

"How did you sleep?"

"Good," he continued looking toward the window, and after several seconds glanced at me in order to discuss our plans for the day. "I was thinking you might want to take a drive outside the city and see if you can't find Timbal."

"That's all right," I answered. "I wouldn't even know where to begin."

"They said he's east of the city. Someone has to know."

I shook my head. "That's OK."

Niles retied the laces of his boots with a mechanical motion of his fingers, and sliding back in his chair repeated, "It's just that I think you should." He ran the back of his hand across his forehead, his features pinched and drawn together. He got up and went into the bathroom where I heard the toilet flush and then the water run. When he came back, he sat again in the chair. I stood near the window, smoking and glancing out at the people passing below: men in long cotton shirts and embroidered gandouras despite the heat, others in suits, women in pale blouses, in haiks and scarves covering their heads. Niles remained in the chair, and staring up at me said, "I was thinking about the man on the train."

"The one with the fever?"

"What he told us about having no choice."

"Crazy."

"No matter what pressure he was under, he still chose to get on the train."

"Exactly."

"And he chose to ignore what his fever was trying to tell him."

"He traveled even though it made him sick."

"He should have come up with a different plan."

"No doubt."

"So you agree a person can choose to do the wrong thing?"

"Of course."

"And regret it?"

"Yes."

"Like your coming this far and not wanting to see Timbal."

"I won't regret it."

"So you say now."

"I came because you asked me to."

"All right, then what about regretting what happened with you and Liz?"

"Niles," I felt foolish for failing to see where our conversation was headed. Up until then, Niles was sympathetic enough toward my situation to refrain from discussing Liz at all, though I knew the exchange was inevitable, and endured further questions as best I could, answering honestly and only when he made reference to the way I chose to play piano did I wave my hands and say, "Enough."

"What?"

"It isn't that simple," I finished my cigarette and discarded it in the toilet, the last of the ash giving way with a hiss as I returned to the front room and sat on the bed. "In the first place, I didn't choose to play as I did. I didn't want what happened."

"You told me not to come hear you."

"I told you not to bother."

"Because you knew you'd fuck up and feared I wouldn't let you."

"That's not it."

"Then I'm confused," Niles shifted forward. "I thought you told me everything is a matter of choice."

"Sometimes, shit just happens."

"How?"

"I don't know, Niles. I suppose once in a while the cumulative effect of earlier decisions just combusts."

"So what went wrong wasn't your fault?"

"I was as surprised as anyone."

"Not more surprised than Liz."

"Hell," I walked to the window, closed the drapes and turned around, thinking myself clever as I tossed the question back. "What about you? Why are we here if you're such an advocate of self-determination? Why can't you simply take control of your nocturnal nonsense and make it stop?"

Niles folded his arms across his chest and sat quietly for several seconds before answering me with a concise, "I can."

Surprised, I came back and sat on the end of the bed, waiting for him to say more, asking, "What do you mean?" but he remained evasive and resumed our conversation by asking yet again, "What about Liz? What do you intend to do?"

"I told you, nothing."

"You're satisfied with how things are?"

"It isn't a question of being satisfied."

"Or happy?"

"Don't start."

"What?"

"She's gone."

"Then get her back."

"I can't."

"Sure you can."

"She's in Spain and I'm here and there's a reason for that."

"What reason?"

"Things are because they can't otherwise help being that way."

Niles shook his head. I watched him tug at the end of his sleeves and continue with, "So what you're telling me is that you plan on treating what happened with Liz the same as everything else?"

I nearly said no, that of course Liz was different from the rest, but then Niles was sure to ask how is she different and in what way could I explain? Wasn't I dealing with Liz's leaving exactly as I always did? As I treated my dissertation and impending dismissal from the university, as I handled my music and the story I created about L.C. Timbal and on and on? How then could I draw a distinction? I sat stone-faced, and repeated my mantra. "There's nothing I can do."

"If you ask me," Niles said.

"Which I didn't."

"But if you did."

"I'm fine."

"Maybe so," he repeated, "but if you did ask me, I'd say your problem is that it doesn't frighten you enough to stay as you are."

I tossed up my hands in such a way as to make it seem the deadeye accuracy of Niles' charge had missed its mark, and smoking a fresh cigarette, knocked a bit of ash to the floor and replied as glibly as possible, "It isn't a question of fear."

"If that's the case," Niles reached toward his duffle and pulled out a thin rectangular envelope that he tossed onto the bed beside me. I stared down, blew more smoke then told him to forget it.

"Think it over."

"I don't have to," I spoke firmly, as I did when one of my students insisted on clinging to an untenable position, and ignoring the ticket said, "I'm not going to see Liz. I'm here because you asked me to make sure you don't carve yourself up at night and that's all."

"You don't want to see her?"

I frowned. "What I want is what I have."

"Who are you trying to convince?"

"You, obviously," I crushed my cigarette beneath my heel, and unable to look at Niles just then, I turned away, stared down at the ash in the wood, at the drapes across the window and the thin ray of light still shining through. I glanced back at the small table between the two beds, and spotting Niles' copy of *A Happy Death,* knew intuitively I was making a mistake, though I couldn't resist and said, "You're forgetting one thing. The risk of being in love only keeps me from being happy."

Niles recognized the line at once, and coming from the chair, picked up the book and flipped to the correct page, scanning down a few paragraphs in order to correct my misapplication of the text. "But Mersault 'realized how easily his certainty could be shaken. His heart was strangely hard. . . . There was nothing ahead of him now except the Chenoua, a forest of ruins and wormwood, a love without hope or despair, and the memory of a life of vinegar and flowers.'" He wiped more sweat from his brow and asked, "Is that what you want? To spend your days in a forest of wormwood?"

"Maybe."

"I don't believe you. Why would you want to do that?"

"Because it's safe."

"Nothing is safe."

"Exactly."

Niles sat back in his chair, his hands folded in his lap, his voice weary and face not quite healthy. He sighed from somewhere deep in his chest. I appreciated his trying to look out for me, understood his intentions for what they were, and still I couldn't keep from sounding resentful. "Why is it all right for you to fly 8,000 miles in search of God knows what and I can't say a word or convince you the whole trip is nonsense, and yet when it comes to me and what I need to do for myself while I'm here, you think to know better?" Before Niles could answer, I decided to defend myself further, and added, "Nothing keeps me out of trouble. Nothing is harmless. You should try it sometime. Just think how much better off you'd be if you weren't always trying to do something. What the fuck are we doing here, Niles?"

He looked at me then, more oddly than before, then stood and slipped his copy of *A Happy Death* inside his pocket. The effects of his walk that morning, the heat outside and whatever else had him appearing fevered, caused his legs to shift awkwardly for a moment beneath him. He recovered quickly however, the color in his face returning, and setting his shoulders back, he hesitated just a second, then said in response to my claim, "I know why I'm here."

"Why?"

He didn't answer, and after another second he turned and gathered up his video camera, wiped a fresh line of sweat from his brow, shooed the fly from around his head, told me to have a good day, and walked out into the hall. The door closed and once again I was alone.

CHAPTER 13

# THE WATER'S EDGE

What is passes, or so the thought occurred to Aziz Zaboud as he surveyed the qasbah with its bins of oranges and pears, the rounds of cheese and mayonnaise jars, the meats and breads and dozens of other staples that just a few short months ago would not have made their way so easily into the country. Since the election many—though certainly not all—of the everyday hardships had diminished. There was still unrest, guerrilla attacks in the countryside, car bombings, and raids on villages. (Just last week seventeen people were killed in Ain Defla Province, less than 80 miles south of Algiers, and three days before the start of Ramadan a bomb exploded downtown at a bus stop frequented by female university students, killing several innocent girls.) The Armed Islamic Group and the Salafist Group for Preaching and Combat seemed to have grown out of the ashes left by the ISF and the history of past insurgencies, and still things had changed.

Aziz swore as much was true as he slipped a juicy pear into his pocket and headed off to the port. As was his routine every morning, he went to the port in order to supervise the incoming and outgoing shipments from his uncle's store. (Gul Ami Zaboud owned a small yet profitable import-export business on the east side of the city.) Sometime before ten an American with slender shoulders and an odd tangle of limbs arrived and paced through the crowd with his video camera aimed at the trains and the ships both moored and moving out to sea. The sight of foreigners was nothing new—they passed through the port as conspicuous as blackbirds—yet something about this particular outlander caught Aziz's eye. More than the camera, which the American failed to realize was already the target of thieves, Aziz was taken by the man's focus as he made his way through the crowd, his machine held firm, his movements both severe and pliant, suggesting the liquid glide of fish.

Aziz finished his work and began following the American around the port, convinced there might be some business the man was there to conduct, a lucrative deal Aziz and his uncle could benefit from. Intrigued by the mystery of the American's filming, he decided to stay with the man as he headed toward the street to catch a bus going west. They rode several miles before the American got off beyond Bordj El Kiffan and Alger Plage, near the beaches of Boumerdes. Aziz trailed behind from a safe distance, hiking up the hillside before stopping in a shaded patch where he sat and watched the American pass through high weeds, eventually cutting across a clearing and striding to the water where he baptized himself in the sea.

The air in the late morning was already quite hot, and as Niles hiked he held his camera bag against his side, alternating shoulders every few hundred yards. The route he took from the port by way of the Enterprise Publique de Transport de Voyageurs skipped the Turquoise Coast that attracted more travelers, and he went instead out toward a secluded patch of beach beyond Bordj El Kiffan and Alger Plage, nearer the white sands of Boumerdes—though not as far as Cap Djinet—where he walked away from the road and parallel to the water.

For a time he thought about Bailey, wondered whether he

made the right decision to leave him alone, if such would force him to come to his senses and either go off in search of Timbal or take up the ticket and fly to see Liz. (Or will he just sit there inside the room?) He considered the core of their argument, how ridiculous Bailey's talk of securing happiness through resistance and avoidance. The attitude was myopic, the notion that doing nothing was ever best, as if happiness was some accidental occurrence one stumbled into and not, as Camus wrote in *A Happy Death,* Man's greatest and most arduous ambition. He considered, too, his own reason for being in Algiers—"I know why I'm here," he said—how he walked each morning, secretly spying and wanting to experience the sense of forgiveness that would allow him to be healed, and yet what was it Massinissa Alilouche had said about human impulse and the plight of being a rebel? What was it that caused him to feel so unsteady now, so weak and frightened and confused?

The path through the hills was a quarter mile from the beach and well above the sea. The grass was dry, rolling across eddies and hollow curves in the earth. Occasionally he was greeted by a stretch of coolness and shade though for the most part he remained exposed to sharp splinters of sun. In the distance, cypress trees appeared to blacken against the rising heat while far out in the water the sea was a darker shade of green. He walked until the muscles in his legs went from weary to an unsteady ache, and staring down he spotted a large stretch of sea absent bathers and descended to the beach where he slipped off his jeans and T-shirt and entered the water in his undershorts.

The warmth surprised him. He was prepared for a chill, but instead was taken in by a new kind of heat, all liquid and clement, fitting around him snugly as he swam out fifty yards or more through the silvery foam. Away from land, he thought again of Bailey and then of Jeana. He swam on, dove down, the water providing an ineffable abyss, the salt in the sea stinging the wound on his belly as he held his breath and plunged further, his feet kicking hard as if he was being chased. When he came up at last, gasping from the full exertion of his dive, he settled into a steady stroke, the muscles in his back and arms springing to life as the muted blue of the distant sky covered him. He swam parallel to the shore, a good distance from the beach, churning on even as his arms and legs began to tire and what may have been the fever he felt earlier returned and scorched his brow. He redirected his strokes, went out another thirty yards, then shifted again and glided further down until exhausted, he rolled on his back and allowed his body to drift with the tide.

The sun caused his eyes to fill with salty tears, and floating aimlessly he absorbed the peacefulness of the moment, the surrounding silence Camus wrote of as weaving together the hopes and despairs of human life. A bird in the sky cast its shadow across the sea and Niles stared as best he could at its flight. (During his own swim in the sea, Mersault contemplated not the sky above but the depth of the water beneath him and all the vast possibilities of the "unknown world . . . and the salty center of a life still unexplored.") Niles turned his head to look toward shore, thought again about the expectations of his trip and of the man whose photograph lay at the bottom of his camera bag. The tide beneath him tugged at his shoulders and hips, his feet sinking further down, forcing him to tread until he could regroup and float once more. He concentrated again on Jeana, pictured the rubble of the Reedum & Wepe still smoldering and the first morning he woke to discover the contusion just above his wrist, followed by a sequence of mysterious welts and burns, bruises and abrasions, all appearing as the progeny of some Immaculate provocation. He remembered that first August and a razor's raw carving of the letter J slashed into his right thigh—

the sixth such noctambulistic dissection to find him—and how his body appeared by the end of winter like a man under attack.

Splayed atop the surface of the deep green sea, he dropped his arms, sank down, came up again and resumed floating. He considered the course of his somnambulistic two-step and how the want to recover, to forgive and move on, and how all of this seemed at odds with a more guttural inclination. He swam on, quit floating, and moved farther from shore. The ache across the right side of his belly where his wound was exposed to the salty sea stung again as he remembered conversations with Marthe, meeting for coffee and dinner and the occasional movie, lunch dates between classes and work. No longer used to keeping company with women, he maintained a certain distance, though eventually she wore him down, cajoled him to stop fighting and learn to relax. He tried, and later that winter—having experienced a hint of happiness otherwise held in abeyance—his affliction took note, released its hold, and fell away.

Niles puzzled over the connection, wondered what to make of this development, found his confusion further tested one night when Marthe invited him back to her apartment. A bottle of wine stood on the counter, a silver corkscrew nearby. Marthe brought Niles into the front room where they sat on the couch, and when she kissed him he shied from her lips, unnerved by her hand on his cheek, her face against his neck, her fingers sliding up his back, kneading through his incertitude. He stopped her and began to explain as she lifted his shirt over his head, but she quieted him as though she already knew, placing her mouth on the freshest scar, covering the bluest bruise, the gnarl of an ancient burn, until his own hands rose and fell tenderly upon her. She drew him toward her then with gentle persuasion, leading him back to the bedroom and across the covering of sheet where he felt himself lose hold, sinking to a point where no measure of resistance could save him, no release but the one his body sent shivering from his hips, trembling as his heart raced on.

He slept beside her, then woke with a start, hurrying to dress even as Marthe encouraged him to stay. Back in his apartment, beneath the floor of Bailey's room and the sounds from his piano producing a soulful rendition of Sammy Gallop's "Maybe You'll Be There," he took the rope and tied his end to the leg of a chair as a false connection, then sat on the side of his bed and wondered about the events of his night. After so much time, was it actually possible this and nothing more was the curative for all his nocturnal nonsense? Was this the mysterious Happiness Camus wrote of, and if so, why did he feel so uneasy? After worrying all this time about the Truth his condition was supposed to reveal, why wasn't he relieved to know the impetus behind his affliction might be rooted in rediscovering simple pleasures? What was it that made him reluctant to believe the gouging of his flesh could, indeed, be dispatched by a course of forgiveness and learning to love again?

He dove once more, opened his eyes, swam as deep as he could before shooting up toward the surface and the glimmering light and air that awaited. If he appreciated anything about Marthe Raynal, it was how her presence empowered him with a will to live, though not nearly as much as Jeana's love once did, and so inspired, he recalled getting up from bed, and thinking of Jeana, went into the kitchen where he removed a knife from the side drawer and in one motion brought the blade through the pale underside of his elbow and down toward his wrist. The cut was deep, though he knew from experience how to tend such wounds without a doctor's care. Three nights later, asleep this time and without being consciously guided, his condition returned of its own accord, a blunt instrument used to punish the arm which earlier held the knife so intently.

Aziz moved down the hill in order to sit on the sands where the American had left his clothes and camera bag. He watched the man in the water floating and bobbing, then removed the camera from its case and studied the American through the lens. In the water, Niles felt the heat of his fever, the wound on his belly breaking the surface of the sea as he floated, his half-healed flesh exposed to the rays of the sun. He remained this way for several minutes before rolling over and swimming off. A second bird cast a shadow across the water while a change in the current brought Niles through a suddenly frigid patch of sea. The drop in temperature caused him to struggle with his stroke, drained him of strength, forced him to fight to keep his movements from seizing up as he switched direction, managed to double back through warmer waters where the chill no longer penetrated his limbs. His panic abated and he made his way toward shore.

Some forty yards out, he began searching the beach for his clothes, surprised to see an unfamiliar figure sitting nearby in the sand. At first he thought he must be looking at the wrong spot, but the rest of the beach was clear. He drew closer, stood in the shallow water and paused to catch his breath as the man aimed the camera in his direction. The sun warmed Niles' shoulders and hair, the heat pushing at him from behind though he was hesitant to move. "Do not worry," the man assured him, pointing the camera still while scanning Niles up and down. "I am not a thief."

Niles came out of the water and stood a few feet away, shifting back on his heels atop the hot sand. Aziz held the viewfinder against his eye, and continuing to record while taking in Niles' scars asked, "What has happened to you, my friend?"

"If you don't mind."

"You have been in an accident?"

"Will you please shut the camera off."

"A car perhaps? Or a mugging maybe?"

Niles reached with his right hand, extending his arm forward and moving his fingers as if to levitate the camera toward him. Aziz pushed the button on the side of the camera and set it back inside the case. "You see, there. Completely safe," he remained crouched in the sand, his knees bent and back arched froglike as if at any moment he might spring forward. "I am Aziz," he said. "And you, my friend?"

"Is there something I can do for you?"

"Please, yes. Perhaps so."

"If you'll tell me then."

"Of course. I have surprised you, that is all, no?"

"I didn't expect to see anyone."

"Or them to see you."

Niles covered his chest with his arms.

"Many apologies," Aziz didn't move from the sand. "You are American?"

"Yes."

"You are visiting?"

"Traveling."

"Indeed," Aziz smiled, a light crease cutting through his cheeks as he did so, disappearing again after his grin relaxed. "But why here?" he patted Niles' pile of clothes, "It isn't always safe this isolated spot, you know. There are men far less friendly than I who patrol just these areas looking for non-Muslims separated from the herd."

"I was hot."

"There are more popular beaches than this for tourists."

"Maybe so," Niles pivoted onto the sides of his feet as the sand began to burn.

"But this place appealed to you?"

"That's right."

"The solitude."

"Yes."

"I see."

Niles took a tentative step forward, unsure as yet what to make of the man, feeling awkward while standing there in just his underwear, and reaching out again, he said, "May I have my clothes, please?"

Aziz leaned to his left and tossed Niles his shirt. A breeze from the water ran up toward the hills and stirred the low brush. The camera was zipped inside its case, protected against blowing sand, and noticing Niles glance in that direction, Aziz said, "Your equipment is safe."

"I see that."

"I did not come to steal from you."

"I never said you did."

"Though this is what you thought."

"I didn't know what to think. You surprised me, remember?"

"If I wanted to steal your camera, why wouldn't I have taken it when you were out swimming in the sea?"

"I don't know."

"Perhaps it is because I'm after more," Aziz stuck his sharp chin out, waited for Niles to react, then laughed. "That's right," he spread his arms. "Always more, yes? It is the American way never to be satisfied. A bird in the hand is not good enough when there is a possibility of two in the bush." He made a different gesture then, opening his fingers flat and extending them toward the camera. "Go ahead. Take it. It's yours," he stood up quickly and brushed the sand from his slacks.

Niles felt himself put oddly on the defensive, and rather than go over and pick up his camera, he bent down for his jeans and shoes. The sun overhead was white and hazed while the surrounding sky glistened in the heat. A second breeze brought a salty scent from the water and for a brief moment Niles was tempted to dive back into the sea and swim again. He wanted to feel as Mersault who left the water shivering and laughing with happiness, but instead, standing there, he felt his fever worsen, his body experiencing both ache and fatigue.

The sun hit Aziz's eyes, forcing him to raise his hand above his brow in order to maintain his view of the American. He smiled again and stepped to the side so that the glow of the sun fell away, and recalling what first caused him to follow the American to the beach—though he had no idea at the time where he was headed—Aziz asked, "You are a businessman?"

"Me? No."

"You are not here on business?"

"I am not a businessman."

"What were you doing this morning at the port?"

"How did you know I was at the port?"

"I saw you."

"I don't understand. Are you saying you followed me here?"

"I admit as much."

"But why?"

"I can't quite tell you. You stood out. I thought your use of the camera involved some business with which I might be of help. I am a businessman, you see," Aziz explained about the work he did for his uncle and why he was at the port that morning. "It is important for a man dealing as I do with merchandise and trade to keep his eyes open at all times for opportunities," he gave a wink, and glancing back at the camera asked, "What then is this filming you were doing?"

Niles finished tying his shoes, pulled his camera bag back over his shoulder, and still taking in this latest bit of news and how the man hadn't stumbled accidently upon him at the beach but followed him from the city, he considered walking off. What was he to make of this confession, after all? "Why did you follow me?" he thought it best to not give ground, only Aziz was equally resistant and answered as before, "I told you, my interest is purely business. I have followed others, have bought and sold goods and services in hotel rooms and cafés, in taxicabs and lobbies but never, I admit, on the beach. As for your filming then?"

"I'm a tourist."

"But your enterprise went well beyond the average traveler. Typically they zip-zip-zip, stealing little pictures for their memory books, yet you were focused for a very long time."

"I'm interested in the city," he said.

"You have been here before?"

"No. I've read, I mean, I like to read Camus. I've studied," he said, and then for some reason he found himself mentioning Jeana, how they used to lay in bed at night and read to one another from Camus' books.

"I see," Aziz looked closely at Niles. "And this woman then, she is your lover?"

"Was."

"My friend, my friend," Aziz gave a deep sigh. The sun placed a streak of gold atop the surface of the smooth green sea, sliding softly toward shore where it disappeared inside the sand. Aziz stepped closer to Niles, eying the American with sympathy while at the same time trying to bring all the pieces of the puzzle together. He thought again about the wounds on Niles' body, and "About this girl then," he couldn't resist asking.

"Jeana."

"This Jeana, yes. She left you for another?"

"No."

"But she is the cause of your being here now?"

"Yes."

"And your wounds?"

"I should be getting back."

"Did she inflict them?"

Niles looked away.

"Ahh, a tiger cat!"

"You don't understand."

"Don't I?"

"I need to be going."

"You are telling me what then?"

"I have to get back."

"Of course. You are right. There's no predicting when the next bus will come," Aziz took hold of Niles' arm and together they walked across the sand and the green stretch of grassy weed covering the hills on the way to the road. The view from where they came to stand created the illusion that the water was just beyond the edge of the hill and if Niles rushed forward and jumped he would land far off in the blue green deep. Aziz remained quiet for a few minutes, knowing there would be time before the next bus passed and hoping the American would feel inclined to talk, he asked again, "About this Jeana?"

"Please."

"It is just that I was wondering."

"Jeana's dead."

"Ahh. I am sorry, my friend."

It may well have been the heat, or the fever, but Niles went on from there to tell Aziz about the Reedum & Wepe, the reference prompting a look of immediate recognition and understanding—"I am familiar with the event," Aziz said—as if a key to a long-locked door had at last been provided. When their bus arrived, they took their seats over the right wheel which rattled and rolled beneath them with great urgency. Sitting no more than a foot apart, bouncing atop the hard metal, Aziz brought his right leg up at the knee and turned his hips so he could view the American better. "My friend, my friend," he said. The bus went down a long slope, picked up speed, and rounded a curve as the sun glistened through the side window and the hillsides rose and fell.

"How are you feeling?" Aziz asked after a time.

Niles sat with his hands resting atop the camera case. "I'm all right," he answered. "I'm due back."

"Yes, of course. You are busy. There is much to do, I understand," Aziz's tone turned sober, and connecting the whole of the American's story while picturing once more the cruel flagellation beneath his clothes said, "You're a tourist and there is much you have to see, though tell me, there is perhaps another reason for your trip?"

Surprised, Niles replied, "No," and placed his head against the window. The bus took another turn and slid down a different path, leaving the sun to chase after the rear metal fender. "It is fortunate we ran into one another," Aziz continued. "There is more than chance involved and how fortunate you are that someone sympathetic to your cause has found you."

"I don't know what you're talking about."

"My friend."

"I'm just here to see the city."

"And while you are here to also?"

Again, "What are you saying?"

Aziz grabbed Niles' wrist and squeezed it hard. "What am I?" he spoke in measured bursts, nervous himself and unsure what he would do once they left the bus, he reached for the camera bag and unzipped the flap, digging around until he'd removed both the photograph of Osmah Said Almend and the knife. "A fine target," Aziz leaned closer, already contemplating the consequence as he whispered, "a fine dagger."

# CHAPTER 14

# SERENDIPITY

What is there to do inside the dark except root about and wait for the light?

With Niles gone, I went down to the lobby of the Sahel and sat in one of the large cushioned chairs. I was put off by his quick exit and the argument we just had, and while I knew he thought abandoning me meant I might reconsider and go searching for Timbal, or possibly fly to see Liz, I remained stubborn and settled back in my chair, looking lazily about the room. Men in dark slacks and long white shirts stood in the cool corners of the lobby while the sun poured through the front window and fell across the weave of two large Persian rugs.

I had Cheever with me, my ticket to visit Liz tucked inside the middle pages for reasons unclear as I had no plans to use it. Just as I started reading, two women walked toward me from across the lobby. Dressed in traditional garments, a dark haik and several layers of equally dark cotton skirts, their faces halfway covered by veils, the younger woman seemed nonetheless lovely. The old mother, in contrast, was as plump as a pumpkin with a large black mole above her right eye, enormous feet, and skin creased like crumpled leather. She was holding the girl's elbow for support, her gait an awkward waddle that caused her to rock from side to side in a state of terminal imbalance. As they drew near, I realized the old woman was not clinging to her daughter's arm for assistance however, but was actually helping her along.

I stared at what I could make of the blind girl's face, and quite by chance, when she passed in front of my chair her veil slipped down, treating me to the handsomeness of her lips and cheeks beneath the dark geography of her eyes. I continued to gawk until the old mother noticed and clicking her tongue, quickened her stride and led her daughter from the hotel.

After another minute I gave up reading and decided to leave as well. I began walking nowhere in particular, doing my best to keep track of my bearings, but I must have turned the wrong way for I soon found myself down a side street of unfamiliar shops, and following a succession of ill-fated maneuvers, became even more lost and with no idea how to get back to the Sahel. I walked on, descended a narrow stretch of road where all the building fronts were connected one to the next and the shops had shallow windows and unusually tall doors. A man in an old brown sports jacket, small white cap, and loose-fitting slacks stood in front of one of the doorways, and when I said, "Le Sahel?" he acknowledged me with a nod and stepped to the curb. I repeated my question, said, "Rue Drouillet?", at which the man pointed through the door and I went inside.

The shop was larger than I imagined from the street, with three separate workbenches covered by pieces of furniture, an electric radio, and black guitar in various stages of repair. Dozens of different tools hung from the walls on metal hooks, implements used for shaping and carving wood, for soldering wires, driving screws, and hammering nails. The proprietor of the shop was a man my age with olive skin covered by flakes of dust and ash, his eyes dark and cheeks unshaved, the sleeves of his

white shirt rolled up above his elbows and brown pants droop-
ing over the points of his hips. He held a pair of thick glasses in
his hands while listening to the music of an old man in a rum-
pled jacket and blue cap who sat on a stool behind the benches
playing a newly repaired mandolin.

Both men glanced at me as I moved inside and stood to the
left of the door. The old musician had knotted hands, huge and
swollen like my father's, his shoulders sloped, his large dark head
bent forward over the mandolin which rested in his lap like a
magnificent cat. He played with surprising agility, the music
both festive and hypnotic, the melody possessed of a unique sort
of lyric, ancient and bucolic. Several other instruments, fiddles
and more guitars, a cello, and handcrafted drums, were spread
around the shop, and seeing them all set out as I listened to the
old man play reminded me how much I missed my own music.
I walked forward, swept up in the performance, and yet all at
once my mind flashed back to the disaster of my recent recital
as arranged by Dr. Kabermill and how disappointed Liz looked
and how despairing and helpless I felt when she left me. Unable
suddenly to listen, I covered my ears and rushed outside.

What a strange reaction. ("What the fuck is going on?") I
turned and hurried up a hill in the direction I hoped was the Rue
Drouillet. What I wanted then was simply the shelter of my
room, and walking on I called out, "Le Sahel?" and "Rue
Drouillet?" I asked directions from an old man sitting on a stoop,
and a woman carrying a basket of vegetables, inquired in an English that elicited no response. Another man in a long brown shirt
and beard went so far as to take hold of my sleeve and drag me
to the end of the block, jabbing at the air with a half-crooked
index finger, but each time I followed his lead, I wound up somehow back where I started, over and over and over again.

Perfect. What could be more fitting? Given a chance to

demonstrate the effectiveness of my ability to be on my own, the best I could manage was to get lost. Convinced my mistake was compounded by celerity, I slowed down, settled into a more deliberate stride. After another few minutes however, I realized I was more lost than ever—if such a state as being "more lost" was even possible—and hurried on. I followed another narrow side street where a large bird passed overhead, its black wings ablaze in the near noon sun, reminding me of a painting in Georges Braque's series of Bird Works, *A Tir d'Aile,* in which an enormous blackbird exploded into an equally black bank of clouds. Reviewers suggested Braque's bird in flight was symbolic of the speed which all individuals rushed toward death, but as I was struggling for a more optimistic view, I refused to believe this was why the painting came to mind and redoubled my pace.

I passed a stretch of unfamiliar shops, breathed deep and tried to convince myself I was no longer concerned about being lost. "What does it matter one way or the other?" Squinting against the sun, I rounded one corner and then the next, increased my pace, oblivious to where I was going, wanting only to wander without interruption, until quite by accident I wound up knocking shoulders with a man coming out of a shop, and stopping to apologize, found myself standing in front of the painter L.C. Timbal.


What chance?

The question can't be answered.

A queer coincidence?

No doubt.

And yet how is it coincidence if it happened?

A short man, just a shade over five foot six, rounded in the middle with a slack chest, thin arms, and stout legs, age had redistributed the weight on Timbal's frame. At sixty-three, his face was lined with furrows drawn at a dozen different angles, his head of yellow white hair wild, dry and waved, jutting out at all points like a bale of straw after a storm. Dressed in an old sports jacket that fit his shoulders and arms loosely, his shirt green, his slacks grey, and sandals brown, he seemed to know I recognized him and immediately walked on.

Surprised as I was, I managed to give chase, and cautious against tipping my hand, asked if he might point me back in the direction of the Rue Drouillet. "It seems I've gotten myself turned around," I said. "The streets wind a bit more than I'm used to back in the States." My comment caused Timbal to glance at me suspiciously before pivoting on his heels and disappearing inside a small café.

I hesitated a second or two, then followed him down into a room several steps below the street. The atmosphere was cool and dark with a series of small silver lamps glowing and shadows snaking their way up the walls. A waiter in black shirt and green pants stood behind a table on which several jars of olives and orange slices were arranged. Unlike the cafés where Niles and I ate, Timbal's retreat appeared to serve liquor, and four other men sat in the back smoking and drinking. "I apologize if I'm disturbing you, Mr. Timbal," I said as I approached the table, admitting then, "I do know who you are, but I'm not a reporter. I'm a student and a teacher and a fan."

"The holy trinity," his tone was cold, and afraid he was about to ask me to leave, I took another risk and made reference to his wife. "I doubt you remember," I said, "but I sent you a letter of condolence." Timbal's expression changed at this, his eyes taking me in with a different sort of interest, penetrative and purposeful. He ordered rum in an Arabic less natural sounding than Niles', and leaning back in his chair, asked my name.

"Bailey Finne, sir."

"Well, Mr. Finne, if you sent me a letter I have no recollection of it. You understand?"

"Under the circumstances, of course."

"Sally," he said, then stopped and folded his hands on the table in front of him. "My wife handled all my correspondences," he continued after a moment. "I'm sure your missive is in a box somewhere. In any event, thank you." Timbal's rum arrived and I ordered a whiskey, sitting down without being invited, overwhelmed still by the coincidence of our meeting and not quite knowing what to say, I stammered out a question. "So, how long have you been in North Africa?"

"Is this where the interview begins?"

"Not at all."

"You say you're not a journalist?"

"No, sir. I was just making conversation. I'm a bit nervous. I'm a great admirer of your work."

Timbal gave a look through the half-light and over the top of his glass. I noticed his hands were small, yet possessed of a firm sort of grace that made it easy to imagine the control he wielded when holding a brush. He took a sip from his drink, his wild hair alive in a style unchanged from the way he wore it in the early '60s when he was working in England with the Young Contemporaries, an American influenced by the Kitchen Sink painters and the Euston Road School. As his work gained a reputation among a select group of patrons and critics, he began fashioning a more independent style that took complex aspects of color and imagery and merged them into preexisting forms of Cubism, Surrealism, and Abstract Expressionism. His most famous works, *Heart in a Hole* and *General Amnesia* to name but two, were absent popular imagery and devoted instead to a sophisticated application of figure and shade. By the late 1970s—

with successful showings in New York and Boston, London and
Barcelona, Los Angeles, Chicago and Rome—a Timbal canvas
commanded as much as $100,000, and in the 1990s he was uni-
versally regarded as one of the modern masters. Looking to
add a new dimension to his art—a way of "diving into a diffuse,
fluctuant, and fluid field of circumstance," as Rothko said—he
decided to alter his style toward a less representational and
more primordial approach, experimenting with muted colors
such that his figures slowly dissolved into vague and mysterious
forms.

In hindsight, he failed to see the ambush coming. Even
before the first showing of his new works there were rumblings
of dissent. Much as scholars attacked Gauguin, Bacon, and van
Gogh in their time, L.C. Timbal's years of achievement generated
an atmosphere for backlash among young critics and academics
looking to make a name for themselves reinterpreting the value
of his art. The summer before last, Timbal exhibited his newest
works in London. Nervous, he entered the evening in an otherwise positive frame of mind and was immediately surprised by
the predisposition of critics who assailed his new creations in
what seemed a perverse collusion. Reviewers insisted he was out
of his element—a post-painterly pariah one such authority
called him—who built a career stealing from the inventiveness
of English artists. As his new work avoided any visceral connection to his past, he was exposed to a completely different level
of scrutiny, one that was not only mean-spirited and divisive but
called into doubt the whole of his career.

The extent of such scathing reviews drove Timbal from his
home in London back to New York, where he shunned all local
media and sequestered himself in the home Sally picked out.
Even as his wife's health began to fail the malicious reviews did
not give way, causing Timbal to retreat further from the public

eye. After Sally died, left alone in the unfamiliar upstate house for which he had no affinity nor desire to remain, Timbal took to traveling, as I came to learn, first to France, then Italy, and Spain where he found little solitude or means of escape, and crossing over one morning on a whim through the Strait of Gibraltar, he wound up in North Africa, where the queer and restless indifference of Algiers suited him and he chose to remain.

Timbal unfolded his hands, glanced back across the table and asked me to continue. I hadn't actually been saying anything, but not wishing to let the opportunity pass, I replied, "I was wondering about your being in Algiers. How are you getting on?"

"Day to day, Mr. Finne," he looked away again, then back at me, and asked a question of his own. "And why are you here?"

"I'm traveling with a friend."

"Another American journalist?"

"But I'm not."

"Yes, yes, so you told me. You're a student and a teacher and all that," he drank again, motioning with his free hand for me to go on. I began with the simplest overview, explaining about Niles' desire to travel, saying nothing more really but enough to satisfy Timbal, who shifted back in his chair, asked a few more questions, then let the subject drop. We finished our drinks, talked about art, with Timbal mentioning the recent deaths of Bacon, Diebenkorn, and Conrad Marca-Relli, "three irrepressible souls," while I brought up the Royal College and paintings by Pete Philips, Boshier and Hockney and Allen Jones, all contemporaries and once coexhibitors with Timbal, which caused him to smile and say, "Such a time before any one of us knew what we were doing, and yet, looking back it seems the only time we knew anything at all." I discovered Timbal had a brusque charm, his coarse demeanor intimidating at first but ultimately benign, and waiting until the moment seemed right, I asked again, "So why Algiers?"

He answered here without hesitation, "I appreciate its absence of familiarity."

"You were looking for something new?"

"No."

"A place to disappear then?"

"I wasn't looking for anything in particular, Mr. Finne. When a man flees into the woods he isn't searching for the perfect tree but for whatever provides a place of refuge. I put myself in flight and this was where the hounds stopped barking." He had a way of speaking in a crisp poetic cadence that mixed naturally with his gruff tone and earthy appearance. I let him know that I knew what happened in London, told him I'd read the reviews, that I saw the film made of the exhibit, and took a bus to New York to view the paintings he agreed to show in the States. I spoke as objectively as possible and said that I found his work unfairly attacked. There seemed little doubt the canvases were first-rate, the quality of artistry and inventiveness beyond most anything being offered at the time. (Nearly all American critics with an opportunity to see the works acknowledged as much in a belated rallying and restoration of Timbal's reputation.) I got only a short way into my response however before he cut me off, no longer interested in my opinion, his thoughts elsewhere, he said, "And you know about Sally? That she didn't just die? That the bastards killed her?"

I made no attempt to answer and waited for Timbal to continue.

"She was my spirit," he said. "More than muse, beyond Aode, Melete and Mneme, Calliope and Clio, and all the rest, she was my love and watched over my progress, offering comment and encouragement, diverting me from periods of self-doubt with gentle and constructive observations. She was the guiding influence of my vision, the sustenance when all other resources failed. She alone provided a third eye for my last work, wondering if I shouldn't try yellows instead of gold, orange instead of red, pointing out when my hand was steering certain forms too far or not far enough. I leaned on her more than was fair and beyond anything I ever understood at the time.

"When the critics saw fit to attack my work, I weathered the assault as best I could and assured Sally everything would be forgotten soon enough, but she took the slight much harder and spent a great deal of energy defending my art, renouncing the reviewers as parochial and nationalistic and far worse when she had the chance. She cursed other artists we once regarded as friends who provided little support and treated me now as an outcast. Ultimately she insisted we move from London. Her health was never an issue before. She was always hardier than I, yet seeing the mistreatment I suffered quite literally exhausted her heart. She lost weight, seemed to age overnight," he stared at the shadows flicking across the ceiling, then back down at his hands. "How these things happen," he said.

Once again, I struggled to come up with exactly the right thing to say. I resisted the impulse to extend further condolence, but was at a loss to offer anything more, and wrapping my fingers around my whiskey glass, the best I could do was note, "And so here you are."

This seemed to please him, that I was wise enough to know when less was more, and he replied in turn, "Here, yes."

"Are you planning to stay?"

"I'm planning nothing."

Of course. "I understand."

The wrinkles around Timbal's eyes appeared as small wounds,

his words a declaration inspiring me to quickly add, "Nothing's good." My comment caused him to look at me curiously again, and sliding his empty glass across the table, he turned his hands over and said, "Nothing is simply that." I was hoping he'd go on, but he fell quiet and I had to start him off with a new line of questions. "How do you spend your days here in Algiers?"

"I do as little as possible."

"And your painting?"

"What of it?"

"Are you working on anything new?"

Timbal observed me this time as he did when we first collided, no doubt wondering exactly who I was and what he should make of all my questions. "No," he said.

"You're doing nothing?" I couldn't resist.

"There is nothing new," he stood then and tossed several DA onto the table, turned and walked outside. I followed after him, past crowds of men coming from afternoon prayer and children who buzzed and dashed about at my knees. For an older man with stunted legs and shoes protruding from the cuffs of his pants like two tethered weights, Timbal moved at a surprisingly brisk rate, and eventually I called out, "Where are you going?" He didn't answer. We rounded a corner and went down a series of side streets with several more shops, then toward an open market where Timbal purchased a copy of both *El Moudjahid* and the *International Herald Tribune,* explaining only as we started off again that his driver, Mullah, was shopping for supplies and should be done by now.

Leaving the market we found Mullah standing beside an old two-door Chevy sedan. Tall and sorrel-colored, his flesh a smooth shade of coffee brown, Mullah was dressed in beige pants and a faded navy blue jacket, black sandals, and a red fez covering much of his dark hair. He greeted us with a half bow, and glancing at me, asked his employer something in Arabic I could not understand. ("*Meen irragill dah, essiyed Timbal?*") The car was box-shaped, lemon-green with wide tires, a flat roof, dented trunk and fender. Several satchels of groceries, paper products, bottled water, and wine along with other assorted supplies were in the rear seat. Timbal answered his driver, then turned to me and said, "If you're free, come for dinner. Afterward Mullah will drive you back." I agreed at once and began helping move much of what was on the seat into the trunk.

We drove south, away from the city for some forty minutes, beyond Tipasa and Blida, angling east off the main road just past Medea, down a dirt lane between a dense cluster of trees and back through open space. Distant mountains filled the horizon, and angling north after a while, we cut onto another road that led to the foothills and a hutch house standing in solitary construct. The supplies were unpacked, the groceries carted in and set atop a thick wooden table, the jugs of water and gasoline lined along the front wall. The house consisted of a single room, a kitchen area off to the right, a tiny refrigerator running on a gas generator out back, the connecting cord slipped through a hole drilled beneath the rear window. A wood-burning stove centered the room, a silver tube rising out of its rear and up through the roof, the shaft supported by wires and bolts. A mattress covered by a blue quilt was laid out in the far left corner, books, paper, and pens stacked nearby, and mosquito netting hanging overhead. A red oil lamp sat to the right of several flat white pillows. On the opposite side of the room was a cushioned chair, a closed sketch pad and box of charcoal, an easel with brushes and paints, and three large canvases turned to face the wall.

Mullah tended to the stove. A pot of marga with chicken and darker meats, carrots and onions, salt and turnips and other assorted vegetables and seasonings was placed on one of the burners to reheat. I thought about calling Niles and looked around for a phone. "The nearest line is in Medea," Timbal said, then produced a cell and helped me get through to the Sahel where the clerk informed me in broken English that Niles wasn't in and jotted down my message. We ate our meal seated at the table, and afterward took glasses of rum outside, where I was educated on the surrounding areas, what villages lay over the hills, their religious and political, nationalistic and historical affiliations. The sky was infinite and as the night darkened filled with thousands of bright white stars.

Timbal leaned against a large rock, his head tipped back, his wild hair tucked beneath a grey knit cap, and staring up at the sky, sipped from his glass. Despite how alternately melancholic and combustible his mood, he seemed now nearly at peace, and envious of his calm, I wondered what it would be like to remain here in the desert. I imagined taking over for Mullah and running Timbal's errands, driving him wherever he needed to go, mastering the language and customs, learning to make myself happy and lick my life like barley sugar, to shape and sharpen it as never before. (My hand at the time was reaching back and touching a residue of stone.) "It's beautiful here," I said to Timbal. "All things considered, finding this spot must be a comfort to you."

My remark did not go over the way I intended, and turning to look at me, Timbal's mouth drew up tight on his cragged face. "Comfort is hardly the right word, Mr. Finne."

"What I mean is, at least you don't have to think about being somewhere else."

He shifted around on the rough surface of rock, his eyes with a sobering look of weary objection. "You're wrong," he said. "I think of being somewhere else all the time," his smile was now sad, and drinking more rum, he set his glass down between his feet and rubbed at the top of his knit cap, his shoulders turned away from me. "You're young," he spoke while rolling his neck back as if his muscles ached, then shifted again and moved closer to me. "Old enough to know better, but naive enough still to think a man winds up where he does of his own accord."

"I understand," I said. "And yet here you are. I mean, you've chosen to be here now."

"Have I? In what sense? Like someone who's lost a leg and chooses to buy one shoe?" he reached for his glass. "Choice is relative, Mr. Finne. The ability to select a course of action is precious, but there is always history beyond the immediacy of our decisions. I'm here now because whatever else I prefer is no longer an option," he placed his heels against the front of the rock and waved his hands once in the air.

I considered what Timbal just said, interpreted his gesture as proof that he, too, was now a disciple of Nothing, and inspired by the rum replied, "It is all history, isn't it?"

"Every tree has its root, Mr. Finne."

I told him then about my father and how his fixation on becoming a musician led to my mother's death. I drew analogy to Timbal's own situation, how his decision to expand his art created a consequence he never imagined, and sipping more of my rum, I confessed my calamity with Liz and how, "Life should come with a warning label: Dangerous Occupation."

"What are you saying?"

"Simply that."

Timbal frowned. "You resent the fact life involves choices?"

"It's not the choice that bothers me, it's the repercussion."

"Guaranties only come at the Five and Dime."

"All the more reason for caution."

Timbal shook his head, bent down once again and set his glass in the sand. He did not say anything for several seconds, did not look at me but stared instead in the direction of Blida. When he did at last address me, it was while coming from his rock, his shoulders raised on his squat frame, his height barely reaching my chin yet somehow looming larger as he removed his hat from his round head, the hairs beneath bursting out in all directions like wild snakes set suddenly free, and asked, "What then do you propose? What is your alternative?"

"Nothing."

"Of course."

"No, I mean not anything. What it comes down to," I tried to explain, "is understanding the nature of the universe and how all things conspire to leave. (Look at Liz, I thought to say. Look at my mother and your wife.) It's a juggling act," I continued. "An endless process of trying to outmaneuver the inevitable. A person can try keeping their balls in the air indefinitely but at some point, despite our best intentions, everything comes crashing down."

"You sound like Chicken Little," Timbal rubbed his head once more.

"Except the bird was wrong."

"And what then? You believe it's better to avoid the tumble than take any risk at all?"

"In the end, yes," I raised my glass. "The trick is learning to keep out of harm's way."

"But you can't go about hiding under a rock and call that living."

"It isn't hiding."

"Mr. Finne. If I behaved for one minute as you suggest I never would have painted a single canvas. What you're describing is a dodge."

"If that's true, then why are you here?"

Timbal's frown became a scowl. "I'm here to recover my wind."

"To do as little as possible, isn't that what you said?"

"I lost my wife. Mourning is a natural course."

"I'm sorry," I apologized for any inappropriateness in my reference. "And still," I said, "you seem to have settled in."

"Is that what you think? Because I'm here you assume I've taken to the void like some anchorite to a new religion? Listen carefully, Mr. Finne. A man can't avoid making history, even if he does nothing. Things happen no matter what. Hindsight is always picture-perfect and wishing my fate might have gone differently will not bring my Sally back, nor does it suggest I was wrong to paint as I did. If all things that might cause us harm were summarily averted, there would be no world to speak of, just ice and sand."

"And still you're here."

"Again with that. I'm here, yes."

"Where the hounds stopped barking, you told me."

"To regather my wits."

"For over a year."

"Time is of no significance."

"Away from everything familiar."

"That's right."

"And eager to appreciate nothing."

Once more, Timbal looked at me as if my statement offended him. He pushed his face closer to mine, his mouth open, pausing in apparent contemplation of what to say next. A second later he turned and placed his knit cap back on his head, reached out and grabbed hold of my sleeve, dragging me into the house. I didn't struggle against his grip, went willingly and in stride as we cut across the floor, past the stove and around the table, over to Timbal's easel and the three canvases propped up with their fronts facing the wall. Timbal released me and set his hands against the sides of the largest canvas, lingering there a moment while catching his breath and murmuring something that sounded almost like a prayer. (The incantation had the rhythm of music, beyond interpretation to my dead ear.) He shifted the painting toward me then and stepped off.

I saw at once an extraordinary work. Within a background of orange and blue, the canvas was centered by the head of a woman painted in a synthesis of Impressionism, Surrealism, and Abstract Expressionism I'd never quite seen combined that way before. The woman's eyes were at once sparkling and mournful, the position of her head tipped back just a bit and turned to the left, her mouth opened as if whispering or blowing a kiss. Her nose was set in a Bacon-like sort of twist that made her face all the more diverting while the color of her cheeks had the density of flesh. I took a single step closer, staring at Sally's eyes while saying to Timbal, "I thought you weren't painting anything new."

"I'm not."

"But?"

"Mr. Finne."

"Why come to Algiers then?" I took another step forward, confused and asking, "What about escaping the hounds and putting distance between yourself and all the rest?" I stared into the center of Sally's face, at her beautiful blue and water-dazed eyes that gripped and gazed out at me with their own sweet warning, and went on to mention the ticket I had to see Liz in Spain and why I wouldn't go, recounting my need for nothing and wanting to forget.

Timbal stopped me there and said, "If you're so in love with nothing, Mr. Finne, I'm confident Mullah and I can accommodate you. A quick smashing of your skull, a hole dug in the hills. It can all be over in no time, if that's truly what you want."

"You don't understand," I dismissed his threat and made another feeble attempt to explain. "I don't believe in the same things you do. It doesn't work for me. Nothing makes me happy," I swore, only the statement sounded specious, awkward and misguided when presented as a vow.

Timbal moved toward me, lowered his voice, forced me to listen while insisting, "It's all excuse," and referring to my ticket said, "At the very least, you have passage. You have an available route." He slumped forward, looking suddenly weary and sad, only to regroup a moment later, and reaching for one of his brushes, brandished it in front of my face. "Nothing is impossible!" he pronounced.

Startled, I backed into the center of the room, almost colliding with the stove, the warmth of which bled through my shirt. "What I'm saying," I began again, distracted as I glanced beyond Timbal's shoulder and caught sight of Sally's face, her lips appearing now to mouth the word What?, I could no longer look away, and seeing me staring, Timbal tossed his brush into its box and went quickly to the painting of his wife.

I wiped my face, a streak of sweat beneath my eyes running down my cheeks as Timbal removed the tacks holding the canvas to the mounting frame, undid the sailcloth and rolled the painting up. "Here," he said and thrust out his arms.

"What?"

"Take it," he pushed the canvas into my chest.

"What are you doing?"

"I'm giving it to you."

"But?"

"Go on, go on."

"You're not serious."

"Of course, I am."

"But why?"

"Because, Mr. Finne. You think you know what you want? You think to know what's best? Go ahead then and spend some time with Sally. Live with her for a while and see what you wind up thinking then."

CHAPTER 15

# ALL THINGS THAT RISE

What the darkness lacks is music.

Oz, in Algiers, performed on bended knee, in the center of a long row of other men drawn at dusk to prayer. Barefoot and head bowed, he repeated the incantations of the imam: "Allah-hoo Akbar. Ashhadoo alla eelaha illa Allah. Ashhadoo annah mohammadan rahsooloo Allah. La eelahha illa Allah. (God is great. I witness there is but one God. I witness that Mohammed is his prophet. There is no God but him.)" All the men inside the mosque shared in the routine, each participating in the ritual in order to confirm their unerring devotion to Islam. Men of such commitment could be counted on in their capacity as humble servants to execute those deeds for which they were chosen. It is the blessed way (Allah Akbar!).

Outside, in the time before Oz entered the iggameh, Niles listened as the elmoazzin called the men to evening prayer. Perched high up on the minaret, the elmoazzin paced around the balcony, his voice rich and resonant, ringing out like a songbird exhilarated by his chance to perform. Aziz sat on the curb beside the American. Unsure what would happen now, he looked at Niles in profile, observed the odd discolor and what appeared a worsening fever, drawn nonetheless by what the Amreekanee said to him earlier about forgiveness and how able he was to sit and observe, waiting so otherwise calm and roosted at the roadside like a child watching a parade. "It is because you are of one mind," Aziz told him, and apologized again for thinking otherwise before at the beach. "It's because you are here in Algiers. Unlike the West where people constantly question their fate, one has a clearer sense of destiny in the East. The focus here is not on the Self but on a greater whole. This is what you are feeling, my friend, the ease of knowing and serenity of being sure."

Niles didn't answer, remained staring across the street at the men disappearing inside the mosque. Much of the afternoon had already been spent in similar conversation, with Aziz going back and forth over every possible concern and Niles assuring him that he came solely to be healed, confining his morning walks to this very spot and how he knelt in his own prayer then and watched Oz come and go. "You don't have to stay with me," he reminded Aziz as the other men enter the iggameh, their holy devotion put on display, and pushing the cuff of his right sleeve up, he stared at the first trace of scar, convinced here, too, was adoration and how much the cleaving and blistering of his flesh was equally a matter of faith.

Just then Oz arrived from the opposite end of the street and entered the mosque. Niles stood and moved from the curb to the street, his fever warming his head, his body all but liquid as if he was once more submerged in the sea. He crossed into the path of men who barely seemed to notice him, shifting only in the last moment as if to avoid a cool shadow, the hint of a specter, the fear of ghosts. The chants from inside the mosque were a steady buzz Niles and Aziz listened to as they stood by the door. Niles' thoughts were mosaic, all dreamlike wisps of visions he experienced there in curious waves. (Jeana's face pressed toward him through a milky pane of glass, her features more irresistible than ever though he couldn't quite get beyond the fog.) After half an hour the votaries completed their prayers, slipped on their shoes, and returned outside. Oz appeared in the middle of a small group, walked a few blocks east with the others, then parted company and went on alone. Although he hadn't planned to do as much, Niles followed from a short distance, Aziz further behind.

One by one they left the main road, crossed through the empty marketplace onto an isolated stretch of street. Soon the route looked familiar, the narrow alleyway Niles had walked to each of the last few mornings, only a few yards from the house where Oz rented a room. Niles closed the gap between them from fifty feet to twenty, more deliberate in his pacing now, drawing near enough to see tiny clouds of dust kick up in the dark beneath Oz's feet. "In a minute, in a second," he thought, his fever causing his shoulders to shake, the contents of his camera bag jostling, the intensity of the shudder inspiring an odd sense of joy, a peculiar pleasure bordering on happiness. It was as if his body, after threatening to betray him, had chosen that moment to conspire with him in a unified complicity, cuing him to stay focused. ("I must be conscious without deception," he quoted Camus, "without cowardice—alone, face to face.") Close enough then to cast his own shadow over Osmah, he thought of another line from the book, an encouraging passage that reminded him that it was, "his own will to happiness which must make the next move . . . all his violence there to help him, and at the point where he found the nerve, his love will (again) join him and fill him with a furious passion to live."

Oz turned and the blade passed through the softest flesh of his throat, an arch that dug and split the top of his breastbone, creating a vacuumlike seal requiring all of Niles' strength to draw out and thrust down a second time with equally deadly force.

("Forgiveness," he called out as the blade descended again.) Osmah bent frantically back, like a wild child dipping beneath a bar, his head tipped to receive Niles' offering as a communicant taking benediction on the flat of his tongue. His shoulders sagged, his hips and knees breaking at an angle that lowered him several inches as his arms flailed at his sides for balance. His face beneath Niles was now that of a boy and nothing else, his expression fearful, as bewildered as Jeana and P. Kelly no doubt in their final seconds, unable to comprehend the nearness of death.

What pity. ("What pity?") Niles cried out louder than Osmah, his sound filled with alarm as the blade glistened and split the moonlight, his fever pitched even higher then as Osmah clutched the air, his fingers catching hold and digging into Niles' arms, both men with knees bent and gasping, then falling as one to the earth, to the cool, cool truth and motionless surrender.


I took Timbal's canvas in a cardboard tube and tied it to the roof with a fibrous brown twine before Mullah drove me back to the city. The stars overhead seemed to fade as we passed Blida, then reappeared as we came again into a clearing and the landscape opened like an infinite sea. We reached the Sahel just after eleven, where I hurried inside, eager to tell Niles about my night. I tried not to think of the argument Timbal made against my want for nothing, preferring instead to clutch at the spoils from my visit, laughing as I imagined my committee's surprise when I gave them a look at the painting. No doubt Dr. Freidrich would let me keep my job in exchange for a promise to write a book about my trip.

I crossed the lobby with the canvas in tow, making a mental note to file a Certificate of Authenticity and Ownership as soon as I got back to Renton, only to stop and turn as someone called my name. I saw a man about my age, thin like Niles only taller, a dark caramel skin and jet black hair, moving toward me from the opposite side of the room. "You are Bailey Finne?" he asked, and when I was slow to answer, he touched my arm in a half-comforting and half-urgent gesture, and said, "I am here about your friend."

Before leaving the Sahel, we went upstairs where I deposited the canvas and this man—Aziz—looked through Niles' belongings, taking away a folder and his copy of *The Rebel.* ("It is best for now you not have these here," he said.) Ten minutes later we were driving back across town, away from the sea and out toward Beni Douala where a community of shops and houses rose out of the sand. I sat in the front seat flipping through the pages of the folder, reading the name Osmah Said Almend, the reality of which limited my ability to reject the story Aziz told me. Still, I tried convincing myself his claim was nothing more than a bizarre fiction, and several times along the way I asked in a confused sort of denial, "What exactly happened?"

Aziz accelerated around a curve, glanced sideways at me as I sat tense and pale, shaking my head with worry and doubt. "It is this," he declared, and repeated it all again.

I tossed the folder into the back seat and looked next at Niles' copy of *The Rebel,* all marked and underlined, and with the name Massinissa Alilouche beside the quote:

The logic of the rebel is to want to serve justice so as not to add to the injustice of the human condition, to insist on plain language so as not to increase the universal falsehood, and to wager, in spite of human misery, for happiness.

These words gave me confidence, and I nearly read as much out loud, only to be shaken by the following highlighted passage:

The consequence of rebellion . . . is to refuse to legitimize murder because rebellion, in principle, is a protest against death. . . . The rebel who, united against death, wants to construct, on the foundation of the human species, a savage immortality, is terrified at the prospect of being obliged to kill in their turn. Nevertheless, if they retreat they must accept death; if they advance they must accept murder.

I cursed and once again blurted out, "But what's happened?" as if this time Aziz's answer would be different.

"My friend."

"This can't be."

"And yet I was there," the rest of the story unfolded the same in a murky sort of confusion, culminating in Niles collapsing to the ground with Oz in his arms and Aziz getting him from the alley to safety. ("The whole afternoon he spoke of forgiveness," Aziz said. "And yet.") I turned on the seat and stared at the man beside me, wondering again what I was supposed to believe, rooting back through everything in search of clues I missed, hints of future trouble revealed in Niles' somnambulism, the fever he exhibited that morning and I failed to take seriously. Still what had happened was beyond anything I could ever imagine. "It's crazy. Crazy," I said again and again until we reached our destination and the car was parked.

Aziz's house was one of several small structures connected in a row of adjoining walls. Inside the house, Niles had been put to bed, Aziz's wife having placed a blanket over him, her intention to have him sweat out his illness. I was taken into the room where he lay, his pale face covered in perspiration though his teeth chattered. His entire body appeared as a soft clay heated, without form, his head resting atop two pillows that folded around his face and caused the warm air to close over him in a discomfiting boil. His eyes remained half-shut, his coloring ashen in the dim glow of the one small lamp. Despite Aziz's warning, I was surprised by how ill he looked. His features were sallow and narrowed to a point where he resembled Odilon Redon's *Marsh Floer, a Sad and Human Head.* I crossed the room, reached down and touched his cheek.

"I have phoned a doctor," Aziz said

"He's burning up."

"He should be here soon. My wife has offered broth but your friend is not interested."

"How about a wet compress?" I didn't wait for an answer, turned in a circle, went into the kitchen and brought Niles a cool glass of water and a damp cloth that I placed on his forehead. Raising his shoulders, I got him to take a drink. The blue of his eyes had faded almost to white, and setting him back down on the pillow, alarmed again by how rapidly his fever had soared, I pulled the wooden chair over beside the bed and asked, "How are you doing?"

He answered in a whisper, his breathing labored, as if passing through lungs half filled by the sea. "Bailey," he said. I leaned closer, examined his face, heard the release of air, the mouthing of words not yet spoken until all would-be sound faded. "It's OK," I said, and offered another sip of water.

Aziz stood just inside the door, his wife a few feet behind, watching Niles as he repeated my name, drawing me close again as he whispered, "I need your help."

"Yes. Of course," I misunderstood and answered at once. "I'm here. It's alright. You're going to be fine. There's a doctor coming and he'll get your fever down." I reached to adjust the cloth on his head while Niles struggled to sit up. I stopped him, insisting, "You need to lie down."

"I can't. I have to go," he made an effort to rise further,

looked past me and searched the floor for his shoes. I came out of the chair, blocked his progress at the side of the bed while assuring him, "It's OK. You're safe here. We'll leave just as soon as the doctor checks you out."

"Bailey," he said again, and it was how he pronounced my name this time, with vigilance and a telling sort of intonation that caused me to stop what I was doing and shake my head. "What are you asking?"

"I need you to take me."

"Where?"

"To *El Moudjahid*."

"The newspaper? Why?"

"Bailey."

"Forget it, Niles."

"I have to."

"No, you don't."

"Take me."

"I won't."

He began slipping his legs out from under the blanket, squirming with some difficulty until he was sitting over the edge, the wheezing in his lungs anchoring every word as he said again, "I need you to do this for me." I circled once around my chair, animated in my resistance. "There's no reason. Stop and think. Oz is dead. You can't change what happened. You need to leave it be." I put a hand on Niles' shoulder and tried guiding him back beneath the sheet. The pressure of my fingers kept him from moving further though the second I removed my hand he continued.

"Wait," I returned my grip. "Just listen."

Niles dropped his shoulder beneath my hold and tried to stand, though even the minor exertion of slipping free seemed to weaken him, and straining to catch his breath, he said, "I can't leave things as they are."

"So what are you saying? You want to confess? Why?" I waved my arms in the air. "A murderer like Osmah deserves what he gets."

"And me?"

"A medal, Niles. You didn't kill innocent people."

He sat with his feet dangling, hesitating before he answered, trying to gather his strength even as the effort of raising his head caused his neck to snap and roll back. His determination remained steadfast, however. "People need to understand what I did," he said. "I have to confess in order not to surrender to the profane," his reference to Camus frustrated me further, and unwilling to debate philosophical ideologies, I answered, "You can't apply any of that nonsense to real life. It's all academic theory, Niles. Right now we need to concentrate on the facts. You're sick. Oz is dead and the only thing important is getting you well enough to fly home."

"Take me downtown," his chin fell forward, then bounced back, his eyes catching mine and holding my gaze until the muscles in his neck sagged again. Aziz's wife stepped into the room, located Niles' shoes and knelt in front of him, slipping them on before Aziz barked at her to stop. ("Tohaf!") Niles watched his shoes being removed, his legs hanging down, and in that moment of confusion I grabbed his ankles and guided him back beneath the blanket, intent on keeping him there until the doctor arrived. "The important thing now is getting you healthy. You've done enough for one night. You need to do nothing else. Nothing, Niles. Nothing. Do you understand?"

———

Niles in recline, said the word "nothing," so soft that the letters barely formed on his lips, were little more than a tease as he thought of what was left for him, of what Massinissa Alilouche warned him about and how unprepared he was back then to listen. "The rebel has only one way of reconciling himself with his act of murder . . ." Truly yes, how impossible it all was to know before. He thought of Oz and then Bailey, of Jeana, and his father, and Marthe Raynal until all blurred together and the final degree of separation faded, leaving him with a single truth, his red-rimmed eyes hollowed as the heat of his fever soared.

He allowed his eyes to shut and there in the dark Osmah appeared once more, the innocence in his face as he spun and stood for all eternity beneath the blade haunting, a perfect incongruity Niles made no attempt to chase away. He trembled then, confronted by a new sense of fear. He was Mersault, smothering under his blankets, cold then hot, struggling to breathe, burning with a great confusion. He remembered being dragged from the alley and brought away from the stones among stones, how surprised he was to find his head filled not with Jeana but Marthe and the night she lifted his shirt and kissed his wounds. He recalled the blade rising and then thrust down, how he shouted with irrefutable knowledge, only to know now it was never love and forgiveness that drove him to find Oz but something else, a condition worse than the nothingness Bailey worshiped, as complete and absolute as death.

When he opened his eyes again, Bailey was gone. He repeated the word—"nothing"—moving his head from the pillow as best he could and staring across the room. A numbness passed through his hands, a chill shooting over his wrists as he looked through the open door. In losing Jeana, he used to assume—as Mersault did—that he was "no longer made for such devotion, but for the innocent and terrible love of the dark god he would from then on serve," and yet now, in the aftermath of everything, how different he knew the answer to be. He thought of Marthe again and said the word "love," in the hope that Bailey would hear. "Love," he tried to shout as an adjuration, but the word was only in his head, the bluish stubble on his cheeks transforming him, a tightness in his stomach passing into his throat like a stone, until his wincing gave way to a different sort of resolve, quieting his limbs, leaving him motionless and becalmed, his mouth already filled with sand.

I walked out to the front room, hoping Niles would sleep, and stared out the window at the dark. It was after 2 a.m. and the stillness of the hour was absolute, the only light from stars clustered in a tenebrous sky. "Where is this doctor you called?"

"I don't know. He's obviously detained. Perhaps we should consider the hospital."

"No," I remained adamant, imagining Niles surrounded by nurses and orderlies and physicians, any one of whom might notify the police about the ill American confessing to a crime near Bab El Oued. The door to the bedroom was open and I glanced back through at Niles laying peacefully beneath the brown blanket. "We'll wait for your doctor friend."

"All right."

"He is?"

"What? *Tabeeb? Sahbee?* He can be trusted, yes."

"And you?" I couldn't keep myself from asking. "Why are you helping us?"

"Me? But what can I tell you, my friend? Because I, too, have become fond of your Niles? But more than that, no? If I left him in the alley with Osmah, maybe someone who saw us together would have connected your friend to me. Or maybe because I am no fan of Osmah, either. Men such as he make it impossible for the rest of us to live. And maybe, simply," he smiled here though not sincerely, "because you are an American, too, and will pay me, of course, for all my effort."

Aziz's wife came from the kitchen with freshly steeped tea. A young woman in tan trousers drawn in tight around her ankles, she was barely older than the coeds I taught, her pitch-black hair combed straight, her head uncovered, a long silk scarf draped over her shoulders and down across her blouse which was blue. She spoke just enough English to understand the conversation between Aziz and me, knew the reason Niles and I were there. "Anah asif. I am sorry," Aziz accepted the tea from his wife, apologized for his anger earlier when he insisted she move away from Niles. "It is like this," he said, and elaborated on what he already told her, discussing the new twist and Niles' desire to confess.

In response to Aziz soliciting her opinion, Mati described what she saw in Niles' face as she knelt before him and helped him with his shoes, how it was clear to her confessing was what he wanted. "Anah mish ahrif layh, Aziz (I do not know why)," she said. "But in that moment—hoowah mab-soot—he was happy."

"Maf-ti-kersh (I don't think so)," Aziz disagreed, and when Mati said again she thought Niles should be allowed to go— "Af-tiker keda (I believe so)," he shook his head. "Anan ahrif ahsan (I know better)." Mati suggested taking Niles to the hospital then—as Aziz proposed not five minutes ago—or at the very least to a clinic.

"La (no)." Aziz assured Mati the doctor would be here any minute and for now they must wait.

I moved from the window and glanced again at Niles who hadn't stirred beneath the blanket and appeared fast asleep. I went to the front door then and opened it, staring down the road, which was unlit and disappeared in the darkness. The air outside was warm and placid, the absence of sound like standing beneath water. I tried clearing my head but found it all too cluttered, and frustrated, I wanted to shout. Aziz joined me in the doorway, aware of my agitation and afraid of attracting the gendarmes, he said, "Sahbee. Let's wait inside." I raised my hands, palms flat as if attempting to push back the dark. "In a minute," I told him, then turned and glanced at Mati who had moved from beside the low table on which she'd set the tea and was standing closer to the bedroom, staring in at Niles. She acknowledged me with a look of sorrow, mouthing the word, "Etfadal (come)," and summoned me with her hand.

I hesitated as Mati continued to signal me. "Etfadal," her arm extended, her expression softening as she noticed the fear in my face. Her milder appeal unsettled me even more however, and I began to back off, colliding with Aziz who was walking then toward his wife. "Ayh elhekayah? (What is the matter?)" he asked her, but I didn't want to hear and covered my ears. Mati took hold of her husband's sleeve and coaxed him toward the bed, and only then did I run with my hands still flat against my ears and my eyes squinting as if to force a great pain from my head.

Niles' face was already a bluish grey. I fell down on my knees and screamed, "We have to get him to the hospital! We have to get him downtown." I began to cry, Aziz and Mati with heads bowed as I flailed my arms and begged for their help. As tranquil as Niles appeared then, I moaned with apology, "Goddamn it, Niles! Goddamn it! It's nothing! It's nothing! It's nothing!" over and over and over again, until the doctor came at last and treated me with an odd-smelling white powder mixed into water, encouraging me to sit in the chair and try to rest. Mati helped with my shoes, removed the blanket from Niles' body, and laid it across my legs before turning out the light.

BOOK III

# AND BACK AGAIN

# CHAPTER 16

# THE TRIP HOME

Under the circumstances, I was ill-equipped to handle the arrangements and relied on Aziz to deal with the authorities and make the necessary preparations for transport. Tests were run to insure Niles' body was not incubating any contagious disease, and only then was I allowed to take him home. I contacted Jeana's family and had Niles buried beside her in Chicago. Elizabeth came from Spain for the funeral, stayed three days then returned. The shock of Niles' death gave her reason to treat me kindly, though the situation confused and ultimately forbid anything further between us. I blamed myself for Niles' death and insisted he'd still be alive if I'd taken better care of him. Elizabeth in turn, who knew only that Niles had caught a fever, assured me with a sentiment I took two ways, "Bailey, there's nothing you could have done."

The night before she went back to Europe, we were sitting on the steps outside her apartment when I thanked her for coming and wondered if we might see one another when she returned. She pushed her hair aside slowly, gave me the sort of look that let me know this was just the question I hoped I wouldn't ask, then said, "I'm sorry for Niles," and before I could ask again, she informed me of her plan to stay overseas through next semester.

"I've taken a leave," she said, as certain opportunities presented themselves and would occupy her through the New Year.

I stood up and looked at the moon, so distant and pale as to appear a kind of brilliant tease. "All right," I said and without amending my gaze, "I understand."


After the funeral I could do no more than sit in my chair, drink whiskey, and smoke whatever cigarettes I could find. I avoided friends who called to see how I was doing, ate pizza ordered from the corner, until all my available cash was gone and I had to go out. My mood was inconsolable. At night I sat by the window, hoping to forget what happened and eventually lose myself in the distant dark.

The problem was, despite my most urgent want for nothing, I didn't quite know how to disappear anymore, and looking for some immediate form of diversion, I got it in my head to write an article explaining what had happened in Algiers. I wanted to present things from Niles' perspective and submit what he would have said had he been allowed to confess. Determined then to commit myself to the project, I cleared off my desk and sat not at my computer but with paper and pen as if composing a personal letter. I worked late into the night, hoping for clarity and anxious for people to understand. I produced a jumble of notes, roughed out my thesis, retooled and altered my approach, ran through a half dozen or so false starts while searching for a coherent voice.

Just before sunrise I fell asleep and had sad dreams about Niles and woke with a stiffness in my back and my head down on a pad of yellow paper. I stretched, then stood and read the pages from my night's effort. The initial result disappointed me as I found my tone overly sentimental, a mewling sort of grief and babble. How could I explain the complexity of Niles' deed, and prove the sacrifice he made was unconditional, if my writing was so biased and over the top? Frustrated that my attempt turned out poorly, I was torn between finding the resolve to sit back down and rework what I wrote and taking every last page and throwing them in the trash. In the end I decided on neither and went to bed.

I got up around noon, waking with a start as I opened my eyes to find Timbal's painting of Sally staring at me from the opposite wall. (I'd unrolled the canvas and fastened it carefully to the brick.) The sun shined through the window, and as I went to close the blinds, I saw a woman dressed in faded jeans, a short-sleeved blue shirt, and red canvas tennis shoes posting an orange flyer on the kiosk across the street. Several people walked by after the woman was gone and occasionally someone stopped to read what she'd left. I got dressed with the intent of going out for something to eat, my last meal too long ago to remember, and in crossing over toward the kiosk, I stopped and looked for the flyer.

Dozens of other flyers were tacked up as well, advertisements for tutorials and bikes for sale, bands playing at local clubs, apartments for rent, health food co-ops soliciting members, and a New Age temple offering spiritual guidance for a fee. I found the orange paper beside a notice for a starving artist's auction and read the five words underlined in heavy black ink: ***IN NEED OF A VOLUNTEER.***

Typed beneath the heading was a brief essay beginning with the pronouncement: "Modern psychiatry has failed. So much talk. Psychologists, psychiatrists, analysts, clinicians, Freudian, Adlerian, Gestalt, Jung. Therapy has become an ineffective fashion, a convenient way to kill an hour in the afternoon with little to show in return. As part of research currently being conducted at the Hatilbee Institute, we believe in a different approach, a unique method that allows the patient to reconnect in short order with the sine qua non of their soul while ridding the mind of all that is harmful and foul. Clean-Slatedness," the treatise continued, "is a new theory on psychological healing, an inventive form of treatment designed to allow the individual to cut through the clutter of past experiences by a process of selective abstinence and sensory deprivation. We at Hatilbee are confident of our findings, and in an effort to confirm our theory, are soliciting paid volunteers." A phone number and address were printed at the bottom of the flyer, along with the name and signature of Doctor Emmitt Speckridge, Hatilbee Institute.

I stepped closer and examined the name just to be sure, then pulled the flyer off the kiosk and took it back to my room where I sat and reread the tract from top to bottom. The writing was curious, its tone at once serious, didactic, and propagandistic, all quite provocative and similar to the Emmitt I knew some eight years before when he was a doctoral candidate in psychology living in the apartment next door. An honor's student with a host of unorthodox and heretical theories incorporated into the outlines of his dissertation—completed at the age of twenty-four and published under the title "Regenerative Self-Healing and Absterging the Mind"—Emmitt often used me as a sounding board for his early work. Our exchanges frequently ended in disagreement where I was accused of faineancy and myopia and worse.

Irrepressible by nature and able to go for what seemed days without any real rest, Emmitt knocked on my door at all hours, his black hair unkempt, his heavy glasses sliding halfway down his nose, his shirttail untucked, and baggy pants bunched about his legs while his arms waved in a constancy of motion. I'd known Emmitt almost a year when he began dating Melissa Dunanne, a beautifully large-boned biology major with a concentration in deoxyribonucleic development. In love, Emmitt proved as indefatigable as ever, wooing Melissa with flowers and candy and entertaining anecdotes about Francis H. Compton Crick and Glenn Seaborg and their early experiments with berkelium and DNA.

That winter Melissa moved in with Emmitt, and so situated, their relationship took its course. I was sitting in my room one night, not three months after Melissa arrived, when Emmitt knocked at my door, all pale and with his right shoulder twitching, his left hand fisted and his dark eyes red. He took long drags from his cigarette, walked to my window and back in front of my chair where he asked for a drink. I wasn't sure how much he'd already had, though I got us whiskey just the same and poured two short glasses with ice. Emmitt sipped from his drink while staring back at the door as if expecting it to open. When it didn't he pressed his glass against his right cheek, frowned at me and said, "She'll be back."

I didn't want to argue, but from force of habit said, "How do you know?"

Emmitt walked in a circle, tugged at his belt, pushed his glasses up with his middle finger, rubbed at his forehead as if an irritant just beneath the surface was prickling his flesh, and answered, "Because I do." He took something from his pocket and put it in his mouth. "You think she won't?"

"I didn't say that."

The twitch in his shoulder became a separate spasm affecting his left eye, the dryness of his lips contrasting with the sweat on his chin as he stepped around my chair, wagged a finger in my direction and asked once again, "What are you saying?"

"I don't know, Emmitt. Maybe she'll come back and maybe she won't. There's nothing you can do either way."

He finished his whiskey, the smoke from his cigarette floating up toward the ceiling as he shook his head. "You're wrong, Bail-bait. From a purely physiological perspective, it's altogether impossible to do nothing. The two words are antipodal. We live in a constant state of action and reaction, are either stilling the waters or making waves. Even someone as seemingly idle as you, is forever reacting to something. Doing is all there is!" he waved his glass, and for emphasis jumped up and down, spilling the ice.

I found his argument both sentimental and specious, and drawn into the dispute, said as much. "Loving Melissa is one thing, Emmitt, but what can you do to insure she'll come back?"

"Let me tell you," he removed his glasses and cleaned them on his shirt, offering me a detailed index of what he planned to do. "There will be changes. Modifications and adjustments," he promised to quit drinking, to keep regular hours and control his moods, to be more composed with Melissa and handle problems before they evolved into crisis. "Change is the essence," he chanted at me. "Everything is a matter of redress and rectification. All that is, is subject to change," he shot a stream of smoke into the air, then distilled it entirely with a backward brush of his hand.

I set my drink down on the floor, and against all better judgement—for what was the point in arguing still?—told Emmitt his riposte was flawed. "You're ignoring the obvious. You can change everything about yourself, from your attitude down to your underwear and ninety-nine times out of a hundred it won't matter at all. Love is like this," I said and flung out my open hand, closed it and opened it, grasping futilely at the air.

Emmitt stared at my gesture and rolling his enormous head from side to side rejoined, "Love is a kite on a string, is that it? Always tugging and ready to take off?"

"Precisely."

"Your opinion evidences a dangerous pathology."

"But we're not talking about me," I refused to indulge his digression, and turning his words around suggested, "Love itself is a pathology. The only reason you think you can perform a metamorphosis is because you're desperate. You're also too much of a control freak to admit the truth. Wanting Melissa back, you're determined to believe you have the power to manipulate the situation but your expectations are unreasonable. Life's a struggle and things rarely work out in direct proportion to what we want."

"How would you know?" Emmitt snapped, beating his heels against the wood of my floor, the soft of his belly throwing waves beneath his untucked shirt. "Since when are you interested in making anything happen? If you're not recoiling from shadows you're backpedaling from ghosts. Everything you can't repress sends you into a panic."

I listened to Emmitt's analysis before walking to my piano and playing six quick bars of "Strange Fruit," stopping in the middle to turn the tables once again and suggest, "If what you say is true about everyone's ability to change for love, then it follows I can change as well in appropriate ways for any woman, including Melissa, and that she'll be equally inclined to fall in love with me as you."

The moment I said this, Emmitt kicked his right leg up as if punting a ball, the red in his face deepening as he hurled himself at me ranting, "That's right, Bailey. That's right!" The space between us filled with heat. I stood and allowed him to push his free hand flush against my chest, then stepping away he dropped his cigarette near a pile of loose newspapers, dashed out my door and disappeared. I saw little of him after that. The rest of my spring and summer went by at a leisurely pace. I spent my afternoons reading and walking through town. I played piano at

Dungee's and tried as best I could to avoid running into Emmitt on the stairs or in the street. Two days before the start of fall semester, he moved out of his apartment. We didn't say good-bye and I had no idea where he was going or if Melissa had agreed to take him back. Watching from my window however, I noticed as he was leaving that his hair appeared cut and brushed, his pants sagged less, and instead of a cigarette he was smoking a pipe.

I put Emmitt's flyer on the bed, considered the coincidence of my looking out the window at the kiosk at just the right moment, and wanting very much to forget everything that had happened in exactly the way Emmitt's treatise promised, I sat in the chair, and after a few minutes of predictable stalling, reached for the phone. The receptionist at the Hatilbee Institute pushed a button and music played through the receiver. (I recognized the piece as John Dowland's "Lachrimae.") A minute later, Emmitt came on the line. "Bailey?"

"Hello, Emmitt."

"Out of the blue, Mr. Finne. It's been what, six years?"

"Longer."

"How are you?"

I answered his question by describing my situation, made general references to Elizabeth and Niles and everything else that led up to my finding the flyer and placing the call. My voice cracked as I told him in more specific terms how desperate I was to try anything, and in an effort to cheer me, he insisted I shouldn't worry, as confident as ever. "Bailey, Bailey. I am the cure."

I invited him to dinner, asked if he was free that evening, and he accepted without hesitation. We met at seven-thirty, at Tyne's on West Jefferson. I was surprised by how well Emmitt looked. Gone were the frumpy pants and baggy shirts, replaced by neatly creased slacks and jacket. His hair was cut short, his stomach flat, and instead of thick black glasses he wore wire-rims that complimented his large head. He was waiting for me in the lobby, not the bar, and greeted me with great enthusiasm. I complimented him on his appearance, while he was polite enough to say nothing of mine.

Over dinner, I learned that just after moving out of my building Emmitt got back together with Melissa. "We've been married for two years. We're living on Belmore. Melissa's in medical school." I congratulated him on his happiness. Emmitt smiled, and after a moment in which I told him more about myself, jumping from one bit of news to the next, from Niles' death—though nothing about Oz—to Liz's leaving, my failed dissertation, and references to Timbal, Roslavets, and Clarence the bird, he nodded slowly and agreed, "I'm glad you found the flyer."

He described to me then the state of his work, how he still subscribed to Eysenck's view that modern psychology missed the boat both in application and approach. "The idea that examining our past will lead us to a clearer understanding of ourselves, and in turn a more constructive life, is egocentric," Emmitt said. "Self-knowledge is unreliable at best and at times a danger. The emphasis should not be on remembering but forgetting and returning to a point where no wounds exist," he tapped the flat of the table with the prongs of his fork. "At Hatilbee, we remove all that's come to infect the individual through a process of teaching the patient how to strip away the negative while ridding the system of unnecessary memory and habit. It's what you called me for, to wipe away the accumulated clutter and all the old undergrowth which does damage to the here and now."

As for the specifics of Emmitt's treatment, I was told, "The process of Clean-Slatedness starts off easy enough. The individual is required to give up something familiar each month and maintain that abstinence for a period of several months. It's important early on for the subject to become acclimated to the process, to let the mind know a journey has begun. Once a patient is ready for the final phase, they're placed in complete isolation. No lights, no sound, no human contact for a period of one month. Locked in with a bed and table, a toilet and shower, they remain in the dark while we feed and guard over them. They have only to give themselves up to their surroundings, to allow everything to flow back through them and be released. It's all quite natural and doesn't require years of wasted energy and expense."

I sat quietly as Emmitt spoke, nodding my head in agreement with each of his contentions, ignoring the gaping holes in his theory, and choosing to believe I was in good hands, repeated my desire to volunteer for his experiment. We set a time to meet the following afternoon and I arrived at the Institute just after three o'clock, was brought into a small room with yellow walls and one square window, where two men and a woman came separately to speak with me for more than an hour. Afterward, I was weighed and measured, my urine sampled and blood pressure checked, my ears, eyes, and throat examined, and my rectum poked. Since Emmitt was not a medical doctor, all of this was done by another man, a very tall and distinguished-looking physician who referred to me impassively as Subject Finne.

I completed the examination and was escorted down to Emmitt's office where we discussed what I might give up to begin my cycle. I suggested red meat, was overly eager and said perhaps additional things could be added in a few days, but my zealousness was frowned upon and Emmitt made clear I was to follow his instructions and grant him absolute control over the experiment. "If not, all treatment will end." I promised to cooperate and shook his hand.

# CHAPTER 17

# THE WEIGHT OF NOTHING

The first month passed without incident. I bought cans of tuna, ate more salad and fruits than ever before. Later that summer I met with my committee, bringing along Timbal's canvas slipped inside the same protective tube I used to travel from Algiers. I explained as much as they needed to know, admitted my original story about Timbal was bullshit and how everything that happened during my trip came about by chance. Dr. Freidrich examined the painting, and over Josh's thunderous protest, came away convinced of its authenticity. "All right, Finne," he returned to his seat behind the desk, "despite my better judgement, I'm going to take you at your word."

I was given an extension on my dissertation, told I could keep my teaching position for the year as long as I produced the paper I promised on Timbal. I agreed to do what I could, explained that I was in the middle of another writing, and in a gesture otherwise unplanned, left Timbal's canvas behind. "Whatever documentation needs to be prepared, I'm sure someone here can take care of it," I said, and agreed then to donate the painting to the university.

Melaine walked me outside. We'd spoken only once briefly since my return—she'd heard about Niles and contacted me with condolence—and looking at me curiously asked, "Are you all right?"

"I'm not sure."

"Is there anything I can do?"

"No, thanks."

"Why didn't you tell me?"

"About?"

"All of it."

"I don't know. I guess," I said, "I didn't know where to begin."

Emmitt and I spoke by phone twice a week and I met with him at Hatilbee at the end of each month. For August, I was instructed to give up reading quarterlies and magazines, and in September to stop listening to recorded forms of music, a difficult assignment so early in the game. I spent several weeks in the silence of my room reworking the essay I still hoped to write about Niles. I resumed playing at Dungee's, taught my classes at the university, ate bowls of tuna, lettuce, and carrots, and before going to bed each night made entries in my journal. (Emmitt provided a notebook, asked me to keep a daily accounting. "Nothing overdone," he said. "For now just concentrate on general observations.") I took a workmanlike approach to the experiment, eager to erase all that affected me adversely, inspired to forever lay old bones to rest.

October and November: motorized forms of transportation, television and movies. I had to walk everywhere, rearrange my schedule and plan my appointments with enough interval between to make it from one place to the next. Despite the inconvenience, I never thought of quitting, the exercise—if nothing else—gave me something to do, and without telling Emmitt, I took on further modifications, gave up tuna and chicken and supplemented myself with soybean and tofu. I stopped using electricity after nine at night and learned to read by candle, limited shaving to once a week, and slept without a pillow for my head.

Looking to test my progress, I took out photographs of Niles and Liz, curious to see my reaction, hoping my emotions would prove less brutal though the result was always the same, disappointing and severe. Frustrated, I put the pictures back in the closet until the next time, for as long as I could.

In December I gave up all fruit and black ink pens, novels written after 1970, music composed by musicians whose last names began with the letters O through Z. My effort was absolute, indefatigable and intense, and still I forgot nothing.

A week before Christmas I received a phone call from an attorney who informed me that Niles' will had cleared probate. I hadn't thought of this before, not once in all the weeks since I was home, such a thing simply never occurred to me and I was shocked to learn that from the trust Niles created for bequeathing sums to charity, he'd arranged to leave me $10,000 a year for life. "A matter of formality now. Just a few papers you need to sign." I went downtown the next day and tried to convince Niles' attorney that I didn't want the money, that I didn't deserve it and wasn't entitled to it, and that he should put the money back into the trust, but he wouldn't let me, said, "The money is yours now. What you do with it once it's in your hands is something else." I signed the papers as he asked and left it at that.

For January I gave up the blanket on my bed and dialed my thermostat down to sixty-three degrees. Liz returned to Renton just after the new year. (Eric Stiles informed me as we happened to pass on the street and I questioned him at length.) Elizabeth's sudden proximity challenged my current ambition, and despite all the months of effort I put into laying the groundwork for Emmitt's treatment, I wanted to go and see her and confess how much she was missed. Ultimately, as a form of compromise, having gone round and round for nearly a week, I waited one day until the mid-afternoon when I assumed Liz would not be in her apartment, and setting the phone atop my piano I dialed her number, allowed the machine to click on, and played Rachmaninoff's "Prelude Op. 32, No. 5 in G."

Following this, I sat in silence for quite some time, wondering what I had done. Around 5:00 p.m. I took out the journal Emmitt asked me to keep and wrote on the page dated January 11, "Forget, forget forget," filling every line back and front, stopping only as the telephone rang and I let the machine answer it. I heard Beethoven's "33 Variations on a Waltz by Diabelli," the left hand alone but clearly recognizable. I listened to the entire piece without picking up the phone, and later that night tried to imagine why Liz chose such a difficult score, not one of her own and a composition which—despite how well she played with her left hand—was nonetheless fractured and only half achieved. I puzzled over this until the next afternoon, then returned her call by performing the right hand to Beethoven's "Variations," the missing half reciprocated in kind.

Early in February, the month I gave up going to galleries and drinking morning coffee, I hit a rough patch in the essay I was writing on Niles. The piece—tentatively entitled "Notes from the Meridian"—had gone well for a time then grew more labored, and looking about as always for a further form of diversion, I decided to review my dissertation. Removing the notes of my most recent draft from its red crate, I read through the material. I didn't expect much, but fell into a surprising groove rewriting what I had, completing my research while rounding off rough edges, and finalizing the whole of my manuscript by the end of the month. I provided a copy to each member of my committee, assuring them, "The article on Timbal's coming," which only added to their shock. I gave no thought to my accomplishment, nor did I concern myself with what would happen now that I'd completed the task and Mel and Josh and Dr. Freidrich each had from me all they could expect.

In March, abstaining from alcohol and wearing only clothes dyed white or blue, I was leaving Dungee's following a night of playing when Marthe asked to speak with me. We went outside, bundled in jackets against the cold, and finding a spot along the wall that broke the breeze, smoked together beneath an absent moon. Marthe stood beside me, silently at first and then wondering, "Do you think he went because of me?"

I expected these sort of questions right after Niles' death and couldn't say what caused Marthe to ask me now. She seemed to have given the matter a good deal of thought however, and rather than respond on reflex and insist Niles had planned his trip well in advance, I took a different approach, and said, "He spoke of you often while we were gone."

"Then why did he go?" she looked at me as if the answer was mine to give.

"He had to," I replied then as honestly as possible, saying nothing about Oz and Jeana and all the rest, and moving my wrist in order to encourage the smoke from my cigarette to swirl in the air like a faint white rope, glanced at Marthe inside her coat with her hood pulled up against the cold, and added, "Whatever confusion you caused him was a good thing. If your relationship caught him off guard, it was also the one reason he wanted to come home. You were with him in the end."

Whether or not she believed me, if there was more she wished to ask and answers she hoped I'd provide, she didn't say, and here I wrapped an arm around her shoulder, drawing us closer together against the chill as we stood silently then, thinking of Niles and Niles and Niles again.

I sat at my piano and worked on a piece of music that had played for much of the week inside my head. I composed quietly from 1 a.m. straight on through until morning when the arrangement was finished, jotting everything down on sheets of composition paper Elizabeth left behind, and setting the pages in front of me, performed my new score with the phone dialed and Liz's machine clicking on.

I ran into Harry Fenton early in April. (Warm showers and eating before sunset were added to my list of abstentions.) Apparently all of Harry's persistence paid off, his investigating the connection between Ed Garmore and Mayor Clabund resulting in a coup as he tracked the money trail from the Union Center development through a network of dummy corporations and bank accounts in the Canary Islands. "Crooked dealings, just as I said," Harry slapped my shoulder and did a little jig. I congratulated his success, was told a grand jury was to convene, that Ed Garmore was already looking to plea out and Mayor Clabund was being pressured from within to resign. Three separate publishers had approached Harry with talk of writing a book, dangling advances large enough to make him laugh.

I walked from campus, thinking more about Harry's achievement and how pleased I was for him. The effect of his perseverance had caused a small corner of the world to undergo change, and as such, I imagined Ed Garmore and Mayor Clabund squirming under the application of Harry's assiduous hand; this quite the opposite of my own lack of industry and how I caused both Liz and Niles to bend, and worse, under the weight of nothing.

At home later that night on my machine was the left hand of Chopin's "Sonata No. 2, Concerto No. 1" in a minor key.

Classes ended the following month. I finished my essay on Niles and printed out a copy, which I mailed to Harry with a note for him to do with the material what he thought best. Two days later I graded my students' final exams and made my way across town to the Hatilbee Institute, covering the three miles at a brisk pace. Emmitt's assistant, Dianne, was waiting for me in the lobby and I followed her down the hall to the examination room where I slipped off my clothes and was given a white cotton sweat suit to wear. The medical doctor came in and had me step on the scale. He was concerned about my loss of weight, and after asking me to cough with his hand on my back, his fingers on my chest and between my legs, wondered how I was feeling. I complained of no physical maladies and assured him that I was fine.

Dianne stood to my left with a clipboard, and after the doctor was gone, asked me several additional questions. These interviews were standard each month, as she wanted to know about my sleep, the pattern of my eating, and any appreciable changes in my moods. As sex was one of the things I gave up in the last ten months, first because of Liz and then, as I raised the stakes, eschewing masturbation as a further show of restraint, I tended to placate my abstinence by looking at women wistfully, and noticing Dianne's rounded shape and liberal fleshiness, found her the sort of admirably plump figure Giovanni Segantini, Raphael, and Rubens loved to paint nude. I imagined myself a painter then and kept the image in front of me until Dianne finished her questions and led me down the hall.

Emmitt and I spoke for approximately forty minutes. He was more animated than usual and kept coming out of his chair to squeeze my arm and poke me with the middle finger of his right hand. He examined the clipboard Dianne left for him, asked his own questions and wrote down my answers with a blue ink pen. "Is there anything you haven't told me? Any particular incident that stands out that you failed to record in your journal?"

I wasn't sure if he suspected me of failing to adhere to the specifics of his schedule, and rather than confess that I had added certain abstentions of my own to his experiment, I shook my head and said, "Nothing, really."

"What about the things you've been doing?"

"What things?"

"You tell me."

I mentioned for the first time finishing my dissertation and how I'd been writing a bit of music. Emmitt came around and stood in front of me again. "Your dissertation?"

"Yes."

"And music?"

"Some."

"And these are things you didn't consider important enough to tell me?"

"I'm telling you now."

He went back behind his desk and wrote furiously. When he finished, I was taken to a room on the west end of the building. The space was approximately fifteen by twenty feet, with a shower and toilet installed in the rear, a single bed with a sheet and green summer quilt, a table to the right where I could eat though, oddly enough, no chair. A plastic pitcher of water was placed on the table with several Styrofoam cups. Food was to be delivered through a lead-lined chute in the bottom of the door, designed so a tray could be slipped in without admitting the slightest hint of light. (The walls were, of course, without windows and the ceiling ten feet from the floor.) The only audible sound inside was the gentle whirl of air being pumped in through vents at a controlled temperature of sixty-eight degrees.

Emmitt spoke with me in the hallway just before I entered the box. Assurances were made that I was not being filmed or recorded with infrared cameras, though for my own safety special devices were installed so those outside could monitor me at discreet intervals. "No more than one or two minutes an hour. Otherwise you're on your own." (I later learned Emmitt lied and a camera was, in fact, rolling the entire time I was in the box.) "We want you to feel completely at ease," he led me to the doorway where I was asked to notice a switch just inside I was to press in case of emergency. "The switch is connected to a yellow light that will flash to us," Emmitt said. "If at any time you feel in distress, you need only flick the switch and those of us in attendance will respond immediately."

"How convenient."

"It's necessary for some. Of course, we're confident you'll go the entire month without any problem at all." He encouraged me to relax, insisting I try and let go. "What you cling to will remain," and here he threw open his fingers, like a sailor releasing the length of a rope. I nodded and stared inside the box. A change of clothes, clean sweats, underwear, T-shirt, and socks, were stored for me beneath the bed. Emmitt folded his arms across his chest. "The key is doing as little as possible," he reminded me once again. "Everything should come and go through you naturally. Allow your thoughts to flow, don't force them or avoid them but let them take hold."

I said I understood, and stepping inside, waved once as the door closed. The last bit of light I saw surrounded Dianne's face as she looked in at me, mouthing the words, "So long, Bailey. So long."

---

The first thing I did was slip off my sweats and crawl into bed. The mattress was stiff but not uncomfortable, the summer quilt soft and cool. My intention was to sleep, if only for a short while, in order to remove all sense of time and disorient myself so that when I woke I'd have no lingering connection with the outside world. I didn't expect to drift off as easily as I did and found when I woke the absolute dark had devoured me completely.

I brought my legs around and put my feet on the floor. After a minute I stood and paced in gradual strides from one side of the room to the other, sliding back and forth along the same path until the route began to feel familiar. I measured the distance from my bed to the side wall, from my bed to the shower, the table and door, then found my way back to the bed again and sat down. I listened to the air through the vents, heard my own soft breathing, concentrated on the instructions Emmitt gave me just before locking me away, and looking to cooperate, I repeated my objective: "To achieve a point of nothingness and return to a natural state of being." The prospect appealed to me, the ability to at last lay things to rest and start over, and extending my hands into the dark, I invited the next phase to reach me.

What memories returned first were surprisingly pleasant as I was visited by my mother and Aunt Germaine. I recalled the pleasure of my music and art, playing piano at Dungee's, and touring galleries and museums. I sat on my bed, got up and paced to the table and back, to the wall and the door. My movement inside the box improved and I developed a reliable efficiency for getting around. I slept on no set schedule and seemed to nap in two or three hour increments. Food arrived through the lead chute, tuna and vegetables, a wheat-based hot cereal. Sometimes there were crackers, at other times cake. I made a habit of eating beside the door and left the tray in front of the chute so it could be retrieved by one of my caretakers.

Time passed and while I was still waiting for the process of erasing to begin, I was surprised that only the most pleasant memories continued to return. In the absolute dark, I could stare with eyes open and watch as life-sized images performed for me on a shimmering black stage. There was Elizabeth in happier days. And Niles. My every recollection proved comforting and welcome and for this reason I was confused. I did my best to remain patient, anticipating the moment everything would change and my more brutal past would emerge and rush from me, and yet none of this happened, not for the longest time.

I ate a meal of soft warm cereal, wondering more and more if Emmitt's idea of locking me away was actually madness and all for show. I had, after all, made progress in the last year, what with my dissertation and music, and why was I here then if the process of Clean-Slatedness wasn't going to help me forget the worst of my past? After the first few days my isolation struck me as nothing but flash added to a treatment that otherwise required month after month of self-sacrifice and abstention and where was the attraction, the selling point and mass appeal in that? If this was a ruse, I thought, then all of Emmitt's instructions were false, and unwilling to wait any longer, I chose to dismiss his warning and conjured a particular unpleasantness on my own.

Sitting there in the dark I traced back to the root of where everything began and saw my mother laid out bluish grey in the snow. The memory caused me to shudder as I looked about to see if the process of erasing might at last begin.

And then it did.

For the next several hours all the bile came coursing through me as I remembered my father, drunk and dancing with an ax around his piano, cursing and crying in the flames. I saw Tyler beaten down at the Haptree Theater, recalled Niles' fever and how I failed him as he lay in Aziz's bed. I pictured Elizabeth equally pale as I purposely botched Roslavet's "Etude," causing her to leave me. I remembered my mother's funeral, and all that otherwise went down with her into the grave. Inside my cell, I suffered through these memories like an addict sweating away his poison, my infected layers scraped away as painfully as peeling muscle from bone. I fought to endure the torment, afraid the torture would never end, and just as I was about to rush for the switch and signal for those outside to end the experiment, my panic abated, my breathing slowed, and the racing of my heart returned to normal.

And then it was over. And everything was gone.


I remained quite still and stared into the darkness, then went and sat on the side of the bed and waited to see what would happen next.

Nothing.

No further memories returned. What's more, aside from incidental information, it seemed I had no memory at all. I could recall my name and what I was doing in the box, though not specifically what led me to volunteer for Emmitt's experiment. I remembered where I lived and how I played piano, that I was unmarried and taught at the university, but when I tried to concentrate on more, a particular day from my childhood, a moment with friends and work, no such images appeared, all memory abandoned me and my mind was blank.

The sensation was not disagreeable at first. There was a great peace in knowing nothing, a tremendous weight lifted. I spent the next few days growing accustomed to the curious calm, doing push-ups and pacing from wall to wall inside the dark. I sat on the end of my bed and relished the wonder of Clean-Slatedness and the luxury of being free of old ghosts, and still it wasn't long before I began feeling uncomfortable with having such an absence of Self. Despite all I hoped to gain, my entire identity had vanished. "Who am I?" I wondered, and received as my answer no reply.

Moored to nothing, I grew disoriented. What once seemed a great achievement made me nervous and unsure. Hours went by when all I could do was ask again and again "Who?" while faltering over and over in my response. Frightened, I walked across the floor, miscalculated my steps and crashed into the wall. I cursed and limped back to the bed where I pulled my knees up to my chest, wrapped my arms around my legs and fell over onto my side. I began to fear without memory there was nothing to keep me from vanishing altogether in the dark, and even when I was eventually released from the box, how was I to know what missteps to avoid if I had no sense of what brought me here? The question exposed a serious flaw in Emmitt's treatment, and trembling, I grabbed for the iron frame of my bed as if to anchor me there. "Who, goddamn it?" I continued to repeat, "Who? Who? Who?" like a ridiculously horrified bird.

I crawled onto my bed and closed my eyes, and while I didn't sleep, I seemed to dream and heard a voice then telling me a story about a man walking along a footpath in a flatland filled with yellow and green grass. The man was quite old. His hair was white and worn long, his beard dangling away from his chin, his whiskers a hoary silver. He appeared healthy, his stride steady. His gait was purposeful and rhythmic. There were other sounds I heard, birds singing, the breeze through the grass and the branches overhead, the man's boots as he moved from path to road and back again, a soft yet constant chant inside my head of "Wait . . . Watch . . . Listen . . ."

He covered several miles. The terrain remained flat and only occasionally did a building come into view. At these times, when a house or small farm or fishing shack appeared, the man would approach the site and immediately be greeted by children and adults alike, all pleased to see him and calling his name. A circle would form around the man who stood in the center and told his story to all that drew near. Four times that day the man stopped at a different place and recounted his tale. His words on each occasion were identical. (I was initially puzzled by the purpose of his routine, but again persuaded by the voice to "Wait . . . Watch . . . Listen . . .") He described his life as a boy, his impressions of the world as they first came to him, how his father had been killed in an accident while mining for gold, and the way circumstance later forced his mother to marry a man she didn't love. He spoke of his days as a student, and of his time in the service and of the war in which his brother was lost. He told of falling in love and starting a family and buying a small farm where one of his children—named Horacio for his brother—had stumbled on a machete carelessly left laying at the base of his field. When the child almost died, the man went crazy with guilt and rushed into the field and cut every last stalk of wheat down until his hands bled and his back hurt so severely he couldn't move his legs for some time. That winter, as his injured child healed and returned to his normal life and kissed and loved his father no less than before, the man was overwhelmed, and more than once dropped to his knees and wept.

During the telling of his tale, the man produced dozens of photographs from a green knapsack. These pictures were passed around throughout the course of his talk and left with the children when he was gone.

Within the man's story, every sort of incident was discussed. He spoke of choices made and not made, of temptations resisted and taken, of good times and bad. He described the birth of his first grandchild and pulled from his knapsack the sweater his wife knitted years ago that he still wore. Moments of delight and infinite sorrow were conveyed with an equal sense of wonder. At the end of the day, after covering many miles, the man arrived back at a small cottage on his farm. The house had a stone chimney and thatch roof, wooden walls inside painted blue, two small windows, a bed and chair with a table, an old-fashioned stove, and a shelf holding many books. Beside the fireplace was a small stack of wood. Photographs identical to those the man carried with him on his walk occupied the mantle, hung also on the walls next to the bed, the windows and door. The man removed his green sack, and lifting three dry logs from the pile of wood, put them in the fireplace. When the fire was strong enough, he sat down in his chair with a book. Each time the light became too dim for him to read, he got up and added more wood to the flame. Afterward, he ate a small meal and stretched out on his bed where he slept until dawn.

In the morning, he went to his garden in back of the cottage where instead of carrots and lettuce, tomatoes and corn, additional copies of the photographs he carried with him yesterday grew in neat rows. The trees, too, were filled with snapshots of the man's children, his wife and parents, and friends. I watched him gather up as many of the photographs as he could carry from the garden and trees and fill his knapsack, before setting out along a different path, passing through forest and wild fields, changing shoulders when the sack on one side became too heavy and he needed a rest.

Here the story ended and the voice disappeared.

I sat up and looked about the dark, waiting and watching for what would come next. A few seconds later I heard a new sound, a soft refrain of notes to a song my mother used to sing, and then my mother's voice from so many years before. "Love me, love me, say you do." I remained motionless on the bed, sitting with my eyes fixed on the ebony pitch in front of me, listening to the music and my mother's voice, the sweet melody drawing closer and closer, until I was entirely embraced and gave way exactly as Emmitt told me. Soon after this other memories returned, filling me completely. Relieved, I dropped to the floor and did a vigorous set of push-ups, then went to the shower where I stripped off my clothes and waited for the water to warm. I stayed beneath the stream and let the water flow through my whiskers, massaging my arms and back, then climbed out and toweled myself dry.

Instead of floating through black space, I felt anchored there by a new sense of gravity, the feeling reminding me of my mother's hand resting softly on my shoulder as I played piano for her when I was a child. In the darkness I performed a rousing rendition of "Brown Penny" with my fingers dancing through the air. As I played, more and more memories returned and I reviewed everything with an eager resolve. Once or twice I wept when working my way inside a particular sadness, though the sorrow I felt was different then and didn't grieve me in the same way as it once did. I dressed and sat near the door, recalling the time I went to a Miró exhibit and stood in front of the weightless white and black figures floating across a hue of diaphanous blue in *Komposition* (1925). I remembered examining the shapes and lines of the canvas, taking in the structure of the work and the relationship between each form, and thought how Miró's genius lay in his ability to display an ethereal sense of order and balance in his childlike abstractions and provide a vision of what could be accomplished through the existing limitations of dimension, color, and scheme. I sat with my head against the wall, my arms relaxed, and my eyes open and staring as I thought everything through, remembered my life in terms of art and not art, saw the way memory recorded my days like a painter working a canvas, with every stroke permanent, each occurrence connecting together, one to the next. Even the false strokes, especially those, the artist had to deal with if he was to keep them from ruining the entire piece.

I finished out the month with no further incidents to speak of, ate heartily, did my push-ups, and slept with little disturbance from my dreams. I was anxious though not for escape, impatient but not to flee. When the time finally came and I heard the clicking of the latch and a small ray of light filtered into the room, I moved toward the door and was handed a pair of dark glasses to protect me from the glow. Emmitt said my name, said, "Bailey?", and I looked about before answering, stared out until all that was there awaiting me came into focus and I was able to say, "I'm here."

In the weeks that followed, I was kept busy with a number of projects. Harry did as I asked and presented my essay on Niles to the press who, in turn, made every effort to verify my claims before publishing the piece to a great deal of fanfare. (I told the truth about everything I knew, though for Aziz's sake, didn't mention him by name.) Three days after the end of my interment, two government agents came by my apartment and interviewed me about Niles and Osmah. I was questioned twice more, found to know nothing beyond what I already explained, and left with a warning to keep my nose clean.

I resumed teaching in the fall, wrote the article I promised on Timbal, whose career, thanks in part to the new painting hanging at the Modern Museum in Renton, underwent a renewed appreciation. Although my trip to Algiers was well documented, I managed to keep Timbal's location a secret and informed those who took up the hunt that I ran into him on my way to North Africa, in Spain, England and Italy, and coming back through New York.

Aunt Germaine retired to Florida where she kept a garden and met a widower by the name of Charlton Filbinger who took her to dinner and taught her how to dance. I mailed her a letter and planned to visit later in the year. In October I phoned my father, and finding the number disconnected, drove the next day to our old house where the new owners said he had moved back to Zenith earlier that spring. I got his address and dropped him a line as well.

I tried to track down my brother Tyler, something I hadn't done for years and years and felt bad about, yet every attempt I made produced nothing but another dead end, and as with everyone I spoke with, I had no idea what happened to him or where he wound up.

Emmitt and I met regularly for much of the fall as he monitored the effect of my treatment. The paper he wrote on our experiment was received skeptically by the scientific community, though he took the reviews from other psychiatrists and psychotherapists in stride. I offered to write a paper of my own and provide my personal account of how the Hatilbee Method actually worked, a suggestion Emmitt seemed to appreciate and promised to ask for my assistance in time.

I continued to play at Dungee's, producing pop and jazz for the crowds, though every now and then I took on a more strenuous assignment and recorded Roslavets, Rachmaninoff, and Chopin for a small label in east New York. The measure of my achievement, if such was the right word, came as Emmitt taught me in the release, and while I forgot nothing, I drew differently from each experience and the weight of that which still had to be endured.

One night, out walking, I stopped at a bookstore and bought a colorful poster of a beautiful stretch of desert set below a bright evening sky. I purchased a flashlight and tacks, and attaching the poster to the kiosk across the street from my apartment, went upstairs and stood by my window, shining the light down. The view was magnificent. The sky glowed with stars a billion years old, while as far as I could see all was clement and calm. The telephone rang as I was staring out, and through my machine I heard an original piece of music. I listened for a minute, then went at last and answered the call.

## ACKNOWLEDGMENTS

Working on my second novel, I fully expected those who were so supportive the first time around to lose interest in indulging me this time, and show a measure of indifference if not antipathy. To my surprise however, the opposite proved true. Not only were those closest to me all the more supportive, they seemed to endure my moods and methods for crafting *The Weight of Nothing* with a greater understanding and willingness to accept what goes into writing a novel. To the usual suspects then: To my father Stan, for his boundless faith and sage eye, ever faultless, I simply can't thank you enough. (This book is for you, Dad. I love you. You will be sorely missed.) Mother Ilene, whose love is unconditional and a sweet constancy. Brother Bob, nonfiction writer supreme, my daily e-mail companion and bridge to my sanity. (Go Stones!) For my agent Henry Williams at McIntosh and Otis, a truly kind and generous soul, indefatigable champion of my work and gifted poet. To the gang at Brook Street Press, James Pannell and Debra Hudak, both of whom saw me through every stage with friendship and generous understanding, thank you. And last but, of course, never least, my family. To my daughter Anna, you are forever my cover girl, heir to my accursed artist's eye; my son Zach, hero for being the calm in all of my storms (except first thing in the morning); and my wife Mary, love of my life, inspiration in every part of my being. How you bear me still is the one mystery I can't ever solve, but I thank you.